"With the top men of the joint military command secured in detention, who gives the orders? *We do.* We deploy and we stand fast. The President is moved out of office, and I make my national broadcast. The American public wants something done. Too many of our people are dying in Iraq. They're tired of the loss of life, the drain on America's resources. We come out of this with right on our side. Plus, our hands on the Iraqi oil fields. Getting control of those would be one hell of a plus in our favor."

Senator Justin picked up the pot and refilled his coffee cup. He sat back and took time to listen as the tight group of men discussed the upcoming takeover of the American government. He saw the earnest looks on their faces, the calm tone of their voices, and he saw they were fully committed to what they proposed to do. They viewed their actions as necessary, something that America needed to do to stay the most powerful nation on Earth. They were prepared to stand against the elected government and the President in order to carry their project through.

God help them all.

DON PENDLETON'S

STONY

AMERICA'S ULTRA-COVERT INTELLIGENCE AGENCY

MAN®

FULL
BLAST

FREEDOM FIRE   BOOK II

A GOLD EAGLE BOOK FROM
WRLDWIDE.®

TORONTO • NEW YORK • LONDON
AMSTERDAM • PARIS • SYDNEY • HAMBURG
STOCKHOLM • ATHENS • TOKYO • MILAN
MADRID • WARSAW • BUDAPEST • AUCKLAND

First edition June 2005

ISBN 0-373-61961-8

FULL BLAST

Special thanks and acknowledgment to
Mike Linaker for his contribution to this work.

Printed in U.S.A.

FULL BLAST

Freedom comes at a high price and requires constant guardianship. Taken for granted, it can slip away all too easily. When the hand weakens and the eye turns aside, the time may come when the resolve needs to be strengthened. And in those times there may be a need for armed conflict to restore the balance. As always, it is the men and women of the Armed Services who must carry that burden. They bear the brunt of the inevitable clash of arms, and they do so in the spirit of the pledge they made to ever defend and protect our peace. Their fight goes on. They continue to suffer and often to make the ultimate sacrifice. They deserve both our respect—and our enduring gratitude.

PROLOGUE

Ho's Island, North Korea

"Did I hear that right?" Rafael Encizo asked.

David McCarter pushed to his feet.

"Yes. You heard it right. It sounds as if our friend Khariza has just gone nuclear."

"Can we discuss this later?" Gary Manning suggested. "I have a feeling company is on the way."

McCarter raised his head and listened, picking up the approaching sound. He heard voices, too, shouting orders back and forth.

"Back off," he said.

Covering one another, they retreated, moving back toward their entry point.

Rafael Encizo helped himself to additional magazines for the Kalashnikovs they had acquired, handing out others to McCarter and Manning.

"Here they bloody well come," McCarter announced.

The distant sound became movement, dark shapes flitting in between the packing cases and pallets of merchandise. Light glanced off weapons. The clatter of autofire sounded. Bullets thudded into boxes. Wood splinters sprayed the air. Some zipped dangerously close to the Phoenix Force.

McCarter paused to pull the pin on a grenade. He hurled the bomb in the general direction of the advancing hostiles. The explosion echoed within the confines of the building, the flash showing the men of Phoenix Force there were approximately eight armed pursuers. The grenade took out one man, who went down screaming, arms flailing as he fell.

Encizo moved into view, a rocket launcher, armed and ready, over his shoulder. He swung the muzzle of the weapon toward the advancing hostiles and pulled the trigger. The missile burst from the tube, trailing a tail of flame. It streaked across the interior and struck a heavy steel-support girder. The explosion sheered the girder, the blast deafening within the confines of the building. Metal creaked and groaned overhead as the girder fell away.

"Hit them again," McCarter ordered.

Manning had lifted another launcher from its box. He swung it to his shoulder and fired, sending the missile in the same direction as Encizo's. The explosion spread its deadly effect across a wide area, scattering the Korean hostiles in bloody heaps.

"We got any more of those?" McCarter asked.

"Here," Encizo said.

"Lay one on those bloody M-1983s."

Encizo followed through, the rocket launcher drilling the missile at the metal pallet holding the heavy machine guns. The damage left the 14.5 mm quads twisted and out of commission.

In the lull that followed, Phoenix Force backed away, still armed with the Kalashnikovs they had acquired from the weapons supply. They helped themselves to more of the grenades.

Manning opened the door and pushed it wide. From where he was standing he could see their plane. He checked out the immediate area and saw no one. The big Canadian knew how quickly that situation could change.

"Let's go," he said over his shoulder.

As the others followed, Manning turned and headed for the parked vehicles they had spotted on the way in. The closest was one of the Jeep-type utilities. Manning leaned in and scanned the layout. He dropped onto the driver's seat and flicked the ignition switch. He jammed his foot on the floor starter. The engine turned over and caught. He pushed the gas pedal down and the engine roared. Manning felt the Jeep sway as McCarter and Encizo clambered in behind him.

The Brit clapped him on the shoulder. "Come on, mate, our plane's waiting."

Manning put the vehicle into first gear and released the handbrake. He stepped on the gas and let out the clutch. The Jeep lurched forward, picking up speed with surprising ease. The ride was hard. The vehicle wasn't fitted with very sophisticated suspension, and every bump and dip in the ground was transmitted through to the passengers. That, plus the still rising wind, made for an uncomfortable ride.

Manning swung the Jeep in under the main wing, turning it so the vehicle stood sideways-on, providing a degree of cover.

Smoke was rising in thick columns from the holes in the weakened roof of the building they had just evacuated, and armed hardmen were starting to appear.

"Keep them busy," McCarter yelled as he jumped from the Jeep and headed for the plane.

The side hatch of the Anatov An-26 was open and the Briton swung himself up into the body of the aircraft. He made his way along the aisle toward the cockpit and had almost reached it when the door swung open and the pilot charged through.

The Chinese was about McCarter's height, broad and heavy. He slammed into the Briton, knocking himself back a couple of feet. The impact also sent McCarter crashing into the seats close to him. He fell back, losing his grip on the assault rifle as he sprawled across the seats. The pilot followed him, large hands reaching out to grab hold of his adversary's throat. McCarter rolled off the seats, landing on his hands and knees. The pilot swung around and made another lunge at McCarter, bending over him. The Briton dropped, turned on his back and swung up his right foot. The sole of his boot caught the pilot under the chin, snapping his head back with enough force to break bone. The pilot let out a strangled yell.

McCarter, pushing upright and avoiding the pilot's lunging blows, grabbed hold of the man's thick black hair. He yanked the pilot off balance, then pulled the man's head down, hard, onto his rising knee. The blow was brutal, caving in the front of the pilot's face, shattering bone and splitting flesh. Dazed and in pain, blood streaming down his face, the pilot tried to hit back, but McCarter had neither the time nor the inclination to continue. He leaned in close, encircled the pilot's neck with his right arm, and put on the pressure, twisting hard. He felt the neck snap. The Chinese went limp in his grip. The Phoenix Force leader let the man drop to the deck. Snatching up his rifle, McCarter pushed through the door into the cockpit. He dropped into the pilot's seat and began the startup procedure.

MANNING HEARD the first of the plane's twin turboprop engines start to turn, coughing as it spit out thick clouds of smoke from the exhaust vents.

"Doesn't he love waiting till the last second," the Canadian muttered.

"*They* don't," Encizo said.

He was watching the tight group of armed men moving in their direction. The North Koreans were carrying assault rifles, and they started to fire once they were in range. The first shots fell short. The following volley was closer, some of the slugs hitting the Jeep that Manning and Encizo were crouched behind.

As the plane's second engine fired up, Manning fisted one of the grenades. He pulled the pin, exposed himself for a brief moment, and hurled the grenade in the direction of the advancing force. The moment it detonated, scattering the group, Encizo followed up with one of his own. The Phoenix Force pair went through their store of grenades, then dropped back behind the Jeep.

Four Koreans had been savaged by the grenade barrage, and another two were nursing wounds. As the sound of the final blast faded, the surviving Koreans began to regroup, opening fire again as they broke into a run.

McCarter slid open one of the cockpit windows and yelled over the rising roar of the engines, "Let's move it, ladies!"

Manning and Encizo ran for the open hatch, hauling themselves inside. The An-26 was already moving, McCarter boosting the power with little regard to any strain he might be putting on the engines. It was to his advantage that the plane hadn't been too long on the ground, the engines were still warm and less likely to stall. He worked the foot controls, using the rudder to swing the craft around in a circle so it was facing back the way it had come. Once the Briton had the plane set on the runway, he pushed the power up and felt the craft moving off. The entire airframe vibrated as the plane fought nature and the drag of the howling engines.

The Koreans opened up with their assault rifles, bullets peppering the fuselage, but none hitting anything vital to the performance of the aircraft.

Out the corner of his eye McCarter could see the heavy swell of the water bordering the edge of the runway. The wind was sending waves crashing against the craggy extremes of the rocky island. He could feel its grip on the aircraft as it picked up speed. Too slowly, he thought as it bounced and hopped its way along the makeshift strip. There was nothing he could do about the weather or the crude runway. It was all he had, that and the aircraft itself. McCarter coaxed and cursed and threatened the plane.

The end of the runway was coming so fast it was on McCarter almost before he knew it. He hauled back on the controls as the last few yards rushed toward him. The aircraft left the island behind, cruising only feet above the cold, dark waters of Korea Bay. McCarter's arm muscles ached from his efforts to hold the controls back, fighting the drag of the air over the flaps. For a moment even the optimistic Briton imagined he was going to end up in the inhospitable waters.

The plane began to lift, gradually, seemingly with agonizing slowness. The black water started to sink below them and the straining engines settled to a steady beat. McCarter held the climb, then leveled off, letting the craft have its head.

"Close," Manning said. "Too close."

Standing behind McCarter during the takeoff, he had witnessed the near miss.

"That's what you get for creeping up behind people," the Phoenix Force leader said.

"Just to satisfy my curiosity, who is the guy back there?"

"The flight attendant. Pushy type."

Manning dropped into the copilot's seat, studying the bank of dials.

"Can you read these? Just asking because they're all in Chinese."

"Most of them."

"How about this one?"

"Fuel. Why?"

"Because the gauge is in the three-quarters empty section."

"Or a quarter full," McCarter suggested.

"Where are we heading?"

"South Korea. Once we get over the border we should be on safe ground. When we land, I mean."

Manning made a sound in his throat, stood and backed away. As he turned, he saw Encizo leaning against the bulkhead. The Cuban had a grin on his face that said he had heard the whole conversation.

"What did you make of that?"

"*Nada,*" Encizo said. "I am only a poor peasant, *señor.*"

"You're as bad as he is."

"Shouldn't we try to contact someone on the South Korean side. Let them know who we are so they don't shoot us down?"

"Good thinking, Rafe. Initiative like that could get you a field promotion."

"Jesus, why don't you two get married?"

"Out of the question," McCarter said. "I'm British and he's only a lowly peasant."

"*Sí,* and I know my place."

"And right now it's working that radio, so get to it."

Encizo took the copilot's seat and pulled on a set of headphones. He picked up the hand mike and began to work his way through the frequencies on the radio.

Peering through the windshield, Manning checked out the coastline on their left.

"How the hell do we know when we're over South Korean territory?"

"It's the part that has electricity," McCarter said cheerfully. "We'll be able to see the lights."

"Tell you what I can see," the Canadian said.

"What?"

"That MiG-23 coming up starboard."

McCarter checked it out. He watched as the drab-colored jet, showing North Korean markings, slid in alongside them, the pilot cutting his speed to match that of the turboprop An-26.

"You don't figure he's come to escort us to safety?"

Manning shook his head.

"I don't think so. The way he's wagging his thumb, I'd say he wants us to land."

"Fat chance," McCarter muttered. "I'd sooner square up to him."

"What with?"

"I've got an autorifle."

"He's got a 23 mm cannon and probably heat-seeker missiles."

"Did I miss that?"

Encizo raised a warning hand. He began to speak into his handset.

"You have? Good. What about our North Korean escort?"

"That better be the good guys he's talking to."

"David, don't be so pessimistic."

"The way things have been going recently, can you blame me?"

Encizo leaned across to tap McCarter on the arm.

"U.S. military command. They've had contact with Stony Man. Apparently they have been monitoring the airwaves for hours. The guy I've been talking to is a

Major Yosarian. He's making contact with a South Korean air patrol. They have a couple of jets close enough to be with us fairly quickly. They'll have orders to escort us to friendly territory."

Manning punched McCarter on the shoulder. "Told you."

"Has anybody told that bloke out there?"

"They're aware of his position," Encizo said. "The patrol will warn him off."

"Why aren't I happy about that last remark?" McCarter said as he watched the North Korean MiG slide away.

The pilot rolled the jet and made a sweep that would bring him up on the An-26's tail.

"That bugger isn't going to wait," the Briton chided. "A few bursts from his cannon and we'll end up shredded."

Manning turned and vanished from sight.

"Where's he gone?" Encizo asked.

McCarter shrugged. He was too busy flying the plane to worry about Manning.

Curious or not, McCarter was alerted by the crackle of the internal com system. He picked up the handset.

"What?"

"This observation blister is quite handy," Manning said.

McCarter had forgotten about the Perspex bubble built into the left side of the An-26's fuselage just behind the cockpit.

"David, he's coming around now. Lining up to hit our tail."

McCarter glanced across at Encizo. The Cuban had a wide grin on his face.

"Always said Canadians had more in them than just the ability to chop down trees," McCarter said.

"I can still hear you."

"Tell me when that sod is steady. And stop moaning."

"Wait…wait…now."

McCarter worked the controls and the An-26 went into a steep dive, dropping away from the MiG a second before the pilot opened fire. McCarter increased power, the turboprop sweeping down in a long curve that ended only yards above the choppy waters. He leveled out and held the aircraft on the same course.

"Pretty good," Manning said over the speaker. "But what about next time?"

"Bloody hell, you're never satisfied. Where is he, anyway?"

"Can't see him at the moment. No, wait a minute. Coming in from your side."

McCarter turned to look out the cockpit window and spotted the dark shape of the MiG leveling out and coming in for the kill. He thought quickly, well aware that evasive action against the jet was not going to keep them out of trouble much longer.

"Okay, chum, try this," the Briton muttered as he hauled back on the stick, kicking on the rudder and bringing the plane around in a turn that set it on a direct course for the hurtling jet. He hammered the throttles wide open and trimmed the controls to get the best speed he could.

"Oh, shit," he heard Manning breathe through the speaker.

The Canadian's exclamation brought a chuckle to McCarter's lips.

"Exactly what I thought," he said.

The seconds flashed by. McCarter held his course, aiming straight for the MiG. He knew that the North Korean pilot might decide to fire anyway. Might even loose off a missile. But at the close range the MiG might easily run into the spinning debris and bring himself down.

"Make your play, sunshine," McCarter said evenly.

The MiG suddenly broke, flashing off to the side, vanishing from McCarter's field of vision.

"That," Manning said, "was daring."

"Bloody mad."

"You are loco," Encizo said.

"That's what it says in my job description. Right next to where it says I'm a clever bugger and prone to being inspired."

"Inspire something else then," Manning suggested.

"How about conjuring up a pair of South Korean F-16s?"

They all watched two F-16s burn the air as they streaked in to confront the MiG, which held out for a time before breaking away and heading back toward North Korean territory. The F-16s fell in alongside the

An-26 and one of the pilots broke in on McCarter's com set.

"Please stay with us, gentlemen, and we will escort you in."

"Thanks, mate," McCarter acknowledged. "I was running out of ideas."

The South Korean pilot laughed.

"From what I saw, you were doing fine. I wasn't sure whether you really needed us."

"Oh, we needed you, pal. Your timing was spot-on. And don't let anyone tell you different."

Stony Man Farm, Virginia

"BEFORE YOU ASK, we don't have a damn thing," Aaron Kurtzman said.

"Phoenix has dropped off the map. If they're in North Korean territory, we're going to be hard-put getting any fix on them."

"I'll save my breath, then," Hal Brognola said.

The big Fed crossed the Computer Room to stand in front of the main wall screen as if he were going to receive some kind of cerebral message that would answer his silent questions.

"All this damn technology and we can't locate our own people."

"How do you think it makes me feel?" Kurtzman growled.

Brognola turned to look at the man in the wheelchair. He knew Kurtzman had been at his station without a break since the China incident. He had refused to give in, relentlessly working at his keyboard and utilizing every sliver of his computer genius. This time it hadn't worked. Kurtzman looked tired. It showed in his face, his movements and his responses. The man was only awake through sheer stubbornness.

"Okay, listen up," Brognola announced to the entire room. "Being the big boss of this facility, as you are always telling me, gives me certain policy-making rights none of you can refuse to accept." He waited as his words sank in. "At least you don't disagree. So I'm making an executive decision here and now.

"You," he said, pointing at Kurtzman, "are relieved of your position and won't get it back until you've had at least twelve hours' sleep. This is nonnegotiable and you aren't allowed to protest. If you do, that coffeepot goes out the window and we get a new one."

"That's hitting below the belt," Carmen Delahunt murmured as she glanced across at Barbara Price.

"I can do worse than that," Brognola said, throwing a withering glance in Price's direction, daring her to put up any kind of protest.

"Hate to think what that might be," Akira Tokaido said.

Brognola lowered his eyes to the CD player Tokaido always carried with him.

"I'd keep quiet," Huntington Wethers suggested.

"You still here?" Brognola snapped at Kurtzman.

Kurtzman held up his hands in surrender. "Just leaving."

He spun his wheelchair and made for the door. No one spoke until he had gone.

"Okay, you know what to do," Brognola said. "Do it. If Aaron shows his face before his twelve hours are up, call in Buck Greene and have him taken back to his room."

"That wasn't a joke, was it?" Wethers asked.

"No, I mean every word. Look, I understand how you might feel I've overreacted. Give me the benefit of the doubt. I've been watching Aaron, and the man is exhausted. If he wasn't sitting in that chair, he'd fall down. If he works himself into the ground, he's no good to me or the job."

Brognola had attempted to make his decision one that had been based on his concern over Kurtzman's work. He'd failed. The cyberteam looked beyond his tough words to Brognola's genuine feelings for Kurtzman.

"We understand, Hal," Delahunt said.

Without another word, the team turned back to their workstations.

Brognola and Price moved across the room.

"Military Command in South Korea is on alert for anything they can pick up from over the border," Price told the big Fed. "The word has come down from the President that we have a team in the north. He's told

Military Command to cooperate with us all the way down the line. I have a contact there. Major Chuck Yosarian."

"Let's hope it's enough. Anything from Able in Hong Kong?"

Price shook her head. "Nothing since their last call. It looks as if they've come up against hard times. They know as much as we do. David's team was taken by Kim Yeo and went off the chart."

"Damn." Brognola ran a hand through his hair. "Nothing worse than no contact. Yeah, I know it's happened before. That doesn't make it any easier. I hate standing around with my di—" Brognola grinned self-consciously. "Sorry. Didn't mean to…"

Price smiled. "Don't go all coy on me, Hal. I know how you feel."

"Any feedback from Gadgets and Jack?"

"They're running traces on Gardener, Justin and the CIA guy, Rod McAdam. High-profile individuals like Gardener and Justin aren't easy to get to without them being aware."

"Call coming through for you, Barb," Delahunt said, holding a phone in her hand.

Price crossed the room and took the handset. She listened for a moment, then smiled. "That's great news, Major. We'll wait for them to contact us. And thanks again."

Price replaced the phone.

"Well?" Brognola asked.

"Phoenix is being escorted into South Korean territory as we speak. That was Yosarian. Apparently his communication team picked up a radio call coming from an unknown source. Turned out to be Phoenix asking for backup. They were airborne but being threatened by a North Korean MiG. There was a South Korean patrol already in the air on routine patrol. They rendezvoused within minutes and the North Korean backed off."

"We need to talk to Phoenix once they're on the ground," Brognola said. "Debrief for both sides."

"Major Yosarian is setting that up now. He'll have a secure connection ready as soon as they touch down."

"Apparently the South Korean pilots were singing the praises of the pilot in the plane they escorted. Just before they made contact they saw him evade the MiG's attack. Twice."

"David," Brognola said without a trace of surprise in his voice.

"Our man McCarter." Price smiled at the thought of the Briton facing off a well-armed jet fighter. "And I'll bet he never even broke a sweat."

MCCARTER'S CALL came just under two hours later. He didn't waste time being polite. Just got down to the facts.

"Henry Lee is dead. But to even the score, so are Kim Yeo and the bloody North Korean who sold Khariza his weapons. The really bad news, and this is going to piss everyone off, is that Sun Yang Ho sent off Khariza's main cargo just after we arrived. According to Kim Yeo we have three nuclear devices en route to Khariza. Just to add to the problem, we don't have any ID on the plane or where it's heading."

Price took in a sharp breath, unsure how to respond.

The rest of the cyberteam paused in its tasks as McCarter's pronouncement reached them over the speakers.

Hal Brognola felt in his pockets for a cigar. He didn't find one.

"I'm bringing you back, and Able from Hong Kong. We need to get together on this, David. Airlift as soon as I can arrange it."

"We'll be ready. Right now I'm off for a meal and then I'm getting my head down. Talk to you later, mate."

Brognola cut the connection and glanced across at Price. "Travel arrangements for both teams."

She nodded and reached for a phone. The big Fed turned to face the rest of the team.

"You all heard that. Let's see what we can pick up. Use all your contacts. Anything and everything. Let's see if we can pinpoint that camp in Chechnya."

"What about Gadgets and Jack?" Price asked, punching in phone numbers.

"Leave them. The more I think about it, the more I get a funny feeling about Gardener, Justin and this CIA guy. Let's see what their muddying the waters brings up."

Washington, D.C.

"THAT WENT WELL," Jack Grimaldi said.

They were in the car that was parked on the street just beyond Senator Ralph Justin's town house. Earlier in the day they had paid an unannounced visit to the senator's office, doing a little probing and pushing with Justin's staff. The senator had walked in during their visit and had reacted just as they'd expected. Showing up at his house later in the day was just putting additional pressure on the man.

Hermann "Gadgets" Schwarz loosened the tie he had been forced to wear along with his suit as part of his role as a Justice Department agent.

"I didn't think that manservant was going to allow us inside. That guy was so stiff he was ready to fold in the middle."

Grimaldi started the car and eased away from the curb. "You think Justin was fooled?"

"Hard to say, but I think we rattled him asking questions about his relationship with General Chase Gardener."

"Just enough of a suggestion that concerns had been raised in certain quarters. Nothing specific. Hints and rumors, but enough to get him interested."

"All we were doing was following up as protocol demanded," Schwarz confirmed.

"He didn't take it too kindly when you told him we couldn't divulge any information Justice had on file."

Schwarz took out his cell phone and contacted the Farm.

"Our friendly senator got a little frosty. I got the feeling he didn't like being spoken to by a pair of lowly Justice agents," he told Brognola. "My guess is he'll be talking to Gardener as soon as he can get in touch. Which is just what we wanted."

"What next?"

"We figure a little desert air is in order. A trip out to Arizona and Leverton."

"The town near Gardener's base?" the big Fed suggested.

"Fort Leverton, home to Gardener's command. We'll do a little prowling around. See if there's anything to stir up."

"Stay sharp," Brognola warned. "If there is something going on, Gardener won't be such a soft mark if he gets wind you're checking *him* out."

"What's he going to do? Court-martial us?"

"Arizona. Big, lonely place. Lots of sand and desert. Easy to get lost out there. Accident or design."

"Come on, Hal, stop dressing it up. Tell us what you really mean."

"Call in when you get there," Brognola directed.

"Will do."

Grimaldi glanced at Schwarz as he put his phone away, noticing the faint smile edging his partner's lips.

"Something funny?"

"Only Hal telling us to be careful."

"He say that?"

"Not in so many words. That's the funny part."

Neither man spotted the plain, light-colored car that fell in line with the traffic and trailed them out of Washington. It followed them all the way to the commercial airstrip where a twin-engined Beechcraft sat waiting for them. The pilot was ready to go. He had his flight plan already filed, and the minute his passengers were settled, he spoke to the control tower and taxied out to the runway.

Razan Khariza's Camp, Chechnya

RAZAN KHARIZA had completed his prayers and as he returned from the small, bare room he used for his devotions, he picked up excited sounds from outside the stone house. The door opened and Wafiq stood there.

They have a prisoner," Abdul said. "Dushinov has a prisoner."

Khariza followed Wafiq outside, pulling on his thick leather coat against the damp chill. He saw Zoltan Dushinov drag a bound figure from the rear of a battered pickup and throw it to the stony ground. When Dushinov looked up and saw Khariza, he raised a hand to beckon the Iraqi to join him, a satisfied smile on his bearded face.

"Didn't I tell you they were looking for you?" Dushinov said. "Now you see I was right."

"I believed you before, Zoltan. Why would I not?"

Dushinov dismissed the words with a shrug.

"This one was found trying to locate the camp. He had a guide. Some local from one of the villages. My men dealt with him. When the villagers find him and see what my men did, they will think twice before selling us out next time."

Khariza reached the pickup and stood over the bloody, huddled figure on the ground. His clothing was torn and filthy. His feet were bare where someone had taken his boots and socks. His arms had been pulled behind him and tied high up his back with a length of rope taken around his neck.

"Who is he?"

Dushinov reached down and caught hold of the man's hair, using it to pull him to his knees. The man's face turned up, eyes meeting Khariza's. He had already undergone a severe beating. His skin was heavily bruised and bloody. There was a deep gash across one cheek, bone gleaming white through the blood.

"He is an American," Dushinov said loudly so that everyone could hear. "One of our enemies to be feared. Look at him, my brothers. Look at him and tremble. This is the great enemy who is going to conquer us all. Are you afraid?"

There was a raised yell of defiance from the gathered men. They moved to stare at the man on the ground, gesturing with their weapons and voicing their contempt.

"Here is your American, Razan. I give him to you as

a gift. If you ask he may tell you why he is looking for you."

"Take him inside," Khariza ordered.

The American was dragged to his feet and taken to one of the buildings. Khariza followed slowly, his mind busy with questions he wanted to ask the prisoner. He wished he had Barak with him. The man had the skill to pull information from anyone. He was patient, thorough and dedicated to his work. And he was extremely loyal to Khariza. But now he was on Zehlivic's motor vessel, *Petra*, somewhere off the North African coast where he was dealing with a matter allied to a Mossad agent named Sharon. The Israeli had been part of the group that had intercepted the team inserted into Israel as part of the strike against the nuclear plant at Dimona. The advance team had been killed, the plane on its way to carry out the attack intercepted and brought down.

The mission to destroy Dimona had been important—planned to demoralize the Israelis—and its loss was a definite blow. Khariza had taken the news badly at first but had pushed aside his disappointment, especially in front of his people. He had to remain strong and to show that defeats had to be borne with strength. Later, alone, he had reviewed the way his plans were going. The strike at Bucklow had achieved its purpose: a significant blow against the Americans. An added disappointment had come with the news that the second MOAB had been retaken by an American strike team and Khariza's men defeated.

Khariza, in his solitary room, had sat facing the blank wall. His mind alive with thought. So many things he was dealing with; ongoing plans, logistics, financial matters. The dealing and bargaining to obtain the Massive Ordnance Air Burst and allied equipment he needed. The endless conversations with his people who were located in many different places. There was a great deal to maintain. So many people to keep updated and at one with their faith. For some, the smallest loss became almost total defeat. Khariza had had to employ his skills as an orator to allay their fears. Persuading, promising, soothing, he became all things to all men, and it was only when he was alone that he found himself questioning and calming his own deep, inner fears.

It wasn't that he was ready to surrender, to call off the campaign that stretched across the Middle East and all the way to the American mainland. Khariza was, if nothing, a man at ease with himself and his objectives. His cause was just. He was doing it for God and for Iraq. Secretly, almost with a little embarrassment, he admitted that he was also doing it in part for himself. Since the capture of Iraq's ex-president, Saddam Hussein, there had been a leadership vacuum. The current structure wasn't proving fully successful. The diversity of tribal culture, of in-fighting and mistrust between interested groups, had led to a continual atmosphere of hostility. The random acts of violence perpetrated by insurgent groups, the destruction and killing, went on.

Khariza had seen all this and the opportunity for someone to step in a take the country back—by force if necessary. He saw himself as that man. The prize was worth the risk.

Stakes were high, of course, so the need for grand gestures and hard action had become the only way. Khariza had no problems with that. The danger held no fear for him. He had lived most of his adult life on the edge, using his power and influence as tools to further his position. He knew and accepted the risks. There was a part of him that kept urging him to accept his fate. To acknowledge that he, Razan Khariza, was the man to step into the void left by Hussein. The former president of Iraq wasn't going to return. His time was over and if the country was to have a new leader it needed someone with the strength of purpose and the will to do whatever became necessary, no matter how drastic.

Khariza believed he had those qualities. He also had the means to boost his credibility, namely the vast amounts of money that had been banked during the Hussein regime. Those funds were now under his control, and they gave him the buying power to gather what he wanted. He already had his three nuclear devices, and as long as they remained in his hands his bargaining was unbeatable. The nuclear gamble, if it paid off, could push him to the top. If it failed and he was pressured into actually using the bombs, Khariza was prepared to take that final extra step. He would deny the country to the enemy, even if it did exact his life as the ultimate price. He was aware of the obstacles in his way. The struggle that lay ahead made him pause, but only for a short time. If he lacked faith in himself, how could he expect others to follow and stay the course? He pushed aside thoughts of defeat and concentrated on the matters at hand.

Entering the building where the American had been taken, Khariza made his way to the room used as a cell and closed the door. The prisoner had been pushed against the far wall. He held himself as straight as was possible, restricted by the ropes binding his arms. Khariza crossed the room to stand in front of the man.

"What agency do you work for?"

The man remained silent.

"CIA? One of the other American agencies? Perhaps you are military? On a covert assignment for the Pentagon? We both know you have to be working for someone. You did not come here on a vacation. So why not tell me and let us get this over with. Cooperate, and I may even let you live. Force me to kill you and we will never know if I might have spared you. As admirable as your resistance is, how would your death profit me?"

"I guess we'll have to find out," the prisoner said.

Khariza gave a slight nod of his head, turning aside so that the two Chechens had room to confront the captive. They used their fists and feet, beating the prisoner until he was unable to stand, then continued when he lay on the floor. Finally they stepped back and allowed Khariza to resume his questioning. The American lay in a pool of his own blood, barely able to raise his head when Khariza squatted in front of him.

"It only begins here," he said. "If you persist, I will allow these men to continue and in the end you will tell me everything I want to know. No man can resist torture forever. I know this because I have conducted such sessions many times. In the end you will tell your most secret things. You will betray all your friends and your country because it will be the only way to end your suffering. If I ask, you will even betray your mother and offer me your wife just so it stops. Think about this, because the next time I turn these men on you there will be no end to it."

The American focused his gaze on Khariza's face. He worked his jaw painfully, finding it difficult to speak because it had been pushed out of its sockets.

"I know...about the bombs...we'll stop you...I passed on the details...people know..."

Khariza barely managed to hold himself back from striking the American. He stared at the beaten figure on the dirty floor, lying in his own blood, and felt anger rage through him. He exhaled forcibly, pushing himself upright. He pointed at the iron ring set in the wall.

"Bind him to that ring. I want him on his feet. Keep him alive but make certain he is uncomfortable. Do what you need to make him speak. I will come back later."

Khariza turned to leave the room. Behind him he could hear the American moan as he was dragged to his feet. The Iraqi stepped outside, turned his face to the sky and breathed in cold air.

Was it true? Had the agent found out about the nuclear devices? If so, where had his information come from? Someone within Khariza's own organization perhaps?

More problems to add to those already plaguing him. Khariza shook his head.

What had he done to deserve such punishment? Was this God's way of testing his faith?

He though about his final strike. The single, most powerful statement Khariza could make. It was to be the make-or-break operation in his bid to regain control over Iraq. If it failed—if *he* failed—then what followed wouldn't only resolve many matters, but would reduce Baghdad and areas of Iraq to a wasteland.

It was to be *the* final word.

If he, Razan Khariza, was pushed to the limit, his retaliation would echo throughout the region. No, it would be heard all around the world, and America would be left with the bloody destruction of a nation on its hands.

DUSHINOV GLANCED up as Khariza entered the stone house being used as their headquarters. The Chechen rebel watched as Khariza crossed to join him by the log fire burning in the open hearth.

"Drink?" Dushinov asked.

He raised the bottle of locally brewed alcohol. Khariza helped himself to a mug of the dark tea brewing in a smoke-blackened pot. Dushinov, grinning, added some of the alcohol.

"So?"

Khariza drank before he spoke. "He hasn't said anything yet except for…"

"Except for?"

"He claims to know about the nuclear devices."

Dushinov grunted. He took a long swallow from the bottle. "Interesting. If he does, you need to consider who led him to this information."

"That has already crossed my mind. I will contact my people and have them do some checking. Maybe we have a traitor in our ranks."

"Do you think this American knows what you intend to do with the bombs?"

Khariza shrugged. "I do not know. But we *will* find out."

"It will help to pass the time."

The Iraqi stared into the flames, his attention wandering for a time. Dushinov sat, drinking, watching the man and wondering what was going through Khariza's mind.

"You have one irritating fault, my friend," he finally said.

"That is?"

"You think too much. It's a mistake to keep going over everything. Create your plan, decide how to make it work, carry it through. Simple. It works for me. Once I make my decision, I send it off and sit down to have a drink. You should try it."

The door opened and Abdul Wafiq entered. He spotted Khariza and went to stand beside him.

"We have had a communication from our people back home. They are asking when the next shipment of weapons is going to arrive."

"Tell them to contact the Syrian base. I had confirmation the weapons were delivered two days ago. We have to be careful. The Americans are concentrating on the border area heavily now. There are patrols. Air surveillance. We have to alter the routes and will only be able to move small consignments for the present."

"They have asked about air-drops. I told them that would be difficult with the Americans and British maintaining patrols."

"I understand their frustration, Abdul, but we have to proceed with caution. We are not in a position to mount a large-scale assault. Our brothers must understand this. Impatience will not serve us in the long run. As long as we continue our isolated attacks, we will still achieve results. Over time, even the Americans will begin to feel the pain we cause. With all their might and their superior firepower they cannot defeat a mobile hit-and-run force. We can deliver telling punishment and be gone before they can find us. Remember this. We are fighting on our own ground. We know the country well, better than they ever will. We have a thousand places to hide. We have support. And we have the will to continue as long as it takes."

Wafiq turned to leave.

"Wait. One more thing. We may have an informer in our group. This American appears to have some knowledge about the nuclear devices. Have an investigation carried out, but make certain it is done carefully. Use only those people you can trust fully. If there is a traitor, it will do no good to alert him. You understand?"

Wafiq nodded and left.

"I must go to the training area to see how the volunteers are coming along," Khariza said, voicing his thoughts.

"It won't do any harm," Dushinov agreed. "Tell them they are important to the cause. That they are going to make a valuable contribution."

"They *are* helping to shape Iraq's future."

"That sounds a little cynical considering your final solution. It's not as if they know about that." Dushinov raised his bottle, teeth showing in a wide smile. "But tell them how important they are anyway."

"Be honest, Zoltan. Am I being rash? Going too far with this nuclear blackmail? Will it even work?"

"My mistake was not putting enough of this in your tea," Dushinov said, waving the bottle in Khariza's face.

"Here, have some more." The rebel leader topped up Khariza's mug.

"We live in changing times," he continued. "To achieve what we desire means taking chances. Ignoring all the rules and challenging the way things are. We can't do that without drastic measures. If we sit around and bleat like mangy goats, nothing will change. Only we can do that. If it takes a nuclear bomb to make the Americans realize they will never be masters of Iraq, then so be it, my friend."

"Would you do such a thing?"

"If it was guaranteed to piss off the Russians, I would press the button myself. Ah, listen to me, Razan. In the end you have only yourself to satisfy. I love my country as you love Iraq. The last thing I would want would be the Americans tramping all over it. Telling me what to do. All they want is to get their hands on the oilfields. Under their control. To put Iraq under their boots and bleed the country dry. They don't care about Iraqi freedom, only U.S. wealth and power. Deny them their oil and see how long they stay then."

KHARIZA'S INSTRUCTOR was a broad, giant of a man called Bertran. He was a mercenary. French-born, he had served in Algeria, but now sold his expertise for a price. A high price because he was good. Khariza had used the man before, in Iraq, to train his own combat squads. Bertran didn't care about religion or politics. He liked his work and the rewards it brought.

He was putting the group through their paces when Khariza arrived. When he recognized his visitor, Bertran put one of the men in charge and made his way over to where Khariza was climbing from the battered Toyota pickup.

"How are they doing?"

Bertran glanced back at the group. "When they leave here they will know everything there is to know about the AK-47, how to set explosives, the best way to kill a man without making a noise. What I can't give them is experience."

"We all have to go through our first taste of combat. Didn't you?"

"I was born ready for it," Bertran said, smiling. "Razan, this is not going to be an easy campaign. You understand what you are going to be facing?"

"And what is that?"

"The most powerful military machine the world has ever known. From a country with so much wealth and material it can sustain this for years."

"And yet they are unable to defeat my people. We use small strikes. Here and there. We worry at them like a small dog nipping their heels and running away before they can respond. Bertran, my friend, what good are a hundred battle tanks and an electronic airforce against a car packed with explosives driven into a building? Or an innocent-looking young woman walking into a crowd with explosives beneath her clothing?"

"You make it sound so easy."

Khariza shook his head. "Nothing of worth comes easily. This is a war that cannot be won by usual tactics. It is intended to wear down the Americans. I will hit them in Iraq. Anywhere around the world American interests are vulnerable. They are easy targets. And most of all, I will hit them on their own soil. These warriors you are training will be my army. I will send them wherever they are needed to carry out the struggle. Here and at home, the American government is going to have to live with the bitter taste left by its foul actions against us. We will see how long the American people and their allies are prepared to suffer as we have suffered."

A chill wind blew in from the north, coming off the timbered peaks and sweeping in over the high cliffs and down into the isolated valley. It brought with it the smell of rain. Khariza huddled into his thick coat.

"We need to step up our attacks. When can you have people ready?"

"Give me two more days with this group and you can ship them out. Razan, are you all right?"

"Why do you ask?"

"You look tired. Take time to rest or you'll not be able to think straight."

"It would be pleasant. But there is so much to do, and I need to be in Syria now that my delivery from North Korea has arrived."

"Your special cargo? Do I get to know what it is? Or should I keep my nose out?"

"When the time comes, Bertran, you will be told. I promise."

"Good enough. Now, let me get back to see if they have remembered everything I've told them."

"I will talk to them before I leave."

Khariza stood and watched Bertran return to the group, taking back his command. His raised voice drifted across the rocky landscape. The wind was increasing, tugging at the canvas of the tents where the group was housed when they were not training. It pulled at Khariza's coat. The first cold drops of rain stung his face and he raised it to the sky. The clouds, heavy and dark, were moving in across the valley.

Razan Khariza saw them as a warning.

There was a storm coming and when it arrived they would all feel its destructive power.

CHAPTER ONE

New Mexico

General Chase Gardener took the thick tumbler of Jack Daniel's whiskey and made his way across the polished wood floor of his spacious study. At the far end of the long room a panoramic window looked out across the ranch and the immense spread of the New Mexico landscape.

Beyond the rolling grass meadows and timbered slopes he could see the jagged march of the mountains clawing its way to meet the blue of a clear and empty sky.

No matter how many times Gardener looked on this view it made him tight in the throat. The sheer magnificence of the high country always took his breath away.

He sat in the massive leather armchair facing the window and sipped his drink.

Whenever he needed to think things out, to work them over in his mind, Gardener would come to this room, with its book-lined shelves, racks holding his collection of pistols and rifles, where the smell of polished wood and leather mingled with the aroma of the mellow whiskey he took.

Across the ranch yard, close to the creek that meandered across the property at this point, he could see the preserved cabin that the first Gardeners had built. They had sheltered under their wagon while they'd constructed the crude cabin, moving into it exactly one month to the day of their arrival. That had been back in the 1800s. Taking residence in the cabin had been their first move in establishing the Gardener dynasty. From that day on they had staked their claim to the great valley, spending the next years putting down roots, fighting and struggling against men and the elements. They had carved an empire out of the raw wilderness, winning and losing along the way, but they had emerged victorious. Wealthy and powerful. A force to be reckoned with.

Always ready to diversify, the Gardeners had moved with the times, changing course on many occasions, and they'd survived while many of their contemporaries had fallen at the wayside. They spread across the country, seeking new ventures. Always ready for a fresh challenge: cattle, mining, oil, manufacturing. In the mid-1930s Gardener Global was formed, a powerful parent company that reached out and took on America and eventually the world. Gardener Global now had affiliates in countries across the globe.

The Gardener clan had always been patriotic, faithful to the country, and their name had always been connected with the military in all its forms. They had served in every branch of the services, being present in every major conflict, and a great many lesser ones.

Chase Gardener, one of the surviving career soldiers, had a distinguished service record. Twice wounded, he carried every major military award there was. Over the years he had fought and won his battles, rising through the ranks by his own efforts. It had been no secret that his journey would have been made easier if he had ridden on the backs of former Gardener warriors. He had known that and because of it he had to prove he could do it on his own. He was respected because of that decision.

He made general early in his career through his determination and his innate military skills. No man under his command would have denied him any of his plaudits. He treated every soldier with respect, never expecting any of them to carry out an order he wouldn't perform himself, and he was known as a commander who refused to even consider using his men for anything that smelled of sacrifice beyond normal expectations. His stubborn defiance in the face of higher authority had earned him a reputation as a tough son of a bitch. His men loved him. They would do anything he asked without hesitation, safe in the knowledge he wouldn't betray them or send them to their deaths on a whim or a political ploy.

Which was why, now, he was struggling with his

conscience, attempting to win himself over to the possibility that he was asking his men to follow him into a struggle that went against everything he had previously believed in.

He had committed himself and his small group of immediate people to a course of action capable of bringing them to their knees. They could all end up in prison.

Or at worst, dead.

And above both those things was the ultimate punishment, something Gardener tried to close from his thoughts.

They could all be branded traitors.

Traitors to the nation they had sworn to protect and defend—the United States of America.

He felt his anger rise when he thought about what he was about to do, anger at the manner in which he had been forced to this decision.

Because of ineptitude, blinkered vision and at times downright stupidity, America was being betrayed by the very people entrusted with its protection, the administrations that had allowed a gradual slide into the fractured society that America was now.

Gardener had a list in his head that detailed all those things that had been allowed to escape notice. Small things in the beginning, but over time they had expanded until they now presented actual dangers. In many cases dangers that were too established to wipe out. At home and abroad, America was losing its way.

Some would have argued that the nation was big and powerful enough to turn its back on the rest of the world and to look after itself, to reestablish that situation of many years ago when isolationism had been the watchword. The two world wars had ended that forever. The 1914-18 conflict had opened the doors. The Second World War had became the flood and afterward it was no longer a world where America could step back and ignore the rest of humankind. Too many things had happened, too many ties had been forged through adversity and dependency. Politics apart, there was an ongoing connection between the U.S.A. and the rest of the world. Gardener had no problems with that in principle.

His concern was with the way America was conducting its affairs. Too much leeway was being given. The guilty weren't chastised enough. The hammer wasn't falling on the hostile regimes basking in America's misfortunes. Not just sitting back and benefiting from those misfortunes, they were helping to orchestrate them. Gardener's own intelligence network had incontrovertible proof that Middle Eastern states were doing everything they could to prolong the disaster that was post-war Iraq. Too many American soldiers were still dying there. The tottering government was failing to get to grips with the internal corruption and the undercurrent of violence that was forever gnawing away at the fabric of everyday life. Gardener had to agree with

Iraqis who were still saying life had been better under Hussein if only from the point that his iron control had kept the country stable. There were no insurgents running around the country blowing things up or assassinating at will. No car bombs. No suicide killers. And all the while there were those individuals from the old regime gathering their forces and preparing to cause more unrest, waiting for their moment when they might attempt some uprising that would push the Americans and their allies out of Iraq and return it to its former masters.

In Gardener's eyes, the American administration was floundering. It was too complacent, still believing that the interminable conferences and the government they were having to support in every degree would become strong and able to rule.

What was needed was a hard line. The time for pussyfooting around the edges had been and gone. It was time for action—in the extreme. It needed someone who saw the truth with unblinkered vision. A man who had the military experience to do it as it needed to be done.

Someone like General Chase Gardener.

He put himself in the spotlight without embarrassment. Not with vainglorious intentions, but with a sound background in the need for strong military insight and tactics. His record spoke for him. He was a man who loved his country, who prided himself on dedicating his life to maintaining the American way. With all its faults, it was the best damn country in the world, and he wasn't going to let the weak and vapid Washington administration sell it down the river. Too much had been sacrificed to allow America to fall by the wayside.

Gardener's brief introspection was interrupted by someone knocking on his study door.

"Yes?"

Behind him the door opened.

"Mr. McAdam, General."

Gardener sighed. He had been waiting for this meeting for the past couple of days. Ever since he had returned from Turkey two days earlier.

Turkey, 2 Days Earlier

"TIME TO MOVE, Khalli," Chase Gardener said.

The man seated at the window nodded slowly, pushing up out of the chair. Tall, lean, with a handsome face and a neat, trimmed beard, he smiled at Gardener.

"I'll miss our times together," he said. "On the other hand I probably won't have all that much too spare for daydreaming."

"If this goes as we planned, you won't have time to do anything except what you're gong back for."

Khalli al-Basur smiled. He picked up his coat.

"Chase, you have offered me more than any man could hope for. My exile has been too long. This is what I have wanted but could never do with Hussein in command—a chance to return to Iraq and make my wish for a united country come true."

"We all want that, Khalli. Iraq has been through a long, bad time. Now we need to bring her back into the light."

"And accommodate ourselves at the same time?"

"No crime there. Iraq has something the world needs."

"Don't you mean, what the U.S.A. wants? And Gardener Global especially?"

"I stand corrected. We understand each other, my friend. No pretending this is going to be easy. First priority for both of us is making the transition to full power. If we pull that off, the rest should fall into place."

"Then we need good luck for both of us."

Gardener considered the word for a moment.

"If luck is the word, it's something we make for ourselves. To be honest, I've never really depended on something as fragile as expecting fate to pass me a winning hand. Luck didn't make me what I am. That came from knowing what I wanted and going for it. Same applies here. We both know what we want. It's up to us to take it in both hands and beat it into submission."

Gardener turned as someone tapped on the door.

"Come in."

The door opened and Harry Masden, the CIA pilot provided by McAdam, stepped inside.

"We're set, General. Plane's warmed up. If we're going, it should be now. Once the weather clears, we risk being spotted."

"I'm ready," Basur said, picking up the small bag he was taking with him. "General, next time we meet it will be in the office of the Iraqi president."

"That's the kind of talk I like to hear, Khalli."

They shook hands. Gardener followed them to the door and stood watching as Khalli and Masden crossed to the plane, leaning into the wind. Dust was sweeping in off the hills. Gardener checked his watch. Given the prevailing weather, the flight would take about two hours. After that, Khalli's supporters would spirit him away to a secure place to wait for the time he would make his appearance in Baghdad.

Gardener stayed at the door until the small plane moved along the makeshift strip. It was almost out of sight before it rose into the air, banking sharply as Madsen set it on the course that would take across the border into northern Iraq.

Renelli appeared, his lean face shadowed as he bent to light a cigarette.

"This really going to work, General?"

"We'll know soon enough, son. Hell, the only way to get things to happen is to give them a kick-start. If we get everything we want out of this, America is going to be in one hell of strong position. Our man in the Iraqi government, making the decisions, and the world's richest oil deposits under U.S. control. If we want to stay on top, we need that oil to keep the machine running. The U.S. military machine is the biggest in the world. We keep it that way, no damn country can stand up to us."

Renelli smiled. "When you move into the White House are you still going to be General Gardener? Or President?"

"Well there's a thing I haven't given much thought to, Rick. It's something for me to consider on the flight home. Let's get out of here, this damn place depresses me…"

GARDENER'S TRAIN of thought was disturbed during the flight back to the U.S. He received a call from Ralph Justin. The senator sounded nervous.

"Ralph, just take a breath and tell me slowly."

"McAdam told me to watch my back until he resolves this problem. I asked him if he'd spoken to you. He said there was no need to worry you, but I think it warrants enough to be on our guard."

"Fine, Ralph. Just tell me what the problem is. I can't comment until I know that."

"There have been some people snooping around. Talking to my staff. Your name came into the conversation. They identified themselves as Justice Department operatives. McAdam checked them out but can't come up with any information. It's like they don't exist. Chase, they showed up at my town house, too."

"Did you say anything?"

"What do you take me for, Chase? Of course I didn't say anything."

"Strikes me these men are just fishing. If they had anything solid, they'd have done more than just talk."

"Who are they? Why is there no record of them on file anywhere?"

"Ralph, you know as well as I do there are discreet agencies in existence. But they can't do a damn thing without proof. As long as we stand firm, they can only guess."

"Aren't you concerned?"

"My only worry is these people wasting our time. Ralph, just carry on as normal. Leave these people to me. I'll look into it. Just remember who you are. If they bother you again, be yourself."

"Myself?"

"Yes. An arrogant son of a bitch. An important man who has better things to do than to have his life invaded by these minor officials. You should be working on what you're going to do with all that oil money coming your way."

Something close to normality returned to Justin's voice. "Thank you, Chase, I'll take your advice. I may see you when you return." He added dryly, "That's if I have time to spare, of course."

"Listen, I'm calling a meeting at the ranch. I need you there."

"There's a Senate meeting tomorrow, early. It'll break quickly because it's Friday and the weekend is coming up. I can fly out as soon as it's over."

"Good. It'll give us time to clear the air. And while you're at the ranch no one can bother you."

Gardener finished the call.

"Trouble, General?" Renelli asked from his seat on the other side of the plane.

"More of an irritant. Justin has been visited by agents who say they were from the Justice Department. McAdam tried to get a line on them but couldn't find anything."

"Could be a cover for some covert agency. I'll look into it when we get back."

"Good. I probably don't even have to say this, Renelli, but if you locate these people and have them in your sights long enough…take them down. I don't give a damn who they work for. If they're checking us out, they're not with us. They're against us. The enemy. So we deal with them. Understood?"

"Taken as read, General, sir."

"Renelli."

"Sir?"

"Change of plan. Tell the pilot we're going straight to the ranch. I'll stay there. You can take the plane and get back to what we talked about. Look into this Justice Department shit and find Jacobi."

"Yes, sir." Renelli half turned, then looked back. "We going to have problems, General?"

"It's how you define the word 'problem.' Things are happening. Whether they become problems as such depends on how we handle them in the short term. It's all to do with strategy, Renelli. Work that out and execute it, the problems become achieved objectives."

"Sounds like a military operation to me, sir."

Gardener smiled. "Exactly, son, because when it comes down to it, we are in a war. And that's how we deal with it. You know the situation with Jacobi. We can't afford to have anyone out there who might make a connection with someone prepared to listen. There's too much riding on this. High stakes. Find Jacobi. Bring him down. Bury him and anything he knows with him." Gardener paused. "Understand?"

Renelli nodded

"Clear, General, sir."

"Damn nuisance this coming now. I need to concentrate on Khalli. McAdam has Khariza to deal with. So it looks like you're going to have to handle Jacobi and the Justice agents, Renelli. Take whoever you need from the unit. Track that son of a bitch and remove him."

"No sweat, General. We'll find him and deal with it."

"This needs swift action. Time's not on our side."

"I'm on it, sir."

Renelli picked up the phone and called the base. He spoke at length to his team and told them to be standing by once he reached them, then went up front to give the pilot his new instructions.

When he returned, he sat across from Gardener and gave him an update on his call to his team.

"We have those two Justice agents under observation, General. I've had a standby team watching the senator. Purely as a security precaution. When those men appeared at his office and then his house, the team put a tail on them, so we might not know who they are, but we sure as hell know where they are. Hope I haven't overstepped my authority, General."

"Renelli, when something like this happens I realize I couldn't have made a better choice. We have to watch for any moves from people like these Justice people. If you hadn't seen fit to cover the senator, who by the way doesn't need to know about our surveillance, then we would not have these people under our watch. Good work, son. Keep it up."

Gardener nodded, satisfied that he had the situation under control. He knew, come the day, that he could always depend on his own people.

They were his people and they would die proving it. What more could a commander ask?

Rick Renelli had been in Gardener's command for more than eight years. He had been a good soldier. But Renelli's problem had been his overenthusiasm and that eagerness to please had proved his undoing. During a covert operation, Renelli had allowed his forceful attitude to kick the rule book out the window. The end result had been the death of three men in his squad and his superior officer badly wounded. On their return stateside Renelli had been accused, tried and discharged from the service.

Two weeks after that he had been contacted and advised that someone had a job for him. A night flight had delivered Renelli to the Gardener ranch in New Mexico and a meeting with his former commander. Gardener had bawled out Renelli big-time, angry at the way he had wasted his military career over a moment of laxity. The dressing down hadn't been so much for the actual misdemeanor, more for the fact that Renelli hadn't managed to extricate himself from the charges. The moment the shouting was over, Gardener sat Renelli down for a meal and offered him a position in the clandestine group he was forming to spearhead his planned coup against the U.S. government and the planting of a Gardener man within the Iraqi government, one who while steering the country toward a new democracy would also smooth the way for Gardener and his global enterprise. As far as Gardener was concerned, the U.S. had to maintain a strong grip on the Iraqi oil deposits. They were vitally important given the way the world was moving. America's strength depended on its military machine and the industrial power base that served it. Allowing that to slide would leave America open to both internal and external threats.

The current administration, with its low-key polices and too much appeasement, was betraying the U.S., opening the gates to allow America's detractors to gain ground, and showing a weaker face to the world in general. Chase Gardener had the vision to push America back to the top, his policy one of standing hard against the people trying to hold it back. Renelli, a man who had previously seen the way Gardener performed, had no argument with the man. He was a soldier, eager to serve under his old commander, and he'd accepted Gardener's offer the moment it was laid in front of him.

While Gardener had his service people and contacts already lining up behind him, there was going to be a need for something off-the-books, a force that could stay away from the military machine as such, while carrying out Gardener's covert operations with the least possible hindrance. Renelli, a combat veteran, was a natural. He could run the covert team, funded through one of Gardener's many financial outlets, without having to concern himself with military protocol. Once the operation moved into gear, time would be a vital consideration. One of Renelli's responsibilities would be unforeseen events. Incidents that might, if left to run unchecked, create difficulties for the main body of the operation. Gardener had explained from the start that due to the fluidity of the Iraq situation and the homeland operation, which would require the ability to be changed at a moment's notice, he—Renelli—would need to be able to operate within that kind of environment. Renelli saw no problems there.

Before dawn the next day Gardener and Renelli had drawn up a list of names of men, all ex-military, who were to be approached. The offer would be similar to what Renelli had been made. The men were to be recruited to be part of Renelli's team. Answerable to him initially, but with Gardener as their ultimate commander. The team was to be provided with anything it needed. Money was no object. Gardener had the ability to procure weapons that could be concealed via judicious juggling of orders and needs. Renelli's team would be paid for by Gardener Global and equipped in part by the U.S. government.

The scheme had been running smoothly until Luke Jacobi had stumbled in on something he would have been better to have left alone. That hadn't happened. A little ball-fumbling had allowed Jacobi to walk out free and clear. Gardener wanted retrieval before Jacobi passed that ball to someone who might run with it.

A LITTLE WHILE LATER Gardener received a call from McAdam himself.

"If this is about the senator, I already know."

McAdam grunted his acknowledgment.

"We're working on it."

"Rod, I have my own people on it. The matter is well covered."

"Fine. That wasn't the main reason I called," the CIA man said.

"So?"

"My contact at the White House has just confirmed

what we talked about yesterday. Time and date as previously suggested."

"Good news, Rod. And your other reason for calling?"

"They picked up Lane in Chechnya. Word just came through. He'd gone looking for that camp Dushinov is said to have running to train Khariza's crew. Some local agreed to guide him in, but they were caught. The local ended up near skinned to the bone. Dushinov's men took Lane. That's all I know right now."

"Did Lane pass anything back before he was captured?"

"No. I hadn't heard from him for a few days. Last report said he had a line on something, but he couldn't give it a name yet."

"Can you get anyone else into the area to try to extract Lane?"

"Not likely. Our station man said the locals have shut down. He can't get anyone to help him after what happened to Lane's guide. This rebel, Dushinov, has the territory out there pretty well under his heel. The guy has kicked the Russians out of his backyard for Christ's sake. He's a scary mother."

Gardener leaned his head against the backrest of his seat, staring up at the curved ceiling of the cabin.

"Chase, you still there?"

"Just thinking. If we can't get to Lane, then all we can do is hope he keeps his mouth shut. Call me sentimental, but I hope he dies quick. If he starts to get a loose tongue, it could have repercussions. Rod, I'll be back at the ranch late tonight. Fly out and we'll have our talk. The senator will be joining us for the weekend."

"I already had the same thought about Lane," McAdam said. "I'll see what I can do about him. Don't hold your breath for quick results. Talk to you later."

Gardener closed the line. He experienced a moment of excitement at McAdam's confirmation of the earlier news. It meant they were going to have to bring their move forward, but he found that stimulating. The sooner they embarked on their plan, the better. Too much waiting around could allow things to go wrong. He was taunted by the image of the man named Jacobi, one of his former soldiers. A man now on the run because he hadn't gone along with Gardener's plan and had then taken it a step further by doing some snooping on Gardener and his people and had actually got them on videotape. Gardener was trying to contain the matter, but the longer Jacobi remained on the loose, the greater the chance he might expose what was about to happen. Having to bring matters forward like this was going to eliminate potential disasters. He called Renelli to update him on the situation.

"Still leaves Jacobi on the loose, General. He could find someone and convince them to look at that damn tape. Word gets out, it would make it impossible for us to go ahead." Renelli paused. "General, you don't think those Justice agents have had contact with Jacobi?

Maybe he got through to them and it's why they've been doing some checking?"

It gave Gardener a moment's concern.

"No, I don't believe so. If Jacobi had told his story and played that tape, we would be locked down by now, wondering what day it was and where we were."

"If that's so, General, we're still clear we need to move fast."

"I agree. I was giving the problem some thought just before you called. So we can't afford to leave Jacobi on the loose where he can do anything to harm us. Can we, Renelli?"

Chase Gardener Ranch—Present

GARDENER STOOD, turned away from the view with a certain reluctance and watched the CIA man crossing the floor. McAdam looked like someone carrying the troubles of the world across the shoulders.

"Good trip, Rod?"

"Nice to see we can keep our sense of humor," McAdam said. There was a slight peevish edge to his words. He pointed to the tumbler in Gardener's hand. "Mind if I have one of those?"

Gardener gestured to the liquor cabinet.

"Help yourself. The large tumblers are at the back."

McAdam took him at his word and filled a tall glass. He took a long swallow then topped up his glass before he turned back to Gardener, who had made his way to his big oak desk. McAdam took one of the comfortable leather armchairs facing the desk.

There was a silence until Gardener waved his own tumbler as an opener.

"And?"

"I managed to get word to one of my people in the area. He's going to try to get a line on Lane. No guarantees. That part of the world is hard to crack. Those Chechens are difficult to deal with. They still operate like the damn Mafia. My guy will do what he can."

"What about these so-called Justice Department people? Who the hell are they?"

McAdam shrugged. He swallowed some of his drink.

"A shrug hardly impresses me, Rod."

"What else can I say? Chase, I have trawled every damn database I can access. There isn't a known intelligence agency in existence I haven't looked at. These guys are so off the wall it isn't true."

"So who are they? Reporters from *Sixty Minutes?* Come on, Rod, there has to be something about them."

"Nothing, Chase. If they're genuine, then they don't have any recognizable remit."

"Well, we need to find out. Jesus, Rod, you work for the fucking CIA. You run a covert black-ops section with carte blanche independence. Right now I am not exactly impressed by its competence. I brought you on board because we've worked together in the past and you think along the same lines as I do. Rod, wake up. I can't afford any slip ups. It's a damn good thing my people have these *Justice agents* under observation."

McAdam didn't even flinch. He swirled the liquid in his glass.

"If it wasn't for me, you wouldn't have had Khalli about to stage a comeback in Baghdad. Call the Agency all you want, Chase, but it was me who got you your info on Khalli. I found where he was in hiding. I got to him and delivered him. So get off my back. And don't think I'm trying to score points, but how's the search for Sergeant Jacobi coming along?"

Gardener smiled. "Good one, Rod. We're still looking. He's been shut out from making contact with anyone. The man is alone with no one to turn to. We'll get to him. Only a matter of time."

"Unless he finds someone who'll listen to him."

"He isn't going to find a sympathetic ear in that direction. The word has been circulated. I'm using up favors on Jacobi. Sooner or later, he's ours."

"Let's hope sooner."

Gardener inclined his head in agreement.

"Rod, your room is made up as usual. Go catch some sleep. You look like you need it. I'll see you at dinner. The others will be here by then. Plenty of time to talk then."

"Yeah, I'll do that. I could do with some sleep. It's been a busy few days and flying always knocks me sideways."

Gardener chuckled to himself as McAdam left the room. The man had only flown in from Langley. Over the past few days Gardener had traveled all the way to Turkey and back, with no more than a few hours' sleep from start to finish.

Rod McAdam, CIA, was an important part of Gardener's group. The man had contacts all over. He had undercover people in place across the Middle East. The former Soviet Union. It was hard to put a finger on places where he didn't have people. His position within the Agency meant that he controlled a large number of operatives and his long standing in black-ops meant much of his control was only known to himself. He was able to intercept and divert, even cancel out information that might point the finger at Gardener and his group. McAdam was an opportunist, tired of his profession and looking for a way out. His tie-up with Gardener meant he would be able to walk away from the Agency with a payoff far in excess of anything the CIA could have provided. The trouble with McAdam was his eternal pessimism. He let himself get wearisome and there were times when Gardener could have allowed himself to lose it with the man. He always checked himself. Bawling McAdam out would prove to be a negative action and Gardener needed the man's access to information.

"WHEN WE ENTERED into this we all knew what we were doing. It was and still is a regrettable decision.

But it has to be done because the current situation demands it."

Gardener glanced around the room. He saw no evidence of disapproval.

"Andy, how are your people shaping up?" he asked an Air Force major.

"I have over thirty percent of my command behind me. The ones who matter. I realize that still leaves a sizeable group who refuse to join us. I have them confined to the base under guard and I have that locked down until further notice."

"It's a pity we have to do that," Gardener said. "This is still a democracy and those people have their rights. But we'll just have to ignore those rights until this situation is stabilized. After that they can make their final choices."

Ralph Justin leaned forward. "A question."

"Ralph?"

"I understand you are communicating between yourselves. How is it no one is picking up your transmissions? Just remember, I'm a plain old civilian."

"It's a good question and deserves an answer," Gardener said. "Murphy, you want to explain."

Lieutenant Harlan Murphy, a communications officer from Gardener's command, nodded.

"We're using one of the Gardener Global satellites. It's out of the military loop and anything going via that satellite is on an encrypted secure channel. We use simple phrases to authenticate who we are to one another. No reason for anyone to even break into our transmissions."

"Haven't I read somewhere that no form of communication is entirely safe from eavesdroppers? Aren't there listening devices in orbit?"

Murphy smiled. "Quite correct, Senator. Listening programs are getting even more sophisticated every day. But they are far from fully perfected yet. Even the Echelon system, as good as it is, has a hell of a lot to deal with. The sheer amount of electronic traffic it has to filter is phenomenal. It can't get everything. And we make certain that all our conversations are limited to a vocabulary that avoids code words or links Echelon might recognize."

"And does that make us safe?"

"Hopefully for as long as we are going to need to be safe," Gardener said. "I understand your concern and the logic behind it. To answer your last question, and I believe Murphy will back me on this, we are vulnerable to a degree. But every gamble has its downside. As far as we are concerned, communication between our units is vital. So we take the chance. And don't worry about Gardener Global. The people running the communications are not going to be a problem."

"So how ready are we?" the senator asked.

"We have equipment and personnel in place, so we're ready to go. The first objective will be to detain the President during his trip to Bucklow."

"Easier for you than trying to deal with him in the White House."

"Just one of those tricks of fate," Gardener said. "Out of the blue he sets up this trip to visit the site and talk with the survivors. We couldn't turn down an opportunity like that."

"Resistance?" Justin asked. "You must have considered it."

"Of course. It may be necessary for us to engage in combat with units still loyal to the current administration. Casualties will be regrettable if they refuse to surrender."

"Killing our own isn't the best way to engender public sympathy."

Gardener turned to face the senator.

"Show me an alternative, Ralph, and I'll use it. If not, I can't afford to go soft over those who choose to resist. Someone is going to get hurt. Possibly on our side, too, but even though I understand that, I have to accept the losses."

"What about my fellow government representatives?" Justin asked.

"Same goes for them. They take it on board. If they don't, they're against us."

"Chase, we're going to need those people."

"Agreed. I don't see a major problem. Ralph, you of anyone in this room should understand the way the people on the hill work. They fight with words, not guns. I don't believe we'll be facing a bunch of Congressmen armed with M-16s, or at best skeet guns."

Justin smiled at the image. "Interesting thought, but I'm sure you are right."

"Ralph, that's where you will come into your own. You've never hidden your opinions about the way the administration has been running the country, or its handling of Iraq since the war. Truth be told, there are enough like-minded on the hill for you to swing the whole damn herd your way. Once we have their backing, we're on even firmer ground."

"Sounds wonderful in theory. But we both know it might not run uphill the way we want."

"Oh, hell, Ralph, you'll have my people backing you. Don't forget that. There'll be a lot of yelling and stamping of feet, but once the dust dies down and they see what we've done…"

"Taking control of key installations? Power, water, broadcasting? Your men at the major airports and seaports?"

"We move fast and we move hard. With the top men of the joint military command secured in detention who gives the orders? *We do.* We deploy and we stand fast. The President is moved out of office and I make my national broadcast. I explain what we're doing and why. The American public wants something done. Too many of our people are dying out there in Iraq. That needs to stop. They're tired of the loss of life. The drain on

America's resources. We come out of this with right on our side. Plus our hand on the Iraqi oilfields. Getting control of those would be one hell of a plus in our favor."

Senator Justin picked up the pot and refilled his coffee cup. He sat back and took time to listen as the tight group of men discussed the upcoming takeover of the American government. He saw the earnest looks on their faces, the calm tone of their voices, and he saw that they were fully committed to what they proposed to do. They viewed their actions as necessary. Something that America needed to stay the most powerful nation on Earth, and they were prepared to stand against the elected government and the President of the United States to carry their project through.

Ralph Justin was with them. He had to be because he walked the same path and held the same reasoning. There was a need to protect their own interests, both political and business.

There was a need to get America back on track, to show that the country still had a grip on sanity in a world that was on the slide. The Iraq situation was one example of good intentions turning sour. The country, far from stepping into the light, had backtracked and was being plagued by insurgent terrorist groups who struck where and when they wanted. By indecision and a lack of consolidation. Razan Khariza was back from the wilderness, engaging in all kinds of subversion.

Doing his damnedest to move back into the power position within the country. The actions of Khariza and his group, trawling in sympathizers from all over the place and setting them free to kill and destroy, had all the earmarks of an attempted return to the old ways.

Chase Gardener didn't want, couldn't allow, that to happen. His own candidate for the position of Iraq's leader. Khalli al Basur had to be the one. An immensely popular man throughout Iraq, Basur had been forced to flee for his life when the Hussein regime, worried by his position in the country, tried to have him killed. Basur had survived three assassination attempts before realizing he would achieve nothing if he died. With great reluctance, he'd decided to go into exile and continue his fight away from Iraq.

Basur had years of experience in the oil industry and it was through this that he had met Chase Gardener. The two men had become friends. They had lost contact following Basur's disappearance from Iraq. Even McAdam had had difficulty locating the man. Basur had done a good job of hiding himself away, unsure of whom he could trust. It had been down to McAdam's black-ops team to find Basur's hideaway, taking him to one of McAdam's own safe bases before McAdam himself had stepped in and delivered Basur to the Gardener ranch, where he had stayed until arrangements were completed to return him to Iraq. Basur would make his return, but as a partner to Gardener rather than the U.S. government.

With the buildup toward war with Iraq and Gardener's growing disenchantment with the way America was being run, the germ of what was now taking place had been born. Both men, now staunch supporters of each other, almost fell into their alliance. It was created through their individual needs and with an eye to the future. Gardener aware of the benefits of having such a popular, influential man as Basur controlling the country and the Iraqi speculating on the long-term advantages of becoming tied in with a man as powerful and long-sighted as Gardener.

The details of their alliance had been mapped out over long sessions that ran each day and into the night. Gardener's intention to move on the President had run parallel to establishing Basur as head of Iraq. That in itself was no easy challenge, but once the word had been covertly circulated among Basur's loyal supporters that he was preparing a comeback, the way opened and unrolled before them like a red carpet.

Always moderate in his views, Basur had wielded unstinting influence among the hierarchy of Iraqi politicians. An overwhelming majority thought as he did, but their views and opinions had been kept hidden during the Hussein tenure, because the former president, aided by his infamous secret police, the Mukhabarat, was always waiting to pounce on the unsuspecting who let slip any such views. Basur had had no illusions concerning his well-being as long as he defied Hussein. His pride wouldn't allow him to simply stand by and allow

Hussein to carry on unchecked. Basur made broadcasts whenever he could, gave speeches and generally made himself an embarrassment to the regime until out of pure frustration the word was passed down that he had to be silenced.

Basur had realized he'd gone too far. His time in Iraq had come to an end. If he wanted to stay alive he would have to put himself into exile, hopefully able to return when the opportunity arose.

Now that opportunity had presented itself. Basur had taken the gamble and returned to Iraq.

Gardener was showing his flag. Determined to make his own stand. He had gathered his people and drawn his battle plan.

The line had been drawn in the sand, and there was no stepping back from it.

Gardener had the military know-how. The ear of like-minded men. He also had a vast conglomerate behind him, a worldwide business empire that had influence in numerous countries. Gardener Global was a powerful weapon in any sense of the word.

Ralph Justin was the political weapon, his knowledge invaluable. Within the Washington corridors of power, he held an enviable position. He could sway opinion with ease. His persuasive skills were what legends were made of. Justin knew he was playing for high stakes this time. The rewards made the risks acceptable.

The CIA had information channels covering the

globe. Rod McAdam's covert team, run virtually as a separate unit within the organization, gave Gardener access to data and locations he would otherwise have been denied. The CIA man, of them all, was less driven by national loyalty and more by what he was going to gain financially. Chase Gardener was aware of that, and he kept a close eye on McAdam while using everything the man had to offer. McAdam's information about the President's visit to Bucklow had been a prize worth having.

GARDENER TOOK a phone call from Renelli.

"Those Justice guys are heading for Leverton. They were followed to a private airstrip where they had an executive Beechcraft waiting. Our boys did some checking. The pilot filed a flight plan for Arizona."

"That pair is nothing but busy," Gardener said. "You know what to do, Renelli. I don't want them poking around at the base. Keep them away. If you have to make them get lost, then do it."

"I'll set it up, sir."

"Do it quickly. I'm starting to get disturbed by these men and their nosing into our business."

"Consider it done."

Gardener banged down the phone and sat drumming his fingers on the polished top of his desk, trying to keep his mind on matters closer to hand. The soft tread of approaching footsteps made him look up.

Ralph Justin stood a few feet away, an inquisitive expression in his eyes.

"Not bad news, I hope."

Gardener shook his head. "More of an irritant. That was Renelli. It seems our men from Justice have decided to take a trip to Arizona. They're starting to annoy me, Ralph."

"Understandably at this stage. I assume you have the matter in hand?"

"Very much so. Fort Leverton is way out in the middle of nowhere, so we can keep matters out of the news."

"Isn't there a town nearby?"

"That's correct. Leverton. It's where the base got its name. The town is small. Isolated. No local law. Just a spot on the map. If needed, my people could keep the place closed up. No one in, no one out."

"Maybe I shouldn't be listening to this, Chase. It sounds distinctly unlawful."

Gardener grinned, raising his glass. "Hell, Ralph, it damn well should sound unlawful. Do you think I'm about to lose sleep over those damn Justice snoopers?"

The senator didn't have to even consider his reply. "The thought never crossed my mind, Chase. Not for a second."

"Taking the President of the United States hostage is going to overshadow anything we do to a couple of government agents."

"Looking at it from that angle, I have to agree."

Justin moved away to rejoin the main group, leaving Gardener alone at his desk. It gave him the chance to consider what was coming. Events were about to take place that would, if it all went to plan, change the face of America. Gardener had to accept that it was a massive challenge. A necessary one, because the way things were going now, the U.S.A. was slowly disintegrating. Future generations deserved better, and if they were going to benefit from America's potential, then getting the country back on track had to be done now. Leaving it would only allow their enemies to gain ground. Once the grip was loosened, it was only too easy for the power to shift. Chase Gardener had too much faith to let that happen. As long as there was the slightest chance he could do something to steer the country back on its righteous road, then he would take it, and to hell with those who didn't like it.

CHAPTER TWO

Leverton, Arizona

"The base is about five miles farther west," Jack Grimaldi said, his finger tracing an imaginary line across the map.

He had parked their rented SUV in the parking lot outside a diner beside the highway that ran through Leverton. It was a dusty town perched alongside a dusty road. Mainly timber buildings, with a few built from stone and even a couple of adobe structures, Leverton sat on the Arizona landscape, small and insular. Its location made it that way. On the far side of the town was a straggling tract of houses and a few trailers.

"Let's go check out the locals and see if they have anything to say about their neighbors," Schwarz suggested. He pushed open the door, feeling the solid heat rush into the SUV's air-conditioned comfort. He opened his jacket. "I hate this place already."

Grimaldi climbed out the other side, using the remote to lock the SUV. He joined Schwarz, and they made their way to the diner. The lot had a number of dusty pickups, a couple of cars and a semi-trailer rig.

"You think when we go in the place the customers will go quiet and all stare at us?"

Grimaldi shrugged. "If the local tough picks a fight I'll let you deal with him."

"Thanks, partner."

"You don't need to thank me."

Grimaldi pushed open the door. It opened with a soft squeak.

"I'll get around to oiling that some day," a female voice said from behind the counter. The woman was in her thirties and attractive. Her hair, a rich chestnut, fell to her shoulders. She wore a while T-shirt and faded Levi's jeans. Her arms and face were brown.

Grimaldi smiled as he perched himself on one of the stools.

"Coffee?" she asked.

"For two," Grimaldi said as Schwarz slid onto the next stool.

Mugs were placed on the counter and the woman brought a pot to fill them. Her gaze kept wandering to Schwarz's exposed shoulder rig.

Schwarz had turned to check out the other customers. When he turned back to the counter, he was shaking his head.

"What?" Grimaldi asked.

"Not a flicker. None of them paid us the slightest interest."

"You watch too many movies."

"I lead a sad and lonely life."

The coffee was rich and hot. Grimaldi leaned over and picked up a menu card, scanning it.

"House special is on the board," the woman said, waving a finger at the chalked menu. "Ham, eggs, fried potatoes, spiced beans."

"That's on here, too. Same price," Grimaldi said, indicating the menu. "What's special about that one?"

The woman smiled. "It's on the board."

Grimaldi thought about that for a minute. "Okay, ma'am, you got me there. Two house specials."

"Be a few minutes."

She turned and vanished into the kitchen area, returning to check their mugs before moving from behind the counter. She went from table to table, talking freely to her customers, refilling coffee mugs. When she returned to her place behind the counter, she topped up their mugs.

"You fellers aren't from hereabouts."

"Does it show?"

"The suits give you away."

"See," Schwarz said. "I said we should have bought those big hats and the fringed shirts."

"Fringed shirts?" The woman chuckled at the

thought. "You boys must be from back east some-where."

"That we are, ma'am. The big, bad city of Washing-ton."

"Oh, my, I feel humbled in your presence," she said, faint mockery in her tone.

"Long time since I humbled anyone," Schwarz said.

"So what are you doing all the way out here?"

Schwarz slid his ID wallet out of his shirt pocket. He laid it on the counter so the woman could see the Jus-tice Department shield and the encapsulated card with his details.

"Agent Tony Ryder," she read, then studied Schwarz's face. "The gun, I understand now. But you don't fit your picture."

Schwarz reached up to touch his cheek. He was still showing bruising from his encounter with Khariza's people at the wood-chip mill outside Bucklow.

"Work gets a little rough at times," he said by way of explanation.

"I guess so."

"Actually he fell out of bed," Grimaldi whispered.

"Yeah? Well, I hope she was worth it."

Grimaldi laughed and even Schwarz cracked a grin.

"Ma'am, I just hope your cooking is half as smart as your sense of humor," Grimaldi said.

"Why do you think I call it special?"

The food, when it came, was good. The Stony Man

pair ate without pause, realizing just how hungry they were after their three-hour drive. The woman, whose name was Louise, kept their coffee mugs filled. By the time Schwarz and Grimaldi had finished, the diner was almost empty. The only customer remaining was the driver of the semi-trailer.

Louise collected empty plates and mugs, ferrying them into the kitchen. She wiped down the tables, then returned to her place and poured herself a mug of coffee.

"You fellers have anything to do with Fort Leverton?" she asked out of the blue.

"Should we?" Schwarz asked, easing his jacket off and draping it on the stool next to him.

"Oh, come on, guys. I'm just curious. You realize how tiring it gets in here listening to talk about cattle and trucks and guns? Jesus, a girl could die of boredom. You fellers come in all suited up, flashing Justice Department badges and guns. What am I supposed to think? Or maybe you've come to check *me* out."

Grimaldi nearly made an inappropriate remark but checked himself.

"Besides," Louise said, "what else would bring people like you all the way out here?"

"You have much contact with the base?"

Louise shook her head. "I get some customers from time to time. Not much. They have everything they need out there. Anyhow, the big muckety-muck, General Gardener, who runs the place, is no public-relations winner. I heard he told his soldier boys to stay away from town. Doesn't like them mixing with us ordinary folk."

"The base off-limits, then?"

"You could say that." Louise smiled. "Don't always work, though. Couple of local girls kind of managed to get Gardener soldiers to date them. Well, you know what kids are like. I can remember when I used to do stuff like that."

"Couldn't have been that long ago," Grimaldi said.

"They teach you that kind of bull at Justice Department training school?"

"He was born under a maple tree," Schwarz said. "He's got syrup in his veins."

"G-men with humor? Never thought I'd see the day."

"Anything out of the ordinary been happening lately?" Louise glanced at him, her eyes showing interest.

"Like what?"

"You tell me."

"This is awkward, fellers. I promised someone I wouldn't say anything in case it brought her trouble."

"If things have gotten to this stage I'd say trouble was already in the frame," Schwarz said. "You mind if I have some more of that coffee?" He watched as Louise topped up his mug. Her hand was shaking slightly. Schwarz reached out and placed his hand over hers. "Take it easy. Okay?"

Louise put down the pot. She glanced across the diner. The trucker was draining his own drink. He stood and crossed to the counter, pulling money out of the pocket of his baggy Levi's jeans. He was a big man, barrel-chested, and could have moved his rig without the aid of the tractor. He glanced at Schwarz's shoulder rig, then the bruises.

"You boys cops?"

"Justice Department," Schwarz said. "Passing through. The bruises come with the job."

The trucker nodded, satisfied, then turned his attention to Louise. "Good as ever, Lou," he said.

"Where you heading this time, Charley?"

"Over to Flagstaff. They got me another load waiting." He counted out the cash and placed it on the counter. He squared his battered Stetson and nodded at Schwarz and Grimaldi. "Is she a good cook or what?"

"You said it," Grimaldi agreed. As Charley turned to go, he added, "Hey, you drive easy, fella. Have a good run now."

"Thanks." He eyed Schwarz. "Next time, try ducking, buddy."

They all waited until he was outside, crossing the lot to his rig.

"Louise?" Schwarz prompted.

She fixed herself a coffee, walked out from behind the counter and crossed to one of the tables. The Stony Man pair joined her. Louise sat and watched the big semi swing around and pull out of the lot, leaving a thin haze of dust in its wake.

"See the other side of the road? Just beyond that mess of brush?"

Grimaldi was the first to spot the dusty shape of a car.

"How long have they been there?"

"On and off the last day or so."

"Obvious question is why?"

Louise glanced across at Schwarz. "Cassie Stone," she said. "She isn't why you're here?"

"Never heard of Cassie Stone. Is she the one in trouble? Maybe you'd like to tell us about her."

"Remember I said about local girls meeting up with soldiers from the base? Cassie is one of them. She took up with this sergeant. Young feller. Real nice guy. Name of Luke Jacobi. This goes back two, three months. I guess they really took to each other. Whenever Luke got time, he'd come in here and see her. Cassie works part-time for me. They met in here first off. Anyhow, things were okay until a week ago. Cassie came to me and said she was scared for Luke. Seems he'd walked into some kind of problem at the base and didn't know what to do. I never saw him again after that. He stayed away. Cassie told me he'd called her a few times. Last she heard, he told her he was really desperate. He was sure someone was out to get him, but he didn't know who he could talk to about it."

"What about his base commander? General Gardener?"

Louise smiled, her expression bleak.

"It was Gardener he was scared of. Cassie told me Luke said it was Gardener behind all the trouble. He'd found something out that had made him a target. He told Cassie he had to get away from the base. She wanted to help, but he wouldn't tell her what he'd found out because it would only drag her in, as well. He said if they came looking for him she had to say she didn't know where he was."

"Did they come looking?" Grimaldi asked.

"Couple of times. They asked her questions. Cassie said she didn't know a thing and to leave her alone." Louise smiled at the memory. "She stood up to them. Told them she wasn't in the military so they had no jurisdiction out here. I added my two cents' worth, and the place was full, so those mutts couldn't do a damn thing. They didn't like it, but what could they do? Shoot us all?"

"So they just hang around waiting?"

"I guess. They try scare tactics. Standing over there taking photographs. I just lean out the door and wave. They generally go away then."

"So whatever else has happened, they haven't found this Jacobi," Schwarz said. "If they had, they'd lose interest in this place and Cassie. By the way, where is she?"

"She took off. Cassie was born and bred around here. Smart girl. She could have made it in one of the big cities. She just loves the country. Photographs wildlife. Paints landscapes. Sells them all over the state. She has a small place a few miles on the other side of town. Used to belong to her gran'daddy."

"So she took off where?"

"You new to Arizona? I guess so. You know how big this place is? Easy for one person to vanish if they want. Forget all your fancy dodads the Army might have. If Cassie wants to disappear, General Big-shot Gardener is going to have his work cut out finding her."

Grimaldi chuckled. "I really get the feel you don't like him."

"Does it show? The guy is a big-time asshole. Okay, so he's a military hero. Good. That doesn't mean he can walk around like he's God Almighty, throwing his weight about and messing up our lives. He comes in here I'll spit in his eye."

Schwarz glanced at Grimaldi.

"Remind me not to upset this lady." He turned back to Louise. "Gardener is the reason we're here, Louise, and from what you've said, Luke Jacobi might be part of the same thing. We need to get to him before Gardener's people. I understand you need to protect Cassie, but she might be our lead to him. We need to talk to her."

"Can you protect her?"

"If we can get to her, we can have her placed in protective custody until this is all sorted out. It's the best thing we can do for her. I wouldn't dismiss Gardener. He's no fool. Cassie may be good but he *will* find her in the end."

Louise considered the implications of Schwarz's words.

"You make it sound serious, Mr. Justice Agent Ryder."

"I can't go into all the background," Schwarz said. "Let's just say this stretches a long way from Fort Leverton and involves a lot of people."

"You know what just came into my mind?" Louise said. "That town in Texas. Bucklow. This have anything to do with what happened there?"

Schwarz had enough respect for the woman to not even try to play coy.

"In a disconnected way, it could have. I'm only telling you that so you realize what we're dealing with."

"Serves me right for asking." Louise placed her coffee mug on the table. "I have a cell phone in the back. Cassie gave it me before she left. Said only to use it if the situation couldn't be resolved any other way. I figure we could say that day's come. I'll call her and set up a meeting. After that, I'm going to trust you fellers. Don't make me regret this."

THE MEETING HAD BEEN fixed by Louise, who had acted as a go-between. Cassie Stone had given instructions, which Louise had passed on to Schwarz and Grimaldi. The meet was at an abandoned gas station twenty miles from Leverton. Schwarz and Grimaldi had been told to arrive and to wait until Cassie decided to show. They had left the diner, watching the stakeout car as they took to the highway. It remained where it was. Schwarz called Louise, as he had promised, and asked her if anything had happened since their departure.

"No. The car is still here. Hasn't moved."

"They could call in backup without leaving themselves," Schwarz said. "We'll just stay sharp."

"You guys look after Cassie."

"That's a promise. Louise, thanks for your help."

"I'm a sucker for a good-looking guy with a badge. You ever get this way again, I always have coffee on the go."

"I'll remember that."

"Hey, sounds like the man made an impression," Grimaldi said.

"Just drive, sonny."

THEY KEPT AN EYE on the highway behind them as the miles slid by. Nothing showed. The highway looked deserted. Schwarz didn't let himself be fooled. If Gardener was as smart as he was made out to be, Schwarz and Grimaldi would be under some kind of observation. Schwarz found himself scanning the cloudless sky.

"If they have airborne watchers, they won't be anywhere we can see them," Grimaldi cautioned.

"Yeah, that's what worries me. Problem is, we don't have any other choice. If we want to speak to Cassie Stone, we have to meet her. Risk or not, it's the only option."

They spotted the gas station up ahead at the twenty-mile mark and Grimaldi eased off the gas.

"I'll go out to meet her," Schwarz said. "Jack, you keep the engine running and be ready for a quick getaway."

Grimaldi nodded. "You got it."

He eased off the highway and ran the SUV across the dusty weed-choked lot. Schwarz opened his door and stepped out. The gas station looked to be in a sorry state. It had been abandoned for a long time.

He walked into the open, feeling the heat bearing down on him, and stood waiting, checking out the area. Nothing moved except a bleached sign swaying gently in the hot, dry wind blowing across the flat landscape. The only sound was the low murmur of the SUV's idling engine.

Schwarz waited patiently. He wasn't going to force the issue. It was Cassie Stone's move.

Sound caught his attention. Schwarz turned to see a tall, dark-haired young woman stepping out from behind the main building. She was wearing faded jeans, scuffed Western-style boots and a cotton shirt. It only took a glance to make Schwarz realize why Luke Jacobi had taken up with her. Cassie Stone was beautiful. Even in her slightly disheveled state, she had the looks to turn heads at any distance.

"Cassie? I'm Agent Ryder." Schwarz held out his badge. "That's my partner, Agent Myers, in the SUV. Louise told us to meet you here."

Stone looked as nervous as she actually was. It showed in her agitated manner. The way she paced back and forth, her eyes on the move as if there were things lurking in every patch of shadow. Behind every object.

"Cassie, tell me what you want to do," Schwarz said quietly. "Stay here or move somewhere out of the area. You decide."

"They'll still find us. Don't you understand that? They've been watching me. Waiting for Luke to make contact. I didn't even answer the phone at home. It's why I moved."

"We can take you away from here. Coming with us will stop them doing anything. And maybe we can help Luke."

The girl didn't appear convinced. Her head suddenly snapped around as a distant movement caught her attention. Schwarz followed her gaze and saw that it was nothing more than the wind stirring dry brush at the edge of the lot.

"Luke said—"

Cassie turned again, peering back along the highway. The intensity of her stare caught Schwarz's attention.

And this time he spotted the pair of dark 4x4s speeding in their direction.

"Damn. I told you," she said. "I told you they were watching."

"Okay, you were right. So let's go. Now."

Schwarz grabbed her arm and pushed her in the direction of the SUV. Grimaldi had seen the converging vehicles and he reached behind him to open the rear door.

The lead 4x4 made a sliding turn off the highway, dust billowing up from beneath the wheels as it bounced across the lot.

"Go," Schwarz yelled as he placed his left hand between Cassie's shoulders and boosted her in through the rear door of the SUV. He heard her startled cry as she hit the seat. He followed her and they were thrown flat as Grimaldi hit the gas, sending the SUV away from the gas station.

The 4x4 slithered to a stop, lost briefly in the swirling dust. The driver hauled the wheel around, powering up and sending the vehicle in pursuit. There was a screech of tires on tarmac as the second 4x4 had to brake to avoid hitting the first vehicle. The brief delay lost the pair of vehicles precious seconds before they took up the chase.

Schwarz climbed into the passenger seat. He glanced in the side mirror and saw the 4x4s pick up speed and fall into position.

"Cassie, where does this road go?" Grimaldi asked.

"Runs through the desert. Nothing around for at least twenty-five, thirty miles."

"I knew she was going to say that." Schwarz glanced at the speedometer. "They going to outrun us?"

"Depends how close they want to get before they start shooting."

"I don't think I needed to hear that," Cassie said.

Schwarz turned to face her. "Let's talk, Cassie. About Luke. Why exactly did he run?"

"He…he said he'd overheard Gardener and some of his people discussing some kind of military take-over. The President was going to be involved some-how. Luke got it on videotape. He got panicky because he was spotted. He called me and said it wasn't safe on the base for him anymore. He had to get away. I wanted to go with him, but he said it was too dangerous. He didn't want me to get involved. He said they might be watching me." She paused, her ex-pression angry and defiant. "He was damned right about that."

"Did he say where he was going?"

"I think he said something about trying to get home. I mean, he was trying not to show it, but he was scared. He didn't tell me anything else. Just somewhere away from Fort Leverton."

"You're doing great. Cassie, did he say anything about reporting what he'd heard?"

She shook her head.

"He wasn't going to say anything because how could

he be sure he wouldn't be talking to someone allied to Gardener? He can't trust anyone. That's why he needed to get away. He needed time to think things out."

"How did he get away?"

"I left my Mustang for him. Parked at the side of the diner. He called me on his phone after he took off to let me know he was clear."

Schwarz fished his cell phone from his pocket and hit the speed-dial number that connected him to Stony Man. He found himself speaking to Barbara Price.

"I need a background check on a Sergeant Luke Jacobi. Stationed at Fort Leverton, Arizona. General Chase Gardener's command. Everything you can pull. Home location especially." Schwarz glanced at Cassie. "Vehicle license plate?" She recited the number and Schwarz relayed it. "Anything you can pick up on that, as well."

"What's this all about?" Price queried.

"Jacobi could be a lead to whatever Gardener's up to. He has some kind of tape evidence. About Gardener and some action against the administration. The President's name was mentioned, too. The way I read it, Jacobi's gone AWOL because he believes his life is in danger."

"And?"

"Right now I have to go along with it. We met with Jacobi's girl and uninvited guests have decided to show up."

"Is it causing you problems?"

"Might if they catch us."

"Gadgets, I never know if you're serious or just making fun of me."

Something clanged against the rear of the SUV. More hits rattled along the bodywork. The tailgate window glass cracked.

"What's that?" Price asked.

"Things just got serious," Schwarz told her, and cut the connection.

JACK GRIMALDI STEPPED harder on the gas pedal. The SUV surged forward, pressing him back into the seat. He held the wheel lightly, feeling the powerful vehicle respond. Grimaldi studied the road ahead. It cut through the featureless desert terrain in a straight line. There was nowhere else to go. Leaving the highway would mire them down in the soft sand that lay on either side. Grimaldi's only course was to keep them on course and ahead of the two pursuit vehicles.

"I don't believe this," Cassie yelled. "They're shooting at us."

"Luke must have walked into something they don't want broadcast," Schwarz said.

He reached down to open the carry-all on the floor between his feet. From the bag he pulled out an M-4 A-1 carbine and a full 30-round magazine. Schwarz snapped the magazine in place and cocked the weapon, flicking the select lever to full-auto. Cassie's eyes widened in surprise when she saw the weapon.

"What are you doing?"

"They call it staying alive, Cassie. Believe me, those jokers back there are not practicing."

"They'd kill us? Just to stop me telling what I know? But I don't really know anything. Luke didn't give me all the details about what he'd heard."

"They don't know that, Cassie. As far as they're concerned Luke could have heard too much and he *might* have passed it to you. And you might be able to guide them to where he is."

Stone leaned across and punched Grimaldi on the shoulder.

"So why aren't you getting us away from them?"

"Lady, if we had turboboosters I would have lit them way back there. I can't make this go any faster than it does."

"Some cops you turned out to be. I need *The Punisher* and I get *Starsky and Hutch*."

Schwarz checked out their pursuers. The 4x4s were closing the gap. Whatever they had under their hoods was proving to be a sight more powerful that the SUV's power plant.

"If you've got anything left, better get ready to use it," Schwarz said to Grimaldi.

Grimaldi had already checked his rearview mirror.

"Where's the Lady when you need her?" he murmured to himself, referring to the *Dragon Slayer,* the state-of-the-art combat helicopter he was normally to be found piloting.

"Cassie, I want you down on the floor between the seats," Schwarz said, his tone warning the young woman he was in no mood for an argument.

As she slid off the seat, Stone heard the rattle of slugs hitting the back of the SUV. This time the rear window shattered, showering the interior with glass fragments.

Schwarz climbed onto the rear seat, bracing his arms on the backrest. He sighted in the M-4 and fired a short burst that impacted with the closest 4x4, scoring burn marks across the hood. He fired again, this time raising the muzzle a fraction, and put his second burst into the windshield. He saw the glass star under the impact of the 5.56 mm slugs. It failed to shatter.

Toughened glass able to resist the force of his shots.

Schwarz swore under his breath. The disadvantage of the short version of the assault rifle was the reduced bullet impact. The carbine version of the M-16 was under capacity when compared to its parent weapon. Not a great deal, but enough to need closer range when it came to penetration.

"I need that son of a bitch closer," Schwarz said over his shoulder.

Grimaldi didn't question the request. He trusted his partner's skills. If Schwarz needed the target up close

and personal, then that was what he would get. The
Stony Man pilot checked his mirror, estimated his
speed, and did some neat footwork with the gas and
brake pedals. The SUV dipped in front as Grimaldi
bore down on the brake, wrestling with the wheel to
keep the heavy vehicle on track. His maneuver reduced
speed without losing control and avoided tire burn. Behind them the 4x4 driver realized he was closing too
quickly and hit his own brake, burning rubber and
throwing smoke up from under its tires.

For Schwarz the looming closeness of the 4x4 meant
a bigger target. He maintained his position, leveling the
M-4 again and this time when he eased back on the trigger, the volley of 5.56 mm slugs went right through the
windshield, filling the passenger area with a hail of
splintered glass. Schwarz caught a blurred glimpse of
startled faces turning to bloody masks an instant before
the 4x4 spun out of control, sliding broadside across the
highway. In the same breath that he called out for
Grimaldi to pick up speed, Schwarz hit the 4x4 with another burst, raking the exposed road wheels. Black
shreds of rubber blew out from the punctured tires. The
4x4 lurched, then began to turn over. Slowly, it seemed
to Schwarz. The second 4x4 ran into the stricken vehicle, the impact helping to flip the already unstable vehicle. It hit on its side, then began to roll, its momentum
taking it along the tarmac, raising a wide tail of sparks.
Fragments of bodywork flew in all directions. The sec-

ond 4x4, its front end crumpled by the impact, came to a shuddering stop and the crew was forced to watch the toppled vehicle crash and burn its way along the highway, coming to rest on its roof, fire starting to lick its way through the crumpled frame.

The final image for Schwarz was of the second crew moving in to attempt a rescue. A short time later there was a burst of orange flame that rose skyward, followed by a pall of smoke. Schwarz slumped down on the rear seat, still clutching the M-4. Stone was watching him from her position on the SUV's floor.

"Are they still following us?"

Schwarz shook his head. "No."

"They meant it, didn't they? I mean, about killing us?"

Schwarz didn't say anything. The expression in the woman's eyes was enough to tell him she already knew the answer to her own question.

"You have to find Luke. Before they do…"

CHAPTER THREE

Israel

"How's the food?" Ben Sharon asked.

T.J. Hawkins glanced up from his plate.

"Not bad."

"Coming from him, that's a compliment," Calvin James said. "Usually if it's not half a steer straight from a barbecue it gets the thumbs-down."

"Sophisticated living," Sharon said. "It's what we're missing."

"Any news?"

Sharon slid next to Hawkins on the bench seat and picked up a slice of bread.

"The security forces spotted an incoming aircraft on a heading for the oasis. When it was challenged it tried to lose them, refused to break off. One of the choppers hit it with machine-gun fire and it made an emergency landing in the desert. Helicopters followed it down. The plane's crew put up a fight. Three were killed. Two were taken captive, one wounded, but not badly. Here's the thing. They were later identified as ex-fedayeen. All they would admit to was acting on behalf of the illegally deposed Ba'ath Party from Iraq. Answering the call to arms from their brothers and we were all under sentence of death."

"It all sounds familiar," James said. "The sad thing is *they* mean it and the mess they're stirring up could lead to everyone in the region being at one another's throats."

"What about the payload on the plane?" Hawkins asked.

"Packed with enough high-explosive to have taken out Dimona. A detonation of that power would have breached the core and let out radiation that would have drifted wherever the wind decided to take it."

James leaned back from the table.

"What the hell next?"

"The Gaza Strip and the West Bank are both up in arms. The Israeli Defense Force is coming down hard because of the recent incidents, and the Palestinians are adamant they have nothing to do with what started all this."

"Could be they're right, Ben. From what we've learned these incidents, on both sides, could have been engineered by Khariza. To achieve exactly what's happening. It creates unrest in the region and it draws attention away from his main agenda."

"I understand that. The problem is getting my people and the Palestinians to accept it. The situation is at its worst level for a long time. We have hotheads on both sides ready to jump in and retaliate, regardless of the consequences. Just what Khariza wants."

"We might have fallen lucky with the bunch out at the oasis," James said, "but it hasn't put us any closer to nailing the mothers behind this Middle East conspiracy."

"There might be a way," Sharon said, "if you guys are willing to step over the line."

"I'm interested already," Hawkins said.

"I had a call from one of my informants. This man is so unofficial I'd be in deep trouble if my people found out."

"Why? Does he have two heads?"

"In some people's view he might as well. He's a Palestinian. I've used him a number of times and he's never let me down yet." Sharon glanced at the Phoenix Force pair. "Okay, there's always a first time. But I trust this guy."

"What does he have?" James asked.

"When he called he said he had a line on people he believes are working for Khariza. Says he can point me in their direction. The drawback is that we have to meet him in one of the cleared villages close to the Strip. Off the beaten track."

"That I'm not so happy about," Hawkins said. "Bad enough in a restaurant, or the back seat of a car. On his ground, away from any friendly backup, I mean…"

"Exactly how I feel. He's never demanded this kind of meet before. We always do it on safe ground for both of us."

"Do you smell something?" James asked. "Like he might be setting you up?"

"I'm cautious. When someone changes their pattern, it's got to have a reason. Doesn't always have to be for the wrong reasons though. Maybe he's feeling unsure. Maybe he has the feeling he's being watched."

"If he does have the right kind of information and someone's found out, could be he's being tailed." Hawkins toyed with his coffee mug. "If we go for this how do you want to run it, Ben? We're in your hands, so to speak, 'cause we sure as hell don't know the area we'll be going into."

"Just the three of us. If we have backup it could expose my contact. I don't want to go in with a full squad behind me. Take a group in and no matter how careful you are, things can go wrong. The more there are, the harder it is to hide them."

"Will your man run if he sees you've brought us?" James asked.

"I'd be grateful if you could watch my back. If this is a setup, I'll feel safer with someone checking the area when I go in."

"No problem."

"How soon do we go?" Hawkins asked. "I'd like to finish this chicken."

"There are few things I need to arrange," Sharon said. "We'll leave as soon as it starts to get dark."

When the Mossad agent had gone, James stood and crossed to the window. From his position he could see a wide vista of Tel Aviv and beyond, the sparkling waters of the Mediterranean Sea. The sun was bright and the colors dazzling. James watched the crowds on the street below, going about their daily business. Even as he took in the peaceful scene James knew it could change in an instant. All it took was the decision to detonate a planted bomb or the action of a suicide bomber, and the calm would be changed to chaos, pain and death. That was all it took. A fleeting second to alter the course of a day, and change it forever. Even when the initial shock had passed there would be those left maimed, suffering from the loss of friends, family, and with a memory that might haunt them for years.

He found his thoughts drawn away from Tel Aviv to a small community in the U.S.A. In Texas. A place called Bucklow. It was a community that would never be the same. The memory of that day was going to be with Bucklow for a long time. James hadn't been there, but he had seen the TV coverage and though it had been sanitized for the television audience there had still been that sense of loss and bewilderment on the faces of survivors. Even the television reporters had been affected by what they'd seen. It was in their voices. In their eyes. It was something a great many people would remember.

Calvin James was one of those people.

If Sharon's meet could throw any light on the people behind the local unrest it might also lead them to the ones behind the Bucklow attack. Not so much who, because they knew that, but perhaps *where* they were hiding out. Khariza and his group seemed to playing an elusive game, directing operations from a distance and letting others take the risks. It was par for the course. The top men stayed behind, while the faithful went out and sacrificed themselves on the altar of whatever cause they were supporting. It was always the same. The leaders hid themselves away and made the gestures in front of TV cameras. The faithful young men and women got themselves blown to shreds. James sensed there was something wrong with that equation. But right or wrong, it would go on until a way was found to neutralize the situation. If ever.

THE SUN WAS SLIPPING behind the horizon as Ben Sharon coasted the dusty, battered Toyota utility vehicle along the rutted street. The village, close to the Gaza Strip, had been cleared by the IDF some months earlier. Despite the damage, with many of the houses and stores being razed to the ground, a number of the occupants had returned, purely because they had nowhere else to go. The IDF made frequent checks to make ensure no hostile elements had taken up residence.

Dust was being stirred by a breeze that had come up in the last few minutes. It gave the already-silent and seemingly deserted streets of the village a dead feel, as if the feet of man had not been making impressions for many years. That was no more than an illusion. Sharon had already made James and Hawkins aware of the possibility that there were people around the place. Maybe even watching as they drove along the street Sharon had been instructed to use. It wasn't difficult to imagine they were being watched.

"There," Sharon said, pointing to a building that had once been a food store. The windows were open and blank. The front door hung on loose hinges, swaying back and forth.

"All we need now is Clint Eastwood to come out of that dust cloud," James said.

He was sitting forward, alert, his eyes flicking back and forth as he checked the surrounding area. He felt the Toyota sway as it slowed and, as they had planned earlier, he and Hawkins would slip out of the vehicle and take cover behind a wall. They each carried 5.56 mm Galil autorifles that Sharon had provided. Both weapons were loaded with 50 round magazines. As the Phoenix Force pair exited the vehicle, Sharon eased it along the street and came to a full stop outside the empty store.

"Any problems, use the com sets," James said before he vanished from the Mossad agent's sight.

Sharon had provided the communication units. They were compact, powerful and would at least allow them to stay in touch.

James raised his left hand and indicated for Hawkins to take the rear. They would work their way to the meeting point and check out the area while Sharon was inside. The moment Hawkins disappeared, James made his own move, staying close to the front walls as he closed the distance between himself and the store. He stopped frequently, scanning buildings across the street as well as those on his side. He took in doorways, checked the rooftops, as well. He didn't resume his advance until he was sure the way was clear. Physical checks were all he had, and from past experience he knew it was close to impossible to cover every spot where someone could conceal him- or herself. There was a point where the eye could be deceived by an expert in camouflage, concealment or just plain hiding. James was aware of that, and he knew Hawkins would be working from the same rule book. Caution was an admirable trait, but it could be used just as effectively by the enemy. *His* task was to reach an intended target by remaining unseen and unheard. To achieve that he was going to employ every trick he knew, and though it could be countered, it was sometimes a case of one skill canceling out the other.

James held his rifle across his chest, gaining some comfort from the feel of the weapon in his hands.

A thin veil of dust drifted across his field of vision, briefly obscuring the street. Some warning sense made him check the rooftops on the other side as the dust began to clear.

A black form had taken the same moment to move, advancing to a better position. James caught little more than a moving image. He knew he wasn't imagining it. There was someone on the far roof, closing in on the spot where Sharon had been told to meet his contact.

James pulled his com set from his pocket and thumbed the transmit button. After a few seconds he heard Sharon's voice.

"Heads up, Ben. It looks like we have uninvited guests. Rooftop on your side of the street. About two buildings away from your position."

"Okay," Sharon said. "I just spotted my gu—" The transmission ended abruptly.

Hawkins cut in. "What happened?"

"Nothing good. T.J., watch your back and check the roof levels."

SHARON'S CONTACT moved out of a shadow into a pale square of light. The moment he saw him, Ben realized something was wrong. The man looked terrified. He was trying to conceal it and failing badly. He was sweating, too, something he never normally did.

"What's wrong?" Sharon asked, but he didn't need an answer. He knew what was wrong.

He picked up a whisper of sound behind him. It might have been the drift of the wind sifting dust against the wall. The movement of a door.

Might have been.

Ben Sharon knew better.

He hunched his shoulders, leaned forward and turned on his heel to confront his attacker. He caught a glimpse of a shrouded figure, clad in a ripple of robes lifted by the errant breeze. The lower half of the face was covered by a kaffiyeh.

The man moved quickly, slashing at Sharon with the combat knife held in his left hand. The Israeli jerked to one side, felt the blade slice his clothing and experienced the keen burn as the tip opened a gash. Sharon's left shoulder banged against the wall, preventing him from moving any farther in that direction. His attacker used the opportunity to step in closer, aiming the knife at Sharon's torso. Back against the wall, the Israeli had nowhere to go. He braced himself and struck out with his own right hand, slamming the hard edge across the attacker's knife wrist. The blow was hard and the impact deflected the blade. Sharon followed through, gripping the wrist and pulling the attacker up close. He clamped his right arm tight against his side, the knife briefly removed from the conflict, pinned against his hip. Sharon brought his left fist around in a short, powerful punch that slammed against the attacker's jaw. The man grunted, dazed from the blow. Sharon hit again, harder, hammering his fist into his attacker's face. His adversary rocked under the ongoing barrage.

Sharon pushed away from the wall, swinging the knife man around and pushed *him* against the wall. He jammed the heel of his hand under the man's chin and slammed his head back until it cracked sharply against the stone wall. Using the folds of cloth as a grip, Sharon kept repeating the action. He saw the man's eyes glaze, felt him sag as the blows weakened him. Sharon caught hold of the knife hand and twisted, turning it against the joint. As soon as the man's fingers loosened their grip, the Israeli snatched the knife free. He yanked the now bloody kaffiyeh away from the attacker's face, exposing his battered mouth. Bringing the knife up, Sharon slashed the blade across the man's throat, cutting deep. The attacker gasped in shock. Blood began to well out of the wound as he was pushed aside.

Sharon turned to find his contact man. As he did, he heard the first crackle of autofire from the street close by. The Israeli yanked his Desert Eagle from its shoulder rig, moved forward and caught hold of his contact's shirt. He pushed the pistol into the man's side.

"You had better have a good excuse for this, Emir."

Emir, lean almost to the point of emancipation, held up his thin hands in protest.

"I had no choice. They forced me. Tortured me. You

must believe me, Sharon. They know about you and your attack at the oasis. It made them angry. They planned this to kill you. To stop you interfering in their business."

Sharon's planned response was cut short as he sensed someone close by. He yanked Emir into the shadow by the wall and turned on his heel, the big Desert Eagle tracking the figure that had appeared behind him. Sharon caught a thin sliver of light ripple along a steel barrel a second before the weapon opened fire. The burst raked the wall, exploding stone chips that peppered the side of his face. Dust misted the air as Sharon dropped to a crouch, his pistol held two-handed. He pulled the trigger as fast as he could, driving a volley of shots at the dark figure. He was rewarded with a stunned grunt, the figure toppling backward, hitting the ground with a hard thump.

Sharon ran forward as the wounded man struggled to roll onto his back, lips peeled back to expose white teeth against dark skin. The downed man was making harsh sounds in his throat. Sharon angled the Desert Eagle and hit the man in the head with a swift double tap.

From the shadows behind him he heard a soft moan. "Sharon…"

T.J. HAWKINS HELD the Galil steady as he laid down a burst. He felt the autorifle jacking out a stream of 5.56 mm slugs, saw them clip the parapet of the roof across the street. The robed figure had been ready to fire down on Sharon's position when Hawkins triggered his shots. The rooftop sniper tried to pull back as the line of shots marched along the roof edging, blowing out chunks of soft stone. He was way too slow. Hawkins had his trajectory adjusted by the end of the run. He raised the muzzle a fraction and his final group of shots hit the sniper in the chest, the impact slapping him down with deadly force. The sniper hit the roof, his weapon spilling from nerveless fingers, leaving him jerking and coughing in a spreading pool of his own blood.

"One down," Hawkins said into his com set. "Heading for Ben's position."

James acknowledged him with a sharp word, then concentrated on his own task. He eased along his section of the street, having seen a dark vehicle edging out of a narrow alley between buildings. The lights were out but he could hear the low rumble of the engine. The timing was off a degree, so the beat of the engine was uneven. The sound rose as the driver applied more gas to compensate for the poorly maintained vehicle.

The Phoenix Force pro brought the Galil into position, watching the progress of the vehicle. It was an open-backed pickup, with crouching figures hunched behind the cab. As the sudden outburst of gunfire erupted from the shadows behind James, the pickup accelerated, swerving from side to side as it made its way along the rutted street.

Gunners let loose from the pickup. James stepped back, hearing the deadly whack of the slugs pounding the dusty stonework shielding him. He waited only long enough for the burst to die away before he leaned out, the autorifle bursting with sound as he stroked back the trigger. He laid his first volley into the open back of the pickup, catching a couple of the men trying to maintain their balance on the lurching bed of the truck. There were cries of alarm and defiance. The pickup veered toward the spot James was firing from. The Phoenix Force warrior held his position and laid a long, hard burst at the cab, concentrating on the driver's area. He saw the side window and the windshield explode, showering the cab interior with glass. Then his 5.56 mm slugs found their target, punching in through the driver's upper chest and neck. The driver lost control and the pickup spun away from James. It sped across the street and slammed head-on into the wall of a building.

As James came out from cover, he saw Hawkins running up the street to join him.

"We still have hostiles in the pickup," James yelled.

He had seen at least three gunners dragging themselves to their feet, bringing up their weapons, searching for targets.

There was a brief, silent pause and then the night was filled with the crackle of autofire.

James and Hawkins had the advantage. They were on their feet, targets acquired before the men in the pickup could do likewise. Some slugs clanged off the side panel of the pickup, some punched through yielding flesh, and it was over as swiftly as it had started.

"Check the street," James said.

Hawkins nodded and swept the area, his keen gaze searching the shadows, scanning the rooftops for other snipers.

James moved to the pickup. The crew in the back was dead, bodies riddled. He pulled away the kaffiyehs, studying the slack faces of the corpses. Then he walked to the front of the pickup and reached in to pull the dead driver off the steering wheel. The man's exposed, bloody face told James all he wanted to know.

"Clear," Hawkins called.

"Stay sharp," James said. "I'm going to check Ben."

He found the Israeli on his knees beside his contact man. Emir was on his back, his thin torso spattered with blood from the slugs that had caught him during the wild moments Sharon had defended himself. Sharon had pulled open Emir's shirt in an attempt to get at the wounds. Once he'd seen the ravaged flesh and the pumping blood, he knew there was nothing he could do for the man. He also saw the dark bruising and the raw burn marks on Emir's body. They confirmed what his contact had told him about being tortured.

"This must be my punishment for betraying you," Emir said.

"Forget that," Sharon said. "You had no choice."

Emir coughed, blood rushing from his mouth.

"I could have let them kill me. Once I had the chance and I could have jumped overboard from that cursed boat."

"What boat?"

"The one they held me on while they tortured me."

"Do you remember what it was called?" James asked, a gut feeling telling him he was going to know the answer.

Emir took a long time answering. His strength was fading and with it his reactions to questions. When he did speak, his voice was little more than a whisper.

"The *Petra*."

IT WAS WELL after midnight when Calvin James spoke to Barbara Price over the satellite link Sharon had arranged for him.

"What did we achieve? Some of the opposition dead. Ben's contact, as well. The poor bastard had been tortured into playing their game to lure Ben into an ambush. The only positive was Emir identifying the *Petra* and some information about visitors."

"Which places Zehlivic right in Khariza's camp. As if we needed more proof after the Bucklow incident."

"He isn't going to be forgotten when we take that damn boat out of commission."

"Your next move?"

"Yeah. This is one piece of the puzzle that needs eliminating."

Price picked up the strain in James's voice. "You guys doing okay?"

James chuckled. "Nothing a quiet, peaceful stretch of R and R won't cure. Put that on the agenda for your next board meeting with the boss."

"I promise."

"This is getting crazier all the time," James said. "The kill team we took out here was a mix of nationalities. If they were trying to pass themselves off as Palestinian, they got the mix wrong this time. They wore the right clothing but underneath I doubt any of them had ever been in the area before. They fouled up because they weren't supposed to end up dead. Ben was the target. He was the one supposed to go down."

"Reports qualify that Khariza is recruiting from a number of sources," Price confirmed. "As long as they're Islamic and have the cause in their heads, he doesn't care where they come from. Don't forget the man has control of enough money to import as many as he needs. And arm them."

"You know what's bugging me? Has been since we got into this?"

"What?"

"Khariza's motives."

"Run that by me again, Cal."

"Khariza was always a big Saddam Hussein loyalist. His return was expected to be aimed at bringing Hussein back. Or at least paving the way. Now that

Hussein has been caught, Khariza must know there's no way he's coming back. The way he's been going about things makes me think he's doing this for himself. Doesn't it rouse your curiosity?"

"When you explain it like that, I guess it does. Maybe you're not far off the mark when you say Khariza might be in this for himself. He sees the chance and goes for it."

"With the kind of financial backing he has under his control, it's a big temptation to go for the big prize. The king is dead, long live the new king."

"Cal, do you need anything at your end?"

"Ben's looking after us. Equipment. Weapons. Right now he's organizing to get us out to Zehlivic's boat."

"How soon are you leaving?"

"Couple of hours. We have a meet with some Israeli security people first. The identification of the kill team has the makings of persuading the Israelis that the Palestinians are not totally behind some of the latest attacks. No guarantees, but it might make them step back from making hasty decisions about reprisals. Ben said they were trying to persuade Palestinian representatives to view the evidence."

"Careful, Cal, you're getting close to politics there."

"Don't remind me. I'd rather face a combat situation any day."

"The way things are going," Price conceded, "that wish is likely to come true."

"Don't I know it."

"Good news for you. The rest of Phoenix is okay. Right now they're talking to Hal over a satellite link from U.S. MilCom in South Korea."

"That's great. I'll tell T.J."

"One thing I already heard that isn't so good," Price told him. "The North Korean supplier shipped a special cargo destined for Khariza. We don't know where it's going, but we do know what the goods are."

From Price's tone, James guessed there was something bad coming up.

"Three nuclear devices."

James absorbed the information in silence, glancing around the room. He saw Hawkins watching him. The expression on James's face warned Hawkins he was hearing unpleasant news.

"Makes our trip to the *Petra* a definite," James said. "We need to cover all bases in case there's information about these devices. Agreed?"

"Yes," Price confirmed.

"Something Ben's man said could tie in with that. About one of the visitors to the *Petra*. He saw him and heard him briefly. Name of Biriyenko. Russian. Check him out."

"Will do. Talk to you later."

"Cal?" Hawkins asked.

"Things just stepped up a notch, T.J."

James told his partner the news he had just received and for once the younger man had nothing to say.

South of France

"IT'S THE *Petra*," Hawkins said, lowering the glasses.

He moved from the window and handed the glasses to Calvin James, who took up the position and scanned the harbor below them. Radic Zehlivic's motor vessel was anchored in the middle of the bay around which the small port town was built.

James, Hawkins and Sharon had arrived earlier that afternoon, going directly to the small villa overlooking the harbor. The Mossad had fed them all the information they had on Zehlivic's current movements. The *Petra* had been in the vicinity for the past few days, with a number of visitors going out to the vessel. Sharon's Mossad spotter crew had managed to get a good selection of photographs of the visitors, as well as shots of Zehlivic himself.

They had also identified the man called Barak.

And once they had seen a woman being escorted along the deck. A photograph had been taken and sent to Stony Man as well as to Mossad and British intelligence. The woman had been identified as Ibn el Sharii's sister, Haruni.

"We'll go in as soon as your people have the transport ready," James said.

He was studying movement on the *Petra*, observing another set of visitors as they powered themselves to the vessel in a small motor launch. The group, four men, climbed the gangway fixed to the side of the *Petra* and vanished inside.

James crossed the room and sat. He picked up his glass of cool fruit juice and took a drink.

"Cal?"

James looked across at Hawkins.

"Just wondering who the latest visitors are."

"Some of them have been identified as Russian," Sharon said as he entered the room. "We ran checks on some of the earlier ones and at least two are Russian Mafia. We're still waiting for data on this one."

He passed over a photograph of a slender, well-dressed man in his late fifties. The man looked more like a banker than one of the Russian Mafia.

"What the hell is the Russian Mob doing mixed up in this?" Hawkins asked.

"Only connection I can make is that they're a good source for weapons. With the Chinese and Koreans out of the frame, Khariza is going to need a new supplier. The Russians are well into arms dealing. Steady supply. And they don't care who they sell to."

"They do a line in nuclear weapons?" James asked.

"Wouldn't surprise me if they supplied the nukes to the Koreans to work on."

Something clicked in Sharon's mind. He turned and left the room. He was gone for a couple of minutes, and when he returned he was holding up the photograph of the slender man.

"Almost forgot. Your people just sent this through," he said to James and Hawkins. "It's the man Emir identified. Fedor Biriyenko. He's a specialist in nuclear weapons. I'll bet he's selling his expertise to Khariza."

"They're leaving," Hawkins said.

Sharon nodded. "No sweat. It's their normal practice. They go out a few miles and drop anchor. Stay out then come back in to allow their visitors to leave. They like their privacy. Makes it harder for anyone to sneak up and check them out."

"That's all we needed to know," Hawkins said.

Sharon smiled. "You can swim, can't you?"

MOSSAD CAME UP with suitable cover—a fishing boat that spent its working life in the area. It was, in fact, a Mossad vessel. It provided good cover for the crew as they spent their days watching and assessing local traffic, gathering and collating information that was passed to Israel via the sophisticated communication equipment belowdecks.

The fishing boat provided James, Hawkins and Sharon with wet suits and snorkels. It would head out to sea, passing the *Petra* at a quarter-mile distance and drop off the trio. They would swim out to the *Petra* under night cover and board the vessel. Each man wore a signal transmitter. Once activated, it would alert the fishing boat and bring it back to rendezvous with the *Petra*.

"Nighttime swims are fine in the local creek," Hawkins observed as he pulled on his black wet suit.

"Halfway across the Mediterranean? Somebody has a hell of a sense of humor."

James was packing weapons into a waterproof bag. Each man had an Uzi, extra magazines for the SMGs and their handguns, which were also going in the bag. They all carried sheathed knives on the belts they wore and in one of the pockets of the wet suits were plastic cuffs. He also placed lightweight tac com units in the bag, closed it and checked that the seal was secure. He lifted the bag and felt its weight.

"Not bad," he said.

Sharon examined the bag, nodding.

"Be easier in the water."

One of the fishing boat's crew leaned in through the hatch.

"Target coming up," he said. "Three minutes, then you go." He looked them over, smiling. "Enjoy your swim."

THE WATER WAS smooth and warm. The fishing boat, traveling at a leisurely pace, maintained its speed. James could see the distant silhouette of the *Petra*, motionless, lights showing at deck level. He followed Hawkins and Sharon to the far side of the fishing boat. They were at the closest point to the motor vessel now. From this position, the distance would start to increase so they had no time to waste.

They climbed over the side of the boat, using the net

that had been hung there for their use. The equipment bag was lowered on a strong cord clipped to James's belt. The moment they were in the water they used their swim fins to push them away from the boat to avoid the undercurrent created by the boat's screws. Treading water, they watched the boat moving on its course, leaving a white foam in its wake.

Goggles in position, snorkel units clamped between their teeth, the trio began to swim out to the *Petra*. They swam steadily, conserving their energy. It helped that the water was warm and calm. The swell was almost gentle. It was a dark night, with virtually no moon. If it hadn't been for the *Petra*'s lights they might easily have overshot their target. They stopped a couple of times to rest, then picked up the pace again.

Nearing the *Petra*, they were able to make out armed men patrolling the deck. They counted three men, all armed with AK autorifles.

The stern deck was lit by angled spotlights that would deny them any decent cover. They checked out the bow, where there was less light and more cover from the hatch projections. Eyeing the armed sentries, the trio swam the closing distance and gathered by the anchor chain. They eased off their goggles and snorkel tubes. James hauled the equipment bag to him, unclipping the cord and looping it around the anchor chain.

"First one on deck hauls up the bag and covers the others until they get on board," he said.

He glanced at Hawkins, turning his eyes upward. Hawkins smiled.

"Looks like I just volunteered."

"Privilege of age," James said.

"I'll remind you about that sometime."

Hawkins took the cord and clipped it to his own belt before he grasped the anchor chain and began to climb. He made good progress, pausing when he reached the top to check the bow deck area. He was in time to see one of the armed sentries make an about-turn and disappear behind the main superstructure. Hawkins raised his gaze to check out the bridge. The interior looked deserted, with only subdued light.

"Here we go."

Hawkins reached up and grasped the bow rail, pulling himself up and over. He dropped to the deck, staying in a crouch and staying close to the side. He made another visual check, then began to drag the equipment bag to him. He lowered it to the deck, broke the seal and opened the zip. He removed the weapons and tac com units and placed them beside him. He took his Beretta, in the Snap-On holster, and attached it to his belt, clipped the power-transmission pack for his tac com on the other side and slipped the headset in place. Then he took one of the Uzi SMGs, freed and checked the magazine, made sure the breech was clear and then clicked the magazine back into place.

As Hawkins cocked the Uzi, James's head and shoul-

ders came into view. Hawkins beckoned and his
Phoenix Force partner slipped over the rail and
crouched beside him. Neither man spoke. James armed
himself as Hawkins had done, and attached his tac com.
Sharon had joined them in the meantime and equipped
himself.

The Israeli had finalized his weapons check when a
figure appeared from behind the superstructure. The
sentry had his AK tucked under his left arm as he pushed both hands deep into the pockets of his black leather jacket. He turned and leaned against the side rail, eyes
fixed on the distant shoreline and the blur of lights from
the harbor. It didn't take a mind reader to understand
what the man was wishing for.

The trio waited, weapons at the ready, hoping the
sentry moved in the opposite direction once he tired of
watching the shore. The sentry glanced toward the bow
briefly when he did move, turning away and walking
back in the direction he had originally come.

"I'll take starboard," James said, "T.J. the port side.
Ben can cover us from the bow. Okay?"

Hawkins, using deck gear for cover, moved across
the deck. James nodded to Sharon and eased along the
starboard deck, his Uzi up and ready.

The Israeli took up position at the bow, hidden from
view behind one of the raised hatch covers.

Within the confines of the *Petra*, as large as the vessel was, contact was bound to be not long in coming.

James found that out within an extremely short time as one of the armed sentries made an appearance just ahead of him.

The Phoenix Force commando flattened against the bulkhead, the Uzi turned in the direction of the approaching sentry. He let the man draw level before he leaned out and delivered a powerful blow, using the upper casing of the Uzi. The sentry slumped against the bulkhead and James caught hold of his shoulder and dragged him out of sight. As the sentry bent over, reaching up to clutch his bleeding face James hit him again, this time across the back of the skull. The man went down with a choked-off grunt. James relieved him of the AK, then tied the guy's wrists and ankles with plastic cuffs, rolling him close to the bulkhead.

"Starboard sentry cleared," he said into his tac com.

HAWKINS ACKNOWLEDGED the call just as his own target stepped into view. The sentry was also armed with an AK and also wore an autopistol in a shoulder rig. Hawkins watched the guy walk the deck in his direction and pulled himself into a hard crouch, ready to move the moment the man was close enough.

"Come on, boy, don't amble," Hawkins muttered to himself as the sentry strolled along the deck.

The Phoenix Force commando saw the man pause, half turn, as if he had heard something. Hawkins knew he couldn't allow the sentry to change direction and maybe walk in on James. He committed himself to action, moving even as the thought entered his head.

The Phoenix Force warrior, aware of time slipping by, pushed to his feet, directing himself at the sentry. The guy sensed the blur of movement on his right and swiveled in that direction. He caught a glimpse of Hawkins's taut features a split second before the younger man delivered his hard punch. It slammed against the sentry's jaw, snapping his head around, blood trailing in a ragged stream. The sentry grunted, stunned, and he was unable to make any effort to prevent Hawkins following up with a palm-edge blow that smashed into his throat. The sentry began to choke. He let go of his AK and grabbed his shattered throat, gagging heavily. Hawkins snatched the pistol from the man's holster and tossed it over the rail into the water.

"Port clear."

SHARON HAD CHECKED the bow section, satisfied he was clear. He picked up James's message, followed soon after by Hawkins's signal. The Mossad agent eased around the bow hatch cover and cut across the deck.

He was in the open, still making visual checks, when a dark shape emerged from one of the hatchways, walked across the deck and looked directly in the Israeli's direction.

Time froze.

The newcomer, a heavyset man with a shaved head

and hard eyes, reacted with surprising agility. He snatched the pistol tucked into the top of his dark pants and fired, all in the same coordinated movement.

Sharon felt the impact as the slug hit the outer edge of his left shoulder. The force turned him aside, so that the shooter's second slug missed by a fraction. The Israeli had stumbled to one knee. He set his teeth against the burning pain in his shoulder and brought up the Uzi, triggering without much target acquisition. His first burst rattled against the bulkhead, inches to one side of the shooter. The man jerked in alarm at the closeness of the slugs. He flipped the pistol back toward Sharon, pulling the trigger and putting a second slug into the Israeli.

Sharon fell back, coming up against the hatchway, which served as a support, allowing him to brace his Uzi for a second burst. This short volley was on target and caught the shooter in midtorso, stopping the guy in his tracks. Sharon fired again, a longer burst that he was able to control this time. He stitched the shooter from waist to chest, the 9 mm slugs punching in through flesh and muscle. The shooter went back against the bulkhead, desperately trying to gain control of his sagging gun arm. His finger, in spasm, jerked against the trigger and sent a single shot into the deck, raising splinters of wood. He raised his head and stared across at Sharon's slumped figure, his mouth moving. Blood was starting to stain the front of his shirt.

"SHOTS FIRED," James called through his tac com.

"Mine," Sharon said. "I took a couple of hits."

"Where are you?"

"I'm stable. Go for it. Pick me up on the way out. Watch your backs."

James swore softly. He knew Sharon had given them the only option. If they abandoned now, they might never get another opportunity. This was a one-off operation. It had to go ahead.

"T.J., we go. *Now.*"

"WE HAVE INTRUDERS."

Radic Zehlivic stared around the cabin, his face draining of color. He had heard the sudden rattle of gunfire, something he wasn't used to, nor wanted. His involvement with Khariza was supposed to be behind the lines, more of an arranger. His purpose was to provide anything Khariza needed materially. He had volunteered for Khariza to use the *Petra* for meetings, as a floating contact center, even as an interrogation base. The possibility that Khariza's dealings might attract opposition forces to his vessel hadn't crossed his mind, and in his moment of sheer panic he realized his naiveté.

Now that it was too late.

He turned to look in Barak's direction. The Iraqi had a smile on his lean face that scared Zehlivic more than the gunfire he had just heard. Zehlivic had always harbored mistrust and wariness where Barak was concerned. Plain and simple, he didn't like the man, but in deference to his friend Khariza he had masked his true feelings.

"Time to deal with these enemies of Iraq," Barak said.

"No..." Zehlivic protested, already knowing his words would fall like dead leaves on stony ground.

Barak motioned to the man who had burst in with the news. "Tell the others. No falling back. Show any weakness, and these men will devour us. Hold these men so I can take Biriyenko to Khariza. You understand?"

The man nodded and turned to leave the cabin.

"This isn't a game, Zehlivic," Barak said. "Pretend all you want, but even you had to realize this could happen one day."

Barak left the cabin, slamming the door behind him, leaving Radic Zehlivic alone with the terrible thought that his own life was out of his hands. Whatever happened now he would have no control over it in the slightest.

He stared around the luxuriously appointed cabin, fitted with the best money could buy, and felt a wave of nausea wash over him. His influence, his power, and least of all his wealth, meant nothing at this moment in time. None of it meant a thing. It wouldn't stop what was about to happen.

It was too late for regret, far too late for apportioning blame.

This time he had become involved in something that could ruin his life and at worst bring about his death.

Zehlivic slumped back in his expensive leather chair. The strange thing was, he couldn't even summon up enough of his faith to draw on. His fear overrode even that. So he sat and listened to the sounds of conflict, and waited for Fate to deliver itself at his door.

BARAK REACHED the companionway that led to the upper deck. He saw the lean figure of Topanov. The Russian was scowling. He reached out to grip Barak's shoulder.

"What's going on? We came to talk a deal. You told us we would be safe here."

"Then I was wrong. I don't think this is the time to discuss it. Do you? If we live, you can shout at me then."

He pulled free from the Russian's grip, reaching up to smooth the soft leather of his coat. There was a look in his eyes that suggested his distaste at being touched.

Two of Topanov's companions joined him, weapons already in their hands.

"Are we under attack?" one asked in Russian.

"I think so. Our Islamic host's security is not as good as he made out."

"I always said these idiots were worthless."

"They are still paying customers."

"Much good that will do if we're dead."

Barak was halfway up the companionway. He crouched at the top, peering around the edge of the hatch, checking out the deck area. He spotted one of the downed sentries, blood staining the bulkhead near where the man lay. Off to his right he heard the thump of boots on the deck as armed men moved in to check out the disturbance. Barak checked his handgun, easing off the safety.

He heard the clatter of the Russians as they came up the companionway behind him.

"Well?" Topanov demanded.

"Nothing yet."

"Sitting here is not going to get us anywhere."

Barak eased to one side, gesturing with his free hand. "Show me how they do it in Mother Russia."

"Bella, take the left. Machek, right. You're with me, Chekov."

The Russians burst from cover, spreading out as they hit the open deck. They raced for cover, weapons tracking back and forth, dropping to their knees the moment they were secure.

Barak watched, a faint smile on his face. All the Russians had achieved was to place themselves in the open, with nowhere else to go. They hadn't even checked whether the enemy was in front or behind them. Russian Bear was a good name for them. Big, physically strong, but with little in the way of forward thinking. The strategy of plunging in was fine up to a point. It was a short-lived move.

Barak only had one thought on his mind—the survival of the man named Biriyenko. Topanov and his heavies were expendable, but Biriyenko carried knowledge that was important to Khariza and the success of the mission. It was of little use to have nuclear weapons in his hands if Khariza was unable to make them work. And Biriyenko was the man to show how to do that. The loss of the *Petra* meant nothing, it had been nothing more than a movable base, a floating, transitional operations center, and they could easily set up another elsewhere.

SHARON SAW the Russians burst from the distant hatch and separate.

"Four out from the fore hatch. Spread across the deck. Stay sharp," Sharon said into his tac com.

The Israeli leaned back against the hatch. He could feel blood spreading across his left side where the second hit had lodged under his ribs. It was starting to hurt now, a dull ache nagging at his nerve ends. Sharon pressed his hand over the wound. He braced the Uzi against his other side and waited, finger touching the trigger.

He heard the sudden crackle of autofire, saw moving shadows farther along the *Petra*'s deck.

As SHARON'S WARNING reached James, there was a flurry of movement along the deck. He crouched, keeping close to the bulkhead. He picked up the bulk of a heavy figure detaching from shadow, the dull gleam of a handgun showing. The shooter paused, twisting to one side, raising the handgun. The muzzle was directed toward Hawkins's side of the deck. There was no time to send a warning. James reacted instantly, bringing the Uzi on line. He stroked the trigger and sent a short burst at the poised figure. The volley punched in through the shooter's chest side-on, coring in and puncturing his lung. The man went down on his knees, then toppled facedown.

James changed position as a burst of fire came his way. He heard the slugs chunk into the bulkhead, splintering wood. Glass shattered. James wriggled forward on his stomach. He could hear shouting. More shots came his way and he heard the follow-up of hard boots pounding the deck.

The rush of bodies alerted James. He pulled himself to his knees, coming face-to-face with a pair of shooters, each wielding an AK. One pulled the trigger and sent a burst that plowed into the deck inches from the Phoenix Force commando. Pale splinters of wood filled the air. James fell back against the deck rail, firing his Uzi and catching the first shooter in the chest. The man went backward, blocking James off from the second shooter. Anticipating the stance of the second man, he dropped facedown on the deck, angling his muzzle up, and as the first shooter fell away, exposing his partner, James already had his target tracked. The crewman fired at the expected target but James had gone. From his prone position, the commando put a burst into the man, the 9 mm slugs rising from waist to chest. The shooter went down hard and bloody.

SHOTS CLANGED OFF METAL in front of Hawkins. He muttered in anger at getting himself caught with only a steel capstan between him and the shooters. He didn't waste too much time debating his bad luck. Instead he rolled away from the scant cover, coming up on one knee, the Uzi already jacking out 9 mm responses.

His target, the Russian, held his big pistol two-handed as he rushed forward, firing as fast as he could pull the trigger. The slugs bounced off the capstan, whining as they flew into the air.

The Russian continued forward even as he felt the hard punch of 9 mm slugs tearing into his torso. He was a fit man, used to long hours working out, and his body bulk was thick with muscle. They reduced the penetration of the slugs a little but not enough to save him from severe damage. Bella kept on coming, breathing hard against the surge of pain.

"Son of a bitch," Hawkins said.

He angled the muzzle of the Uzi and laid a longer

burst into Bella's broad chest, the rounds carving a bloody path through flesh and bone, tearing aside anything in their path until they reached the Russian's heart. Distorted from contact with bone, the jagged slugs ripped the beating organ apart and Bella was dead on his feet as he took his final steps, a look of surprise etched across his face. He fell, almost into Hawkins's arms before the Phoenix Force commando stepped aside and moved on.

BARAK SAW the Russians go down. The fact that he had been correct did little to alter the situation. There was serious opposition on board. These were skilled operators. The Iraqi immediately thought about Mossad. The Israeli force was well-known for its fearsome image. But the covert team that had already clashed with Khariza's organization had also proved its worth. Barak knew they were still in the game. Under fire they had showed themselves to be strong adversaries.

He pulled back down the companionway, closing the hatch as he did and securing the doors from the inside. It wouldn't hold back any attacking force for long. Barak wasn't going to need long. He had a backup plan already worked out for such an eventuality. One of the reasons for Barak's longevity was his forward planning. He had always insured he had a back door available, a means of escape. It had saved him on a number of occasions and was going to do it again now.

Barak was a survivor. He saw little profit in martyr-dom. He wanted to do his living in the world around him, not in some imagined paradise. His faith kept him secure in the reality of the present. He would go to God when his time came, but he had no intention of bring-ing that moment forward.

He moved quickly through the *Petra*, making for Biriyenko's cabin. The man had insisted on his privacy. That was over now. Reaching the cabin, Barak pushed the door open. Biriyenko was seated at a fold-down ta-ble, his papers spread out and a laptop open in front of him. The Russian was hunched over the keyboard, his fingers busy with the keys. As Barak pushed into the cabin Biriyenko looked up, startled.

"What do you want?" he asked in English.

"Can't you hear what's going on up there? We are under attack. We have to leave. Now."

Biriyenko stared at the Iraqi. "Who…?"

"Mossad. American commandos. It doesn't matter. They are not here to sell you life insurance. Now move and bring your information with you."

Biriyenko snapped the laptop shut. He reached for his jacket and pulled it on. Turning back to the table, he scooped up the laptop and snatched at the papers strewed across the table.

Barak, at the door, gestured anxiously.

"Come on. Now. Before those boarders get down here."

"Where is Topanov? The others?"

"Alongside my people. Buying us time. Now move quickly."

Biriyenko followed the Iraqi out of the cabin, clutching his belongings to his chest, panic starting to overwhelm him.

The sounds of the gun battle going on overhead remained at the bow of the vessel. It was what Barak had hoped for. He needed only a few minutes at the opposite end.

Pushing the complaining Biriyenko ahead of him, he emerged from the stern hatch, staying low and edging to the rail, peering over. A small motor launch hung suspended from its davits. Barak leaned back and pressed the control button. The electric-powered davits began to lower the small craft.

"Get in," he ordered, and Biriyenko, still mouthing soft protests, almost fell over the rail and dropped into the launch. Barak climbed over the rail and into the boat closely behind the Russian. He maintained a watch on the rail as they were winched down into the water. He released the davit clamps, pushing the boat away from the *Petra* into the darkness beyond the motor vessel's spill of lights. He used one of the emergency oars to maneuver them farther away. Any noise he made was drowned by the furious gun battle. Only when he was fifty feet from the vessel did he sit at the stern and power up the outboard. He lowered the motor into position and felt the spinning screw push him forward. Taking the rudder, Barak turned the small craft away from the *Petra*. Biriyenko sat on the forward seat, head down as if it would make him invisible. He was out of his depth. In his ordered life these things didn't happen. He took an assignment, carried out the terms of his contract and returned to his safe existence while his fee sat in a secure account earning interest. The only thing going through his mind at the moment related to whether he ought to ask Khariza for extra money. Compensation for this unnerving experience.

The gunfire continued for a while after Barak had powered the launch away from the *Petra*. He dismissed the vessel from his mind. The event was in the past already. Barak had never been one for hauling old concerns around with him. His job now was to get Biriyenko to safety, contact Khariza and arrange for them both to be picked up and taken to wherever Khariza ordered.

The only thing that lingered for a few minutes was the regret that he wouldn't be able to continue his association with Ibn el Sharii's sister, Haruni. She was still on board *Petra*. There had been no time to bring her along.

Barak smiled to himself as he thought about the young woman. He had been devising such exquisite plans for the two of them. Haruni might not have agreed with his views, but then, that didn't concern Barak. Women had no say. They were there for only one purpose. He wished he had been allowed more time so he could have showed her how that worked....

THE STRUGGLE on the *Petra* was brutally short. With the Russians out of the picture the remaining resistance came from Barak's men. They fought fiercely but without the skills of seasoned combatants, making the simplest of errors and leaving themselves open to the superiority of James and Hawkins. The Phoenix Force warriors faced them down and took out four of the six defenders before the survivors surrendered.

The rattle of autofire died. An odd silence descended over the vessel, broken only by the soft moans of injured men.

James hit the button on his signal transmitter. It would bring back the trawling fishing boat. He and Hawkins made a tour of the deck, removing weapons and disarming the survivors. The confiscated weapons were disposed of by the simple expedient of throwing them overboard. The men who had surrendered were quickly cuffed, the wounded also secured.

The half dozen men who comprised the *Petra*'s crew were quick to show they had no involvement with the Iraq or Russian shooters. The captain himself, a quiet-spoken Italian, offered his help and set his crew to work tending the wounded.

With Hawkins supervising this operation, James went to check out Ben Sharon. The Mossad agent had remained where he had been since getting shot, one hand pressed over the more serious bullet wound.

"Your fishing boat should be on the way back," James told him. "Stay where you are, Ben. As soon as your people come on board they'll look after you."

Sharon nodded. He had shed a deal of blood and was feeling weak.

"I mean it. Take it easy."

"No arguments from me," Sharon said.

JAMES SAW that Hawkins had the situation under control. He told the younger man to inform the Mossad about Sharon as soon as they showed, then he made his way belowdecks, his handgun out, and began to check out the cabins. In the second one he found Haruni el Sharii.

The dark-haired young woman was chained by one ankle to the fixed leg of the cabin's large bed. The chain allowed her to move around the large bed but no further. The first thing he saw was her naked state. The smooth skin of her slim body showed bruising, as did her face. She glanced up as James stood in the open door of the cabin, looked at the weapon in his hand and then at his face, doing nothing about covering her exposed body.

"Haruni?" James asked gently.

She nodded.

James moved into the room, looking around until he saw what he needed. Picking up the blanket from where it had been thrown on a chair, he crossed to the bed and draped it around her shoulders, pulling it over her nakedness.

"We'll get that chain off as soon as we can and get you out of here."

He bent to brush stray hair away from her face. The gentleness in his touch freed the emotion inside and she began to cry softly, tears coursing down her bruised cheeks.

"I'll be back," James said.

"Who are you?"

"A friend."

"Do you have a name?"

"Calvin."

"Please…"

James turned back to her. She reached out to touch his hand.

"Thank you, Calvin. I was beginning to believe I would never leave this place alive." Her grip tightened. "Is he still on board? Barak? The one who brought me here?"

"I'll find out."

James couldn't recall seeing anyone who looked like Barak. The man's photograph had been in with all the other information Ben Sharon had shown James and Hawkins during their briefing before they had left Israel. The assassin's face had been one James wouldn't forget.

"Do you have any news about my brother?"

"He's alive. In the U.K. Part of my team located him and took him away from Khariza's people. Haruni, he was hurt, and shot, but the place they took him is good. He'll recover."

"Will I be able to see him?"

"It can be arranged once this is all sorted. I promise." James hesitated, then asked the question forcing its way to his lips. "Barak—did he hurt you?"

The young woman raised her head and stared James in the eye.

"If you mean, did he rape me, yes. More than once. I did not make it easy for him. As you can see. Which only made him angrier."

"We'll find him, Haruni. I promise."

She only nodded, reaching up to pull the blanket closer around her slender body.

James felt a bump against the *Petra*'s side and guessed that the fishing boat had arrived. He went up on deck and watched as Sharon's Mossad team came on board. Hawkins moved to intercept them, pointing out where Sharon was. The medic went immediately to attend to Sharon while the others dispersed across the deck. James asked if one of them could free Haruni from her chain and a Mossad agent went below.

Hawkins followed James belowdecks where they carried on with the search of the cabins. James briefed Hawkins on Haruni. They moved through the vessel, opening doors, checking each cabin.

They found the cabin Fedor Biriyenko had been using. Something in its appearance suggested it had been abandoned in a hurry. There were signs of occupancy. A chair pushed back from a fold-down table, a thin power cable still connected the wall socket. A half-drunk cup of coffee. Still warm.

"Cal," he heard Hawkins call.

Hawkins was standing in the open door of a cabin at the far end of the companionway. James joined him and looked over Hawkins's shoulder.

"Zehlivic."

James recognized the man from the images he had seen in data files.

Zehlivic was pushing up out of his chair, a sudden attack of fear forcing him to make some kind of resistance. He stared at the two Americans in defeat, knowing that his association with Razan Khariza had brought him to this. He didn't regret that association. Khariza had been, still was, a good friend. Zehlivic couldn't blame him for this occurrence because he had willingly entered into the game. His only disappointment was that he would be removed from any further dealings with Khariza and anything else he might have offered would be lost.

He moved to face the Americans, lashing out with his fists in a vain attempt to break past them.

James avoided the futile blows. He swung his left hand in a wide arc that connected with Zehlivic's right cheek, the blow stopping the man in his tracks. Zehlivic stumbled awkwardly, pain filling his eyes with tears. As he stepped back, he knocked into his chair and lost his balance. He fell to the floor of the cabin, groaning on impact, and lay staring up at the Americans

"You like travel?" James asked.

Zehlivic frowned at the question.

"I only ask because it's likely you'll be doing some soon. There are people who want to talk with you back in the U.S. About your involvement in the attack on Bucklow. You've heard the name I'm sure. Seeing as you own a business out there."

A chill invaded Zehlivic's body as he listened to the American's words.

"Channeling money through a business in your wife's name isn't going to get you off this," Hawkins said.

"Stay with him, T.J.," James said. "I'm going to find the radio room. Call in and let them know what we've got."

Stony Man Farm, Virginia

"THE REST of Phoenix is shipping out to join you in Israel," Barbara Price said.

James was speaking from the radio room, using the satellite radio link. He had given his status report, laying out what had happened on the vessel.

"It looks like Barak *was* on board, along with this Russian we identified, Fedor Biriyenko. The guy is probably here to give Khariza's people the lowdown on these nuclear devices. Just before I linked up with you we found out a small launch is missing. Barak must have taken off along with this Biriyenko character while we were engaged with the shooters."

"You can decide what to do once the rest of Phoenix arrives. Listen, Cal, do you think there'll be any problems with the Israelis over Zehlivic? The government is going to want him back here."

"They can be bloody-minded if the mood takes them. Hal will need to talk to the President if they do. Maybe his clout will straighten out the Israelis if they dig in their heels. What happened at Bucklow is going to weigh pretty heavy in our favor."

"Let's hope so."

"Any luck pinpointing that camp in Chechnya? If we can locate it fast enough, maybe we can catch up with Khariza."

"Nothing yet. Our satellite scans haven't come up with anything. Let me know how Ben is when you touch down in Israel."

Price disconnected and turned away from the desk and watched the activities of the team. They were all at their workstations, bent over keyboards or scanning monitor screens for some small scrap of data that might widen their current search parameters. Even Kurtzman was back after his enforced rest. He had grudgingly admitted it had been worthwhile. The first thing he had done on his return to duty was to check that his treasured coffeepot was still available.

While Huntington Wethers and Carmen Delahunt

concentrated their search for the rebel camp in Chechnya, Tokaido was digging into the Gardener-Justin connection. There was a degree of arrogance in the attitude shown by Senator Ralph Justin. His stand was strong where it came to condemning the U.S. administration for not doing enough to seal American control in Iraq. The attacks against U.S. interests and military personnel, which Justin only saw as increasing, wasn't being dealt with. He made no attempt to conceal his distaste at the deaths of American soldiers. On more than one occasion he had issued challenges to the administration to stand up and do something.

Gardener, known for his extreme views on how to deal with both internal and external problems, remained less vocal. There was a line he couldn't cross when it came to making criticism of the President. As a serving military commander, Gardener's views and feelings had to stay his own—in public at least. What he did or said out of the public view was another matter.

Wethers was tapping in coordinates, his monitor showing a changing display of maps and satellite images as he cross-referenced items. He had been working steadily, deep into his task, until he suddenly sat upright and banged his fist on his desktop.

"You have something?" Delahunt asked, swinging her chair to get a closer look at Hunt's screen.

"Maybe," he said, his attention focused on what he was doing.

Delahunt backed off, not wanting to distract him. She watched as his screen split, showing two different images, then began to scan in another that overlaid the first. Wethers transferred his findings to one of the big wall screens.

"This is a region that lies along the foothills of the Caucasus Mountains. Pretty isolated area. Nothing much to shout about. But there's a village, or what used to be a village, right here. It's been deserted for years. Everyone moved out a long time back."

Wethers enlarged the big-screen image. The aerial pictures, courtesy of the SARS satellite infrared cameras, zoomed in on the topography. The distant shot came into sharp relief as Wethers manipulated the digital imagery. He brought the picture into full-screen and the shapes and outlines of a number of buildings could be detected. Some in derelict condition with roofs and walls collapsed. Other in better condition.

"The one to the left has smoke coming from the chimney. If you look between the center buildings, there's a pickup parked there." Wethers flipped the image. "Twenty minutes later. Two men moving across the clear area. Both carrying assault rifles."

"Pretty sharp, Hunt," Delahunt said. "But is it Dushinov's camp?"

Wethers smiled, unflappable, as he leaned forward and tapped in more instructions.

"Always save the best until last. Had to wait until I

could use the satellite again. Did a full sweep of the village. More activity this time. The pickup had gone, but there was an old truck parked near one of the buildings with boxes being unloaded and taken inside some kind of dugout. See there. It's been carved out of that ridge just beyond the last building. Even looks like a machine-gun emplacement in front of it."

Delahunt stared at the screen, eyes flicking back and forth as she watched the silent activity the satellite's cameras had picked up and transmitted back to the Stony Man data banks. The clarity of the images was startling, given the distances involved. Wethers's diligence had paid off.

Especially when the camera moved in for a shot of a large, bearded figure directing the unloading of the truck. The man, unaware he was being observed from a satellite orbiting Earth, had little reason to conceal his identity. More than once his face was caught by the camera. There was no mistaking who he was.

Zoltan Dushinov.

Wethers had frozen his image and placed it on screen against a library photograph.

"How did you settle on this village?" Delahunt asked, her curiosity getting the better of her.

"I read through Dushinov's family background. Looked for the obscure rather than the standout stuff. There was a reference to the village Dushinov's grandfather came from. Told how it had been abandoned years ago because there was no means of keeping it going any longer. It was pretty isolated, near the foothills of the Caucasus Mountains. The place had been almost forgotten about. Dushinov is a Chechen patriot. He believes in its past. His family ties are in this region. I just took the gamble he might figure the old family village would be a good place for one of his hideouts."

"Smart thinking," Kurtzman said.

"Okay, Hunt," Price said. "Get a package together for Phoenix. Coordinates they can feed into a GPS unit. I want them fully briefed before they head into this place. I'll arrange for transport. We need to make sure they have everything they might need."

CHAPTER FOUR

Pennsylvania

Luke Jacobi sat behind the wheel for long minutes after he woke. Despite the severity of his situation he had been forced to stop and rest before he fell asleep at the wheel.

If he hadn't been scared, he would have thought more rationally and would have figured out the fact much earlier.

Jacobi could feel sweat soaking through the back of his shirt where he sat pressed up against the seat. His palms were wet where he gripped the steering wheel. All in all, he was a mess, which was to be expected. He had put himself in an unenviable position. Walking out the way he had, because he couldn't go through with what Gardener was planning, meant he had painted a target on his back that said, "Shoot me, I quit."

HE HAD KNOWN General Chase Gardener for a good few years. He had always looked up to the man, not just because he was Jacobi's commanding officer, but more for his leadership qualities. There was something about the man that inspired loyalty way above the norm. In that respect Jacobi had been in line with every other man under Gardener's command—until he'd become aware of just how far-reaching and devastating the general's operation was. Being a sergeant in one of the company squads, Jacobi had led his team into numerous engagements under the general's command, including the Iraq War to topple the Hussein regime. The company had seen action, had stayed on for a couple of months after the conflict, eventually being rotated back to the U.S. and finally to Fort Leverton, Arizona. It was in the months following the war that Jacobi sensed a change in Gardener. The general had started to withdraw from his men, which in itself was odd. He had always been an approachable commander, there when his people needed him. Always with a good word and always keen to help if one of his men was in trouble. His manner became noticeable. No one questioned the change. Gardener's men were well aware of the strain of command. He had a lot to deal with.

Jacobi, who had been assigned to a position in equipment and supply procurement at Fort Leverton, had seen Gardener regularly. He'd also become aware of the

increased number of meetings taking place, of the un-
familiar faces visiting the HQ and vanishing into Gardener's inner sanctum. Happening on a regular basis for
a few weeks, the visits generated base gossip among
men with too much time on their hands. When they
were on the base, the newcomers used a barracks hut
set apart from the main area. Jacobi had picked up some
of the talk as he went about his business, but hadn't paid
much attention at first. Then he'd heard that word had
come down from on high for the talk to cease. The suggestion was that these newcomers were on special assignment for the general, and he didn't want idle talk
being generated. There was a security clampdown. Jacobi had seen no profit in getting caught up in the matter, so he'd concentrated on his job. He hadn't wanted
to jeopardize his chances of getting off the base so he
could go see his girl, Cassie Stone, in nearby Leverton.

That was until a sheaf of documents had landed on
his desk, along with the usual daily clutter, and caught
his eye when they reached the top of the pile. Jacobi
scanned the documents, skimming through at his usual
speed. Something had made him pause, flip back
through the sheets and reread, this time taking in the information at a slower rate. He'd absorbed the facts,
more facts than he needed to in one sitting. By the time
he'd reached the end of the document file he wasn't sure
what he was looking at. All he did know was that the
items he had seen in the documents suggested someone

was working up to starting a war. The equipment ranged from ordnance through to Hummers and heavy transport. There was communication equipment. A mobile command center. It was a great deal of equipment to be taking in when the base was already well stocked. When he ran the equipment reference through his base computer data file he couldn't find it. Jacobi checked a number of times. Nothing. The equipment on the manifest wasn't on the database. The chances that so much equipment hadn't been logged was odd. The odd few items could sometimes go adrift, but not this much. And there was no record of the procurement having been officially issued by Leverton.

Jacobi felt sure he had seen the equipment and when he thought about it he recalled where. It was housed within a fenced compound, set apart on one side of the base. It was under a restriction order and under constant watch. Jacobi's interest had been roused, simply because it was unusual for something like this to occur within Gardener's province. He had taken the sheaf of orders to the HQ office, having words with the admin clerk. The moment the clerk had seen the paperwork he had asked Jacobi to wait while he went through to the main office.

A couple of minutes later Gardener himself had appeared, smiling that disarming smile of his and asking Jacobi to follow him. They had walked all the way through to Gardener's own office.

"Close the door, Jacobi."

"General."

Jacobi had closed the door and turned, expecting to see Gardener seated behind his large desk. Instead the general was standing at the window, looking out across the busy camp. He remained there for a moment before turning around.

"Sorry to be so dramatic, Jacobi," Gardener said.

"Sir?"

"Don't tell me you're not curious about all this? Bringing you in here just because of a supply manifest?"

The general reached out to take the sheets of paper, holding them loosely in his left hand. After a moment he turned and casually dropped the manifest on his desk.

"Must admit I was a little surprised, sir."

"Hell, son, I would have been disappointed if you weren't. Not like one of my boys to let something suspicious slip by."

Gardener had crossed the room to stand in front of Jacobi. The general was an impressive figure. Tall, broad-shouldered, his face tanned from constant exposure to the elements. There was a faint, pale scar just above his left eye, a reminder of an old wound. His neatly trimmed dark hair was starting to show flecks of gray, but there was nothing to suggest the man had lost any of his stature. He faced Jacobi with the unflinching stare that had made armed men back down. Gardener could be totally intimidating when he wanted. Jacobi had seen the general use that stare in the middle of combat to break the hostile intention of an enemy.

"Jacobi, we've been through hard times."

"Yes, sir, we have."

"The U.S.A. is going through one of those hard times right now, son. You understand that?"

"Yes, sir."

"Relax, son, I'm not going to come down on you. Jacobi, just because we came back from Iraq doesn't mean the war is over. You understand that?"

"Yes, sir."

"Hell, you saw what those fedayeen did in Bucklow. Here, son, on American soil. They brought the war home to us. You know what that does to me, Jacobi?"

Jacobi faced the general, eye-to-eye. He saw the rage in Gardener's expression. It lasted for no more than a few seconds. That was all it took for Gardener to regain his control.

"I guess it makes you angry, sir."

"You've got a hell of a grasp on understatement, Jacobi. It makes me a damn sight more than angry. I want this put right, son. I guess you've been wondering, along with the rest of the troops, about the people I've had coming and going over the past weeks. Those boys are the best there is in any man's army. Same with the equipment in that manifest. It should have landed right on my desk, son. Not yours. Someone made a mistake. Now I'm counting on you, Sergeant Jacobi, to let me handle this. You go about your business and we can forget this happened. I have to keep those men and that equipment out of sight and out of mind, Jacobi, because there are certain parties in higher command who wouldn't go along with what we have to do here if they got wind. You with me, Jacobi?"

Later Jacobi would decide his reaction had made the difference. If he had responded instantly, giving Gardener the answer he'd expected from a loyal member of his command, nothing would have changed. He might not have found himself on the run, trying to stay alive while Gardener's *specialists* were doing their best to kill him.

His slow response, measured in seconds, made the difference. Jacobi had been unsure of Gardener's implications, a slight doubt in his mind when it came to figuring out who those "certain parties" might be. His loyalty toward Gardener had been rock-solid when he had entered the office, but taking in the undertones in the general's words had tipped Jacobi off balance, albeit slightly. He couldn't shake off the reference to people above Gardener who might not be in favor of his plans; if that was the case, Jacobi's loyalties became disturbed. Loyalty to Gardener seemed to be coming at a price. There was no way Jacobi could ignore his main loyalty, which was toward the Army, the nation and the

President, who was his commander in chief. It wasn't in Jacobi's nature to be duplicitous.

He became aware of Gardener's full-on stare. The gleam in the man's eyes was hard to avoid. Jacobi knew he had committed an error of judgment. He should have said yes to the general's question without pause, then got out of the office. He had not done that and now it was too late.

"I…yes, General. With you, sir."

The expression on Gardener's face told Jacobi he had spoken too late.

Gardener took a sharp breath, nodding slightly. "That's all, Jacobi. Carry on, soldier."

Jacobi snapped to attention and gave a salute. It was returned with a flick of Gardener's hand before the general turned on his heel and went back to his desk.

As Jacobi closed the door behind him, Gardener leaned across his desk and picked up a cell phone. He tapped a speed-dial number. When it was answered, he spoke quickly. "I need to talk to you. My office now."

He clicked off the call and replaced the cell phone on his desk. Swiveling his leather chair, Gardener stared out across the camp—*his camp*—seeing the activity but not really taking it in. He remained in that position until a gentle tap to his door made him turn the chair back to the desk.

"Come in."

The door opened to admit a lean, sun-browned man

in his early forties, pale blond hair cut short. He wore military fatigues and moved with the ease of a seasoned soldier. No hurry, moving lightly, his appearance relaxed. His eyes were constantly on the move, restless, missing nothing.

"Did you see the sergeant who just left? Luke Jacobi."

"I saw him. Is he causing problems?"

"He *is* the problem," Gardener said. He held up the manifest Jacobi had brought to his attention. "Somehow this landed on his desk along with regular paperwork and he decided to bring it to me. He's a good soldier, but I think he'll have difficulty with what we have in mind. He's a regular kind of individual. Not used to extreme measures. I ran something by him and his reaction gave me cause for concern. Renelli, if he starts to think about what I said, he might decide to do some digging. Maybe even take it elsewhere. At this stage we don't need complications."

Gardener allowed his words to trail off, watching the other man's eyes. It took no time at all for Renelli to accept what the general was saying.

"Leave it with me, sir."

"Handle it, Renelli. I don't give a damn how. If he shows any more signs of going loose, do what's needed. We can't afford to have anything raising concerns at this stage. He's made himself expendable. Understand?"

"Understood, sir."

ON HIS RETURN to his office Jacobi was unsettled. He couldn't put a finger on it, but something was off center. He paced his office, often stopping at the window. From it he could see the secured compound. He stared across the camp and asked himself if maybe he was overreacting. Maybe the manifest hadn't been as important as he had first believed, and his imagined feeling about the general himself.

What had the man done that was so...Jacobi answered that without much thought.

Gardener had acted out of character. His manner altering, maybe slightly, but enough to make Jacobi uncomfortable. That had never happened before, under any circumstances. There *was* something odd going on. Gardener's command was one of the best. His individual teams, specialists to a man, were some of the finest. So why was Gardener bringing in outside personnel? And why so closemouthed about all the extra equipment?

At his desk Jacobi tapped into the base data system to do some more digging. He was trying to locate information about the specialists Gardener had brought on the base.

The first thing he found was the absence of Gardener's new intake. They weren't even listed as being at the camp. That did surprise Jacobi. Knowing the Army as he did, the sergeant knew nothing ever happened without there being some kind of record about

it. The movement of personnel was one of those things.
Where were the men's movement orders?

Why all the secrecy about them?

Like Gardener's equipment, these men were also off
the books. They weren't supposed to exist.

JACOBI WENT ABOUT his business the next day. On the
surface the base appeared normal. Nothing to suggest
there was anything wrong. The sergeant couldn't accept
that, not any longer.

He called Cassie a couple of times, using his cell
phone. He explained he was troubled about things on
the camp and wasn't sure what to do. Cassie, always
levelheaded, told him to go above Gardener's head if he
wasn't sure about the man. It sounded like good advice
at the time. Once he was back in his office Jacobi had
second thoughts. If General Gardener was involved in
something illegal, how was Jacobi to know how far it
extended. Put simply, who could he trust?

He was walking back to his barracks that evening
from the PX, having spent a couple of hours trying to
relax, pushing his worries to the back of his mind. Even
a couple of beers had failed to console him. He spoke
to Cassie again as he made his way through the darkness between buildings and after finishing his call he
had turned to cross the road.

The Hummer had come around the side of the building, engine roaring as it swept in at him. Jacobi stood

rooted for a moment, shielding his eyes from the full glare of the lights as the powerful vehicle came at him. It would have struck him head-on if Jacobi hadn't lunged to the left, throwing himself full length across the tarmac. He rolled, feeling the rush of the vehicle as it swept by him. By the time Jacobi had climbed to his feet the Hummer had vanished.

Jacobi had no illusions. It was no accident. Not at the speed the vehicle had been driven.

Someone had tried to run him down.

BACK IN HIS OFFICE the following morning the sergeant acted as if nothing had happened. It was obvious that the incident had been engineered so that Jacobi had been alone, with no witnesses around. He sat at his desk, staring at the monitor screen of his computer, determined to get some answers.

Even that was a failure. When he tried to enter the base personnel data bank as he had done previously, he found he was locked out. His instructions were ignored and the screen threw up the information that he wasn't permitted to access the database.

It was as if someone was telling him to back off, that his inquiries weren't welcome. As nervous as he was, Jacobi began to get angry. All his shadowy adversaries were doing was to increase his curiosity. He knew something was wrong, and he wanted to find out what. Pushing him away was the wrong thing to do.

Which was the reason he found himself watching General Gardener's private quarters that night. He never quite understood what moved him to do such a risky thing. Regardless of the possible consequences, Jacobi made his way through the darkness, taking the long route that led him around the perimeter of the officers' bungalows and the final stretch that brought him into sight of Gardener's larger, isolated quarters.

Jacobi was calling himself every kind of a fool as he worked his way in close, using the very skills he had learned under Gardener's training and which he had employed during actual combat missions. It wasn't that Luke Jacobi was a coward. Far from it. But his previous exposure to this kind of situation had been in the face of a true enemy. One he could identify. Here he was stalking an enemy with a face he had once looked on as friendly.

Everything was telling him he was taking a risk, one that could get him killed. Jacobi ignored his misgivings. He had to satisfy himself one way or another as to Gardener's behavior. He allowed himself the brief indulgence that he might be mistaken, that Gardener's reaction to Jacobi wasn't prompted by some wayward plan move against the government. That it was something Jacobi had misread. Wasn't that possible? And maybe that near accident with the Hummer had been exactly that—an accident. His probing the computer database? The simple explanation was that he needed a higher security rating than he held. Looked at that way, Jacobi had to accept it held some credence. So had he overreacted? Allowed himself to build a fantasy built on misunderstanding?

Jacobi considered that angle. And dismissed it. He saw the possibility of it being true but had to see it from a realistic viewpoint.

He found himself crouching in the shadows at the rear of Gardener's bungalow. The sliding-glass doors leading to the yard were open and Jacobi could see into the room. There were a number of men gathered inside. It looked harmless enough. A social gathering. Jacobi recognized faces. Officers from Gardener's command. Others he didn't know.

He reached into the carry bag belted around his waist and took out the camcorder. He hadn't been sure what he was going to find at Gardener's place, but a nagging thought had insisted he obtain some kind of record— proof of his suspicions—and a digital videotape would certainly provide that proof.

He checked the camera, set the video and sound and raised it to his eye. He focused in on the distant room, panning from left to right to cover as many of the people he could see.

Three figures detached from the main group and drifted outside. As they moved through a patch of light, their faces were revealed: Colonel Chase Gardener, and one of the men who had come to the base as a specialist, Rick Renelli, the third man was a stranger to Jacobi. Sandy-haired, he carried himself like a civilian. There was nothing military about the way he looked or moved.

Jacobi eased back, settling the camera on the trio. He could feel his hands start to shake and had to steady himself. He felt a calmness descend as he focused the camera on the three men.

The threesome stood in a loose group. Gardener was doing most of the talking, his authoritarian voice carrying clearly to where Jacobi crouched.

Gardener: "We stick with the program. Too much has been finalized to change now."

Renelli: "Then we have to deal with Jacobi, General."

Gardener: "If your man hadn't screwed up we wouldn't even be having this conversation."

Renelli: "He made a mess of it, General. I won't even pretend to cover for him."

Third man: "Can we forget the mistakes and move on? What's over is finished. For Christ's sake, Renelli, he's one man against all of us. Just find him and put a bullet through the back of his fucking skull. Bury him in the desert. There's a hell of a lot of it out there. Do it before the little shit goes on the run."

Gardener: "Do it, Renelli. No more waiting. Choose your moment. I don't want him taken down in front of the whole company. Let's just agree that Sergeant Jacobi is history as far as we're concerned. Now, Rod, when are you going to give me the President?"

Third man, Rod: "I can't just walk in and ask. The details will be issued in time for us to organize. This is the President of the United States we're talking about. His travel arrangements aren't there for Joe Public to see. We'll have them but I can't get pushy otherwise somebody is going to get curious."

Gardener: "All right, I get the message, Rod. We wait. I hope the President doesn't change his plans at the last minute. We'll only get one shot at this. If we screw up the whole damned exercise could fall apart. We have to take him before we go ahead."

Renelli: "We'll get him, General."

Rod: "Is everything prepared for his stay?"

Gardener: "He'll be well cared for."

LUKE JACOBI'S earlier flight of fancy concerning Gardener's intentions was completely shattered by what he had just overheard. He stayed in the shadows, half listening to the conversation, letting his camera continue recording. Not that he needed to know more. Gardener and Renelli and the civilian had drawn a neat, if chilling, picture of what they were considering. Not just the disposal of himself, but a plot against the President of the United States.

Jacobi finally lowered the camera. He ejected the cassette and dropped it in the carry bag, his mind racing as he tried to work out what to do. One thing was certain: he couldn't remain here on the base. Fort Leverton was his prison at the moment, with Gardener the governor and Renelli the chief warden. If he stayed around for much longer, he would end up dead. That much had come across loud and clear. It left him with a single option. To leave Leverton now that he had his evidence. As far away as possible so he could clear his mind and work out what to do. His first move was to leave the vicinity of Gardener's bungalow and get out of the camp.

And then what?

Jacobi didn't own a car. So gaining distance between himself and Fort Leverton was going to be a problem. The answer sprang into his mind in the same instance.

Cassie.

She had a car. And he knew she would let him borrow it.

He turned to move off. And a dark figure, carrying an M-16, loomed large and blocked his path.

"What the fuck are you doing, soldier?"

The challenge was loud enough to reach the ears of Gardener and Renelli.

"What's going on there?"

"Looks like we got a snooper, sir," the armed man replied.

Renelli ran forward, his gaze fixed on Jacobi as he stood.

"It's Jacobi, General. He's got a camera with him."

"Goddamn. Bring him here."

Panic was Jacobi's initial reaction. Just as quickly, it dissipated. He realized his life was going to end if he allowed himself to be taken captive. With that in mind he did the only thing he could under the circumstances. He turned and struck out at the armed sentry. The guy hadn't been expecting Jacobi to retaliate, and he was caught briefly off guard. Before he could recover, Jacobi swung the camera on its strap and hit him under the chin, snapping his mouth shut with a solid impact. The sentry bit down on his own tongue, blood welling up from the deep cut. In his moment of pain the guy was left immobile and Jacobi kept up his attack, closing in on the man. His bunched left fist arced around and struck the guy across his right cheek, knocking him off balance. Dropping the camera, Jacobi reached out and gripped the M-16, yanking it from the sentry's fingers. As the weapon dropped into his grasp, Jacobi spun, finger slipping over the trigger. He lowered the muzzle and triggered a burst that laid 5.56 mm slugs in the ground just ahead of Renelli.

"You can't go anywhere, son," Gardener said, moving up to stand next to Renelli.

"Watch me."

"You'll do what I tell you, Jacobi. Remember who I am."

"I know who you are now, you son of a bitch."

Jacobi sensed movement close by. He turned and lunged to the side as the sentry, recovered enough to launch an attack, reached out to grab him. Jacobi butted him with the M-16, dropping him to his knees, then turned back and laid down more shots to keep Gardener and Renelli back.

"Don't try," Jacobi said.

He turned and ran, away from the light and into the darkness. Behind him he could hear raised voices. He knew he had little time before Gardener organized a full hunt for him. His free time was limited. He had to use it well.

JACOBI REACHED his quarters and went directly to his room. He had left the M-16 outside, behind a trash bin. He didn't waste time. He grabbed a bag and threw in civilian clothing. He also dropped the videocassette in the travel bag. The only other things he took were his service pistol, a spare clip and his wallet. He made his way back outside and cut off across camp, searching for a vehicle. He spotted a couple of Hummers parked outside one of the admin buildings and climbed into the first one. He fired up the engine and drove off without hesitation. Whatever he did from that moment would be against every military regulation. He turned the vehicle along the road that led in the direction of the camp entrance.

Jacobi kept checking behind him, expecting to see the lights of vehicles in pursuit. He was coming up to the guard post where a car was just rolling to a stop,

waiting for the barrier to be raised. Jacobi slowed the
Hummer, easing it to one side so the car could drive in
alongside the guard post. The post sentries were standing beside the car. Jacobi gauged the gap and decided
he should be able to get by the car and through the barrier before it came down. He dropped into gear, pushed down on the gas pedal and sent the Hummer forward.
He spun the wheel, swinging in alongside the car, then
around its rear. He felt a slight nudge as his vehicle
caught the back end of the car. Out the corner of his eye
he saw the post sentries break into movement. They ran
around the car, arms waving as they watched the Hummer speed away from the barrier, dust swirling from under the tires. Jacobi felt sure he heard a crackle of
autofire as he picked up speed.

A couple of miles down the dusty road he worked
his cell phone out of his pocket and called Cassie.

"Luke?"

"It's me. Cassie, listen. No questions. I need to borrow your car. I have to get as far as I can from the base.
They'll be coming to find me anytime. Gardener and his
people. I overheard them tonight. Something about the
President. Some plan against the government. No shit,
Cassie. It's true. I've got it on videotape. They want me
dead and buried. I have to get away so I can try to figure out what to do next."

"Whatever you want. Luke, maybe I should come
with you."

"No. No. I don't want you in the line of fire if this gets out of hand. Trust me, Cassie. I'll keep in touch and let you know what's happening. Right now I just need to get as far away as I can."

"Where can you go?"

"I'll figure something out. I don't know. Maybe back home. Just leave your car with the keys in it outside the diner."

"It'll be there, Luke. Hey, be careful. I don't want you getting hurt…Jesus, Luke, this is crazy. Are you sure…"

"I'm sure, honey. I'll call when I can. Just be careful what you say. They'll come to question you."

"I haven't seen you for days. Right?"

"I'll see you, Cassie."

HE ABANDONED the Hummer a couple of miles outside Leverton and slung his bag over his shoulder. He took a shortcut across country that brought him to a point by the main highway from where he could see the diner. It was set back from the road. There were a few vehicles in the parking lot out front. Lights shone in the windows and Jacobi could see people moving inside. One of them would be Cassie. He shrugged off the desire to go inside to see her. He waited instead until the highway was quiet, then crossed and skirted the front of the diner. Cassie always parked her car around the side. As he moved in that direction he spotted the dusty Ford Mustang, its orange paintwork faded by the Arizona sun. Its worn appearance concealed a well-maintained vehicle, with a powerful, dependable engine. Jacobi reached the car and opened the driver's door. The keys were in the ignition. He tossed his bag inside, slid behind the wheel and fired up the engine. It caught instantly, the throaty sound settling quickly. Jacobi swung the Mustang around and drove slowly out of the diner's lot. He hit the highway, heading east and pushing into the darkness beyond the diner.

JACOBI HEARD the insistent sound repeating itself. He glanced around, unable to figure out what it was. Then his eyes caught movement in the rearview mirror.

A police patrol cruiser.

Panic gripped him for a moment. Had he been identified?

Gardener had far-reaching influence. It was possible the police had been informed about him and were working on Gardener's behalf. The son of a bitch had even drawn the law into his conspiracy.

Jacobi leaned forward, reaching for the ignition key. He paused before he touched it. Ease off, he told himself. You don't have any proof about the police working for Gardener. The cop behind him had most likely pulled in because he had spotted Jacobi's car parked on the side of the road and wanted to check on him. It didn't have to have sinister overtones.

Despite his self-assurance Jacobi remained on high alert, conscious of the cop's appearance. He kept a close watch in his side mirror as the cruiser slid in behind him. The officer stayed in his seat, leaning forward as he ran a check on his in-car computer. That worried Jacobi. The vehicle registration would come up as belonging to Cassie Stone. That would flag suspicion in the cop's mind and might cause him to run further checks. It was possible that Jacobi might be identified as a known associate of Cassie. If Gardener had any kind of links to the law-enforcement database, he might pick up Jacobi's location. The more Jacobi extrapolated, the more his worry grew.

He saw the cop climb out of the car. Before he moved, the officer reached to loosen his holstered handgun. He walked toward the Mustang, caution in every step, the way he held himself.

Taking the M-9 from his belt Jacobi eased off the safety and worked the slide, pushing a load into the chamber, then slid it under his left thigh, close to the door, where he could reach it quickly if he needed it. He powered down his window. He could feel himself starting to sweat again and realized he was going to give himself away if he wasn't careful. He placed both hands on the steering wheel, in plain sight, hoping to present a nonaggressive attitude.

The cop stopped alongside the driver's door, a few feet back to give himself space if he needed to move quickly. He leaned forward so he could scan the car's interior.

"Any problems here, sir?" the cop asked.

His eyes examined every detail of the car as he spoke.

"No, Officer. I just pulled over to rest. Been driving for a while. I felt tired so I figured it safer to stop for a while."

"Not the best place to stop, sir. You should have looked for a rest area. Pulled right off the road."

"I realize that now, Officer."

"This your vehicle, sir?"

"Er, no. Belongs to a friend. She loaned it to me so I could visit home."

"Who is the owner, sir?"

"Her name is Cassie Stone. Leverton, Arizona."

"You've come a long way."

"Yeah."

"You work in Leverton, sir?"

He knows who I am. He checked me out on the fucking database. If I lie, he's going to know. But does he know why I left Leverton?

"I'm in the military. Based at Fort Leverton. It's near the town. I took some leave to visit home."

"That is?"

Jacobi gripped the wheel. He was trying to stay cool, but the persistent questioning was picking at the edges of his patience. He almost snapped back his reply but held himself.

"Lansing. I got an uncle there. Haven't been back for some time. You know how it is."

The cop didn't reply. His silence clawed at Jacobi's nerves. The silence seemed to go on forever though in real time it was no longer than a second or two.

"You sure there's no problem, sir?"

"Should there be?"

The cop let his right hand move closer to the butt of his holstered handgun, fingers curling slightly. It was a slow move, deliberately easy so as not to alarm Jacobi. The effect it had was the opposite. Jacobi's troubled mind interpreted it as an entirely hostile move, a precursor to the cop taking aggressive action.

"Keep your hands in sight, sir, and step out of the vehicle."

The order struck fear in Jacobi. The cop had made him. There was no doubt in his mind now. The computer check had told the cop everything there was to know about Sergeant Luke Jacobi. That he was AWOL and had to be detained so that the military could come and pick him up. What the database wouldn't have revealed was the fact that if he was picked up by Gardener's men he would end up dead, or vanish from sight. He would *not* reach Fort Leverton. General Gardener had him nailed down and ready for the firing squad.

Well, the hell with you, Gardener.

Jacobi lifted his hands from the steering wheel and turned his upper body in a show of compliance with the cop's instruction. He could feel the sweat peppering his forehead as he contemplated what he was about to do. But he had no choice. If the cop got him into the cruiser, locked in the rear, possibly cuffed, it was all over. He couldn't let that happen.

He placed his left hand on the door, reached out with his right to work the interior handle. His fingers moved on down beyond the handle and curled around the butt of the M-9, where it sat just under his thigh.

The cop's hand was resting on the butt of his own weapon now.

Jacobi made his decision and acted on it without further hesitation. He brought the M-9 up from below the window and leveled it at the cop.

"Don't…" the cop said, his voice rising despite trying to stay calm. "No. You don't—"

The cop's hand dropped, fingers closing around the holstered gun. It was more of a self-protective, reflex action, but whatever the intention it was the wrong thing to do in the face of someone in Jacobi's state of mind.

The M-9 fired a single round. Jacobi was never able to recall actually touching the trigger.

The crack of the shot was deceptively loud within the confines of the car. It reverberated in Jacobi's ears. His hand jerked in recoil.

The cop twisted sideways as the 9 mm slug took him in the right shoulder. It hit high, shearing a wedge of flesh and tissue on its way out. The cop fell back, losing his balance and hit the ground, his handgun bouncing from the holster as he rolled.

Jacobi stared at the weapon in his own hand, down at the stricken cop, then jerked back into movement. He threw the M-9 on the seat beside him, reached for the key and fired up the engine. He took off in a burn of smoking rubber, the Mustang fishtailing until he got it under control.

He put his foot down hard, blinking away the sweat that was running into his eyes. It came back to him in a sudden shock.

He had shot a cop.

Everything Gardener would be putting out about him would be assessed on what he had just done. It would reinforce Gardener's accusation that Luke Jacobi was a deserter from the Army and had further shown his contempt for authority by shooting a cop. He had walked right into Gardener's hands. No one would believe a word he said now. Trying to denounce Gardener would sound as though he were simply trying to justify what he had done.

Now he was truly on his own. His name and picture would be on every law-enforcement database very soon. He would have cops in every town just waiting for him to show.

He was Sergeant Luke Jacobi—AWOL. And now he was a fugitive. A criminal on the run.

Jacobi slammed his foot hard on the gas pedal. He

was well over the speed limit. So what? That was the least of his worries.

He thought about the car. He would need to ditch it. The entire Pennsylvanian law-enforcement machine would be on the lookout for it. So he needed to hide it and find an alternative means of transport to get him to Lansing.

The signs ahead warned he was approaching a town. Jacobi slowed the Mustang and he took a narrow dirt road off the highway, driving into the deep undergrowth until the car was well hidden. He didn't have the time to do anything else. He pulled on his coat, tucked the M-9 into his belt and grabbed his bag. It took him less than a couple of minutes to return to the highway. Jacobi headed for the town, keeping his eyes open for a bus stop. When he reached one, he dumped his bag on the ground and sat on it, waiting. For once his luck changed. A bus appeared within twenty minutes. He flagged it down and climbed on board. He checked with the driver and found he could get to within a couple of miles of Lansing. There were only three other passengers. Paying his fare, he made his way to the empty rear of the bus, sitting close to the emergency door in case he needed to make a quick exit. The bus jerked into motion as he flopped into the empty seat. Jacobi made sure the M-9 was safe. He eased the gun to one side, fastening his coat.

He tried to stay awake but exhaustion overwhelmed

him and he began to doze. He had a final clear
thought—how badly injured was the cop?

THE BUS DROPPED HIM OFF a couple of hours later. Jacobi stood at the side of the highway, turning up his coat
collar against the rain that was slanting in off the hills
and crossed the blacktop, heading for the side road
sign-posted Lansing. He knew exactly where he was.
This was home ground to Luke Jacobi. The place he had
grown up in. The town lay some eight miles back from
the main highway. The wooded landscape acted almost
as a shield, cutting off the small community from the
mainstream. It had thrived once as a mining town,
where its inhabitants lived and breathed coal that was
mined and shipped out by rail. Those days were long
gone. Only a small percentage of production still ex-
isted, employing a minority of the men who had refused
to move on. Lansing was a shadow of its former self,
many families having chosen to leave.

Jacobi made his way along the road leading in the
direction of the town. He didn't stay on it for very long,
cutting off into the encroaching forest, tramping
through the wet undergrowth until he merged with the
trees. Once deep in the forest, the rain was prevented
from reaching the floor by the high canopy of treetops.
He knew his way. Taking the forest trail would also
shorten his journey.

Lost in memories of his youth Jacobi found a mood

of peace descending over him. Here in this green world, the events that had followed him all the way from Arizona and Fort Leverton faded into the background. He was aware it was only a temporary condition. Like taking painkillers that dampened the effects of an injury. The real hurt was still there and once the calming effect of the drug wore off it would return. He didn't allow that to spoil his moment of calm. For a while, as he relived his growing days in this peaceful backwater, Jacobi imagined it might stay like this. He could hide away in the hills, staying away from human contact, find himself a place to camp and survive on his skills as a hunter. In his youth he had helped feed his family, going out with his rifle and tracking down wildlife. He smiled at a fleeting recall, memory of his lost years when life, though hard, was pretty good. Then he had friends, family. A couple of local girls he had been involved with.

He stopped, threw his bag to the ground and leaned both hands against a thick tree trunk, head hanging. The reason for being here came in a rush. It took his breath as he felt it wash over him, destroying the images from his past. Leaving him shaking with true fear. He was fooling himself. There was no way he could stay safe. Even out here, Gardener and his powerful military machine would hunt him down. The general had no choice; Jacobi was a threat that had to be eliminated.

Luke picked up his bag and moved on, in a more sober mood. He wondered what the police were doing. The wounded cop would have been picked up by now. The camera installed in the police cruiser would have picked up the shooting incident and recorded it on tape. He was known. So was the car. Had they found that yet? And what would Gardener have to say about the incident? No doubt he would be using his authority to try to take over the manhunt. He would want *his* men on Jacobi's trail, not the local law-enforcement agencies. Gardener wouldn't want witnesses if his people picked Jacobi up. Chase Gardener was a powerful, influential man, with far-reaching contacts. Senator Ralph Justin was an example. Jacobi knew about their relationship. It had been reported in the media before. Between them they might be able to close out the police and conduct the pursuit on their own terms. It wouldn't have surprised Jacobi if Renelli, or at least part of his team, were already in the area.

He made the edge of town just after midday. Jacobi crouched in the shadows of the treeline, studying Lansing. He found the town had changed hardly at all since he had been here last. A little shabbier. Not as many people around. Beyond the town, the forested hills rose in green ranks. Nothing changed up there.

It was still raining. Jacobi was feeling the dampness in the air. His clothing had soaked up the rain, as well. All he wanted was a place to get dry, somewhere he could get food and drink. It wasn't an indulgence. His

Army training had drilled into him that the active body needed nourishment to keep it going. Denied food and drink, like a car starved of fuel, the body would start to slow down. The reactions and the ability to fight off fatigue would decrease. If Jacobi was to keep going, he needed to build up his resistance.

Edging toward the road, Luke walked in the direction of the narrow steel bridge that spanned the old rail tracks. He remembered the long trainloads of coal trundling beneath the bridge, the grimy diesel locomotives sending out their mournful wails as they hauled the cargo away from Lansing. Passing over the bridge, he looked down at the rails. There were a lot of weeds growing alongside and between the rails. Another sign of the town's decline.

Entering the main street Jacobi looked for the diner. It was partway down the street. He paused at the entrance. The diner hadn't changed much except for looking shabbier. He pushed open the swing door and entered. It was warmer inside. Jacobi glanced around the place. Most of the booths were empty. Just a couple were occupied. Heads were raised when he stepped inside. If anyone recognized him, they didn't show it. He made his way over to the counter. The guy standing behind it was a total stranger to him. Jacobi dropped his bag on the floor and eased onto a stool.

"Coffee?"

Luke nodded. He watched in silence as a thick mug

was filled and pushed in front of him. He picked it up and drank. The brew was strong, not the freshest but Jacobi wasn't about to raise any objections.

"You want something to eat?"

The counterman's were words clipped.

"Ham. Eggs. The works," Jacobi said.

The counterman's question had made Jacobi realize he *was* hungry. Now was as good a time as any to eat. The opportunity might not arise again.

The order was called over the man's shoulder. He moved to the far end of the counter without another word, picked up a creased magazine and began to read.

Luke drank his coffee slowly, savoring the hot liquid. He heard movement behind him. A figure appeared at the counter. It was one of the customers come to pay his bill. He left without a word, the door creaking shut in his wake. Jacobi settled back to his coffee. He managed a refill before his food arrived. It might not have been the best-cooked food but it was plentiful and Luke ate without pause. He pushed his empty plate aside and caught the counterman's eye, lifting his mug for more coffee.

"You got a phone?"

The counterman nodded toward the rear of the diner. Jacobi slid off the stool and located the phone. He picked up and dialed the number. His call was answered after a couple of rings.

"Evan? It's Luke."

"Where are you?"

"Close. Evan, you had any visitors? Strangers?"

"Damn fool question. Why do you need to know that?"

"Because it's important."

"No visitors. Luke, what's this all about?"

"Tell you when I see you. Evan, just be careful."

Jacobi ended the call. He returned to the counter and took his seat. His mug had been refilled. Jacobi drank. Silent, hunched over his mug, thinking ahead. He needed to speak to Evan. The man might not be the most sociable person alive, but he carried a sound head on his shoulders. He would listen to what Luke had to say and then offer his advice. It was something Jacobi needed. Another opinion. A fresh perspective on the situation.

Luke finished his coffee, settled his bill and picked up his bag. He stood for a moment, scanning the clouded, rain-heavy sky. Then he moved off, heading along the sidewalk, collar turned up against the rain that suddenly seemed colder.

As he neared the intersection of the road that led to his uncle's place he heard the low wheezing of an old truck. He turned and raised a hand to the driver. The truck rolled to a stop and Luke opened the passenger side door.

"Any chance of a ride?"

"Where you going?"

"Evan Jacobi's place. He's my uncle. I'm just visiting."

"I'm passing nearby there. Haul your ass inside, boy, and close the door. It's getting wet in here."

EVAN JACOBI SAT STARING at the telephone after he had replaced it on the cradle. The conversation with Luke puzzled him. The boy had seemed genuinely upset about something. And what was all that about strangers? Being careful?

Evan pushed up out of his swivel seat and crossed the small office. He peered out the streaked window. The yard of his haulage business was silent, deserted. His three heavy trucks were lined up on the far side. His crew would be back at work tomorrow. Business was slow at the moment, and Evan had to lay off his people at least one day a week; it was hard but it was the only way to keep his business going. He hated the look in the eyes of his crew each time he told them to stay at home. There wasn't much he could do about it.

Beyond the yard, on the far side of the chain-link fence, was his house. He could see his battered Dodge 4x4 parked next to his wife's Plymouth.

There was a third vehicle there now. A black SUV. New-looking. Something about the vehicle stirred an uneasy feeling in Evan. He couldn't explain why he thought it was linked to the phone message from Luke.

"You had any visitors, Evan? Strangers?"

Evan turned back across the office and reached behind the old wooden filing cabinet. He pulled out a

Remington SP-10 shotgun. He slid open the top drawer of the cabinet, reaching inside to pick up a couple 10-gauge cartridges. He loaded them into the shotgun's magazine. With the weapon ready for use, Evan scooped up more cartridges and dropped them into the pocket of his thick coat before he left the office and crossed the yard.

Misty rain was still sheeting down off the wooded hills that surrounded the property. The ground underfoot was soft, glistening puddles dotting the uneven surface of the yard.

Evan reached the main gate and paused, scanning the area that led up to the house. The SUV had dark windows so he couldn't see whether anyone was inside. It just sat there, big and black and ominous.

Damn, he thought, this isn't right.

He stared at the house and saw that the front door was wide open. Evan clutched the shotgun to his body, finger sliding against the trigger. He felt a stirring of fear rise in his stomach, that greasy, sick feeling that accompanied the sense of dread, and he knew at that moment things were not right.

"Angie?" he yelled.

He stepped forward, pushing his booted feet hard into the soggy ground. Rain slicked against his face, chill against his skin.

"Where are you, Angie?"

CHAPTER FIVE

"That's Jacobi," Schwarz said, leaning forward to peer through the rain-streaked windshield.

Grimaldi checked out the lean figure, coat collar turned up against the chill wind gusting along the street. Rain had followed them in from the main highway, to this small town perched at the foot of wooded hills. Outside the town, a mile or so north, was the open cast mining site that provided the town's sole industry. Still operating, on a smaller scale than during its heyday, the mine only produced small tonnage. It managed to pay its way. That was about all.

"With everything that's happening," Grimaldi said, "makes you wonder why he's come back here. The people looking for him aren't going to be far behind."

"People in trouble, with nowhere else to go, need somewhere they can go back to. Home is a base to touch. It has substance. Roots. Where else can Jacobi go?"

"Guess you're right."

They sat and watched Jacobi climb into the truck he had just hitched a ride with.

"Let's wait until he's clear of town and had his ride. We don't want too many civilians getting caught up in any confrontations," Schwarz said.

Grimaldi fired up the 4x4 and waited until the truck had moved off before he fell in behind, keeping a good distance behind. He had no trouble tailing it. The truck driver took his time.

"What do we know about family or friends here?" Grimaldi asked. "Did Stony Man come up with anything?"

Schwarz had been speaking to Barbara Price only minutes earlier as they had approached Lansing.

"They pulled Jacobi's file, military and civilian. The only family left here is his late father's brother. Evan Jacobi. The guy lives a half mile out of town along this road. He runs a local haulage business and has contracts with the local mine. He has a wife. No kids."

"Has there been any contact recently?"

"Nothing in the recent past."

"Jacobi's military file would have all his contacts. They'll know he has family here."

Schwarz nodded.

"One other thing. Earlier today Jacobi had a run-in with a cop. Seems the officer stopped to check because Jacobi was parked at the side of the highway. When he went to speak to him, Jacobi panicked and shot the cop. Shoulder wound. Then Jacobi took off. He abandoned the car Cassie had lent him and must have caught a bus to bring him the rest of the way to Lansing."

"He shoots a cop and still comes here?"

"What else can the guy do, Jack? Bet your last dime he feels cut off from the rest of the world. He can't go to the military because he doesn't know who to trust. Now he has this cop shooting hanging over his head. He's suddenly out in the cold."

"These people who work for Gardener? Are they legitimate military? Or are they ex, gone mercenary?"

"That's being checked out now. I have a feeling the ones doing all the running are off the books."

"YOU LOCATED HIM?" Renelli asked, impatience crowding his words. "Don't disappoint me, Deke."

"He's on his way. It all checks out. After he shot that cop he dumped the Mustang. Far as I can figure, he must have hitched a ride to Lansing."

"So where is he now?"

"We monitored his uncle's phone. Jacobi called a short time ago. And the guy confirmed it."

"He just up and told you?"

Deke hesitated.

"He had to be persuaded. Fuckin' idiot tried to take us on with a shotgun. We had to—"

"I get the picture. Can he ID you?"

"Not anymore."

Renelli sucked in a sharp breath. "He have any family?"

"He had a wife is all. Hell, Rick, I couldn't leave her around to point the finger, could I? You said—"

"Just don't let Jacobi get away. If he finds out you totaled his family, he's going to keep running. Make it happen, Deke. Christ, if you hadn't fucked up with that Hummer back at Leverton, we wouldn't be in this mess. The general isn't going to be best pleased if I tell him Jacobi skipped out on us again."

"Yeah. Message received."

LUKE JACOBI WALKED the last quarter mile, coming up to the house from the east. He pushed his way through the brush-choked trees to crouch at the edge of the tree-line so he could see the house.

Unzipping his bag, he reached inside and located the videocassette. He pushed it into an inside pocket of his coat, then stowed his bag at the base of a tree, covering it to prevent rain getting through. He took out the Beretta and checked that it was ready for use.

The sight of the pistol brought the memory of the incident with the cop. Jacobi regretted his action. He didn't make excuses because he didn't have any. The only thing in his defense was the fact he had been scared. Unnerved. Mistrustful. Those strong emotions had caused him to lose it during the encounter with the cop. It was how he had been affected by Gardener and his crew.

Jacobi made sure he had his spare clip in his pocket before he moved off. He eased out of the trees and started for the house.

He had traveled no more than a few yards when he came face-to-face with an armed figure.

The guy wore civilian clothing and carried a squat M-4, the black webbing sling over one shoulder, steadying the weapon as he walked. He had a lean, tanned face, his dark hair cropped close to his skull. Jacobi had seen him back at Fort Leverton with Gardener and Renelli.

"Hey," the man said, starting to pull the M-4 on target. "End of the line, Jacobi."

Jacobi remembered the Beretta in his fist. He lashed out hard, using the pistol like a club. His first blow caved in the other man's nose, crushing it. It was like opening a faucet. Blood burst from the guy's nose, squirting in bright fountains that flooded down the man's face. He let out a roar of pain in the instant before Jacobi struck out again and again, and kept hitting until the guy went down. Jacobi was sobbing with rage and fear and as the man dropped to his knees. He hit him one final time, across the back of his skull. The solid blow pitched the guy facedown on the wet ground.

For a long moment Jacobi stood over the motionless figure. The rain was cold on his face. When he moved his gun hand he could feel the sticky cling of the man's blood on his fingers where it gripped the Beretta's butt.

He wanted to take the M-4 but it was pinned under the guy's body, the strap still wrapped around his shoulder, and it would have taken too much time to free it.

Jacobi knew he didn't have time to waste. The presence of this man proved that Gardener's people had reached Evan's house first. And Jacobi knew without having to see for himself that Evan and his wife, Angie, were either dead or close to death. He was under no illusions as to that. Gardener wanted to silence Jacobi. He would use any and all means to achieve that end. Which meant that Jacobi could not go anywhere near the house. He had to keep moving. To make distance between himself and Gardener's people. The moment they had him in their sights he was dead.

He turned and retraced his steps to the tree line, thinking he would first pick up his bag, then head up-country and lose himself in the densely wooded hills. He needed time to figure out what he was going to do next. A fleeting thought crossed his mind. He wanted to speak to Cassie, to let her know he was still alive. He dismissed that thought. Gardener would have that end covered. He was pretty certain the general would have all communications to and from Leverton being monitored. Jacobi couldn't risk contacting Cassie. He had no right to put her life in danger. As he had Evan's. He realized that his call to his uncle had probably been monitored, too. That was why Gardener's people had been at the house waiting for him.

He caught a glimmer of movement off to his left, heard a distant shout. Jacobi turned to see two armed figures running from the house.

They had him spotted.

Forgetting about his bag, he turned and ran, cutting across open ground, his intention to reach deep cover before his pursuers could get within range and open fire.

The rain-sodden ground under his feet made running difficult. The same would apply to his pursuers, but the thought did little to comfort Jacobi. They were equipped with longer range weapons.

As if to qualify that, he heard the harsh crackle of autofire. The vicious snap of slugs chunking into the earth came uncomfortably close. As he labored up a long slope, he slipped and went down on his knees. He almost lost his grip on the Beretta. He pushed to his feet, throwing a quick glance over his shoulder. His pursuers were still there, having as hard a time as he was trying to close the gap to gain target acquisition.

Jacobi spotted the black SUV behind the pair following him. As it came alongside, a man's head and shoulders appeared at the passenger window. He was shouting orders to the gunners. One waved in response and they pushed on as the SUV swerved aside, moving off across country.

They were trying to cut him off, get him in a loop, shut off his escape routes.

Jacobi topped the slope and went down the far side.

Let them try, he thought. This is my home ground.

GRIMALDI SAW the black SUV break out from behind the thick brush and pick up speed. He followed it and spotted the pair of armed men in pursuit of a lone figure struggling up a long slope.

"There," Grimaldi said, pointing toward the rising terrain beyond the house. "Jacobi?"

They could make out the distant figures against the green landscape.

"Let's find out," Schwarz said. "And fast. I don't want him ending up like those two at the house."

They had arrived at Evan Jacobi's place only minutes earlier and what they'd found only confirmed their earlier fears. Chase Gardener's pursuit team was determined to find its man. Regardless of whether Evan and his wife had known anything worthwhile or not, their deaths had placed the final stamp on the ruthless intent of the trackdown of Luke Jacobi.

Leaving the house, the pair had checked the area and picked up the fresh tracks left by the SUV as it had joined the pursuit.

"Let's move, Jack."

They had donned the tac com units so they could stay in touch if they were separated. Schwarz activated his and Grimaldi did likewise.

"You leaving me, buddy?" he asked.

"Don't worry, it isn't a divorce."

Schwarz was studying ahead. The undulating terrain was slowing their progress. Grimaldi was having difficulty maintaining a constant speed.

"I'm going EVA," Schwarz said. "I'll cut across that ridge. See if I can circle around. You stay on Jacobi's tail from this end."

Grimaldi managed a smile as he stared out the rain-streaked windshield.

"Like he hasn't already gone," he said.

Jacobi had vanished from sight, concealed by the rugged terrain.

"Damn," Schwarz grumbled. "Okay, I'm out of here. Keep in touch, Jack."

"Keep your butt covered, pal."

Schwarz opened his door and dropped from the 4x4, turning aside to start his flanking movement.

THE TWO-MAN PURSUIT TEAM had lost Jacobi, too. They cast around, peering through the rainy mist, cursing the weather and the ability of Jacobi to lose them.

"Son of a bitch is playing fucking games," one said.

His partner sleeved rain from his face. "He knows the area, is all."

"A fucking big area. And don't forget this is no civilian. He's been in combat with Gardener's command."

"Am I supposed to give a shit? We're talking about one of the general's goddamn dog soldiers here. Come on, Pete, give me a break."

"Hey. Over there."

The man named Pete turned and brought his M-4 into play as he made out a figure emerging from cover yards to their left. His partner, muttering something about dog soldiers, followed his lead and opened fire.

SCHWARZ DROPPED to a crouch as the M-4 crackled. He brought up his Beretta and triggered a fast shot that hit the shooter in the left shoulder, kicking him back a step and breaking his concentration. The Able Team commando followed up with a second shot that hit the target dead-center in the chest. He went down hard, dropping his weapon and clutching his chest. The instant he fired, Schwarz went full-length on the wet ground, below the muzzle of the second man, who jerked his weapon down to regain target acquisition. He didn't get the chance as Schwarz thrust out his arm and triggered the Beretta, punching a trio of 9 mm slugs into his body. One tore through between his ribs and emerged under his arm. The others cut in deep, cleaving his heart and dumping the guy dead on the ground.

Schwarz pushed to his feet, turning away from the scene and continued trailing after Jacobi and Grimaldi.

GRIMALDI PUT HIS FOOT down hard. He felt the 4x4 slide before the wheels gained traction. The big vehicle surged up the slope, bouncing over the undulating surface. Thick geysers of dark soil blew out from beneath the tires. Grimaldi worked the steering wheel, fighting the 4x4's natural inclination to broadside. He watched the way ahead as he drove, weaving in and out of the tangled scrub and the wiry trees that dotted the lower slopes of the hills. Low branches scraped across the vehicle's roof, slapped at the body sides. Partway up the slope the left side wheels dropped into a trough, the 4x4 tilting dangerously. Grimaldi used all his skill, kept the heavy vehicle upright and gunned the engine the second he cleared the trough.

He caught a glimpse of a moving figure in the thicker stand of timber off to his left. He recognized Schwarz. Grimaldi's partner had his handgun out as he trailed Jacobi. The fugitive soldier had a good start. There was also the fact he knew this part of the country better than the men hunting him, or Schwarz and Grimaldi. It gave him an edge, but it wouldn't save him ultimately. Sooner or later the hunting crew was going to outflank him, and when they did, Luke Jacobi was a dead man.

Grimaldi, like Schwarz, had no illusions on that score.

The hunters would close in and put Jacobi down like a trapped animal. They had no concerns over ending his life. They had already proved their intentions. The dead couple back down the road bore mute testimony to that. Grimaldi was forced to delete that image from his mind. It took some doing and he knew they would come back to haunt him in the quiet dark of night.

The tac com unit spoke to him. It was Schwarz.

"Jack, I have him eyeballed."

"Give me a location."

"Three hundred yards ahead. Your one o'clock."

Grimaldi tracked the position.

And saw the lean figure as Jacobi rose briefly, silhouetted on a rise for a mere second before he vanished down the far side.

"I got him. You want a pickup?"

"Uh-uh. Better I walk drag for you, keep my eyes skinned for any opposition coming on your back. I took out two but there may be others. Jack, go get him, and don't take no for an answer."

Grimaldi hit the gas pedal and felt the powerful engine surge. He saw a relatively smooth stretch leading to the rise over which Jacobi had plunged. It came up fast, Grimaldi braking as he swung the 4x4 broadside-on, checking out the long slope below him.

He spotted Jacobi easily. The trees had petered out, leaving open terrain, except for curling grass and clumps of brush. The slope ran for almost one-third of a mile, then bottomed out to a spread of waterlogged, marshy ground. On the far side lay a stretch of dark water.

"He's in sight," Grimaldi reported.

"Go," was Schwarz's response.

Grimaldi swung the 4x4 around and hit the downslope, pushing the pedal to the floor. He overtook Jacobi halfway down the slop, swinging the big vehicle around and coming to a rocking halt. Grimaldi was out of the vehicle the moment it stopped, his Beretta in his right hand. He threw up his left hand, palm out, as Jacobi brought himself to a stumbling halt, going down on one knee.

"What the hell. I can't run anymore. You'd better shoot me. Wouldn't want Gardener to be disappointed."

"Listen, Jacobi, we're not with Gardener. My partner and I are here to get you to safety."

"Bullshit."

"Mister, don't get me started. The sooner we get you out of here, the better for us all. Now get in the damn truck."

Jacobi looked beyond Grimaldi, eyes widening with alarm.

Grimaldi threw a look over his own shoulder as he picked up a sound he was more than familiar with.

The rising beat of helicopter rotor blades.

As he turned, he saw the dark shape of a chopper swinging into view from beyond the ridge. Angling down to match the drop of the slope, it came at Grimaldi and Jacobi.

"You said…"

"I know what I said, and those aren't my buddies. Now get down beside the truck."

The helicopter, dark-colored and without markings, turned sideways-on. The open hatch was blocked by a man cradling an M-16. He pulled the rifle around to cover Grimaldi and Jacobi and the moment he had them in his sights he opened fire. Grimaldi heard Jacobi grunt as he took a round in the left shoulder. The hit pushed him against the side of the 4x4.

Grimaldi reacted, raising the Beretta. He punched out three fast shots at the hatch gunner, saw at least one hit. The gunner jerked back from the hatch. Grimaldi switched his aim, going for the pilot. He emptied the Beretta's magazine at the side panel in line with the pilot's seat. The 9 mm slugs cored in through the light alloy, ripping holes, some of them fragmenting as they went through. The pilot jerked as something tore into his thigh. Hot fragments of metal that shredded his flight suit and gouged his flesh.

As Grimaldi ejected the empty magazine and slid a fresh one in place, he picked up the crackle of pistol shots and saw Schwarz firing up at the chopper. He was going for the engine casing. His shots punched in through the metal and somewhere they hit something vital. The tone of the chopper's engine changed. A thin trail of smoke issued from the cluster of bullet holes. The pilot, suddenly aware of his vulnerable position, ignored his bloody wound and concentrated on keeping the chopper stable. He worked the controls, moving the chopper away from the firing line, his retreat followed by more shots from the men on the ground. Smoke trailing, the chopper pulled back to level ground and moved away.

Grimaldi reloaded for the second time, then turned his attention to Jacobi. The man was on his knees, bent forward, one blood-streaked hand clutched to his shoulder. He still held his Beretta in his bloody fingers. Schwarz appeared at Grimaldi's side.

"First-aid box under the passenger seat," the Stony Man pilot said.

He eased Jacobi's hand away from the wound. "You're lucky," Grimaldi said. The slug had penetrated the shoulder just below the bone, tearing in through the muscle near the armpit and wedging there.

Jacobi raised his head. He was deathly pale from shock.

"Swap places with me and see if you still want to say that."

"I meant, it hasn't hit the bone."

"And there I was believing it's been a bad day."

Grimaldi had to smile at Jacobi's response.

"Here you go," Schwarz said, passing down the plastic box to Grimaldi.

The ace pilot opened the kit and went through the contents. It was basic, only intended for minor support.

He located sterilized pads and after opening Jacobi's shirt, pressed a couple over the entry wound. The puckered hole was bleeding slightly, the flesh showing purple bruising around the puncture. He bound the wound, using the bandage to immobilize Jacobi's arm against his chest, then pulled the shirt back into place.

Schwarz had been keeping watch. The chopper had vanished completely. It didn't mean the opposition had quit. Now that they had Jacobi's location, they would keep coming.

"Jacobi, what's the best way out of here?"

"To where?"

"Back to town."

"East from here. Along the base of the hills. Takes us through some forested country. It'll bring us into town by the back road."

"Okay," Schwarz said. "I want you on the rear seat with me. Keep that arm still until we can get you some medical help."

They climbed inside the 4x4, Schwarz joining Jacobi in the back. Grimaldi gunned the engine and turned the vehicle east, following the terrain under Jacobi's direction. After a few miles they reached the forested area. There was a faint trail winding its way through the trees. The canopy of foliage cut out a great deal of the daylight and the patches of forest floor lay in deep shadow.

"They won't quit," Jacobi mumbled.

He was starting to react to the shock of his wound. Schwarz checked him. The fugitive was sweating, his pale face glistening.

"Don't worry about them," Schwarz said. "Let us do that."

"Yeah?"

His voice faded and Jacobi lapsed into unconsciousness, slumping against the backrest.

Schwarz pulled out his cell phone and speed-dialed Stony Man. The connection seemed to take forever.

"Talk to me," Barbara Price said.

"We have the package. He took a shoulder hit. We're en route back to town. We need to locate a medic, unless you can get us some help."

"The rest of Able is on the way to your location. You guys okay?"

"As of now, but we haven't seen the last of Gardener's crew. They're around the area somewhere." Schwarz hesitated. "You said the team is on the way?"

"Yes."

"They get tired of vacationing in the Orient?"

"I think they miss your charming personality. They could be with you anytime now. Gadgets, you have any numbers on the opposition?"

"Nothing specific. Let's just say more than enough."

Price paused. "You'll have to hang in there." Her voice was giving out orders off the phone. "Can you improvise?"

"Right now I'm not sure I can even spell it. Hey, we'll manage. Just tell Ironman to haul his ass out here fast."

"He'll probably give you a call himself."

"Oh, great. I'll point the phone at the bad-guys and he can yell at them."

"Has Jacobi told you anything?"

"Not really. We reached him about the same time as Gardener's crew. Things got a little hot and then he caught one in the shoulder so he hasn't been in a talky mood since, if you get my meaning. Another thing. Gardener's crew got to Jacobi's relatives first. Husband and wife. We found them both dead and they weren't easy deaths."

"I understand. Keep me updated."

Schwarz put the cell phone away.

Grimaldi had been listening to Schwarz's side of the conversation. It didn't take a genius to fill in the gaps. He got the message. They were on their own until the rest of Able Team showed up. Grimaldi accepted the situation. It was strictly par for the course. The usual compromise between what should have been and what was. He and Schwarz were going to have to keep Jacobi away from Gardener's squad until reinforcements arrived.

The Stony Man Pilot concentrated on keeping the 4x4 moving hard and fast, wheeling along the narrow, overgrown trail and hoping it would eventually bring them back to civilization.

A few miles farther on Grimaldi began to see where the trees were thinning out. To his left were dark hills. He caught the gleam of water off to the right. The river that skirted the edge of town?

He took a look in the rearview mirror and saw something else. The shape of a black SUV behind them. Coming up fast, bouncing and swerving along the trail as it was pushed hard to close the gap.

"Gadgets. Behind us."

Schwarz twisted in his seat. Through the streaked rear window he saw the vehicle tailing them.

"This is getting to be a habit with these guys. I thought we were getting off too light," he said.

A man's head and shoulders leaned out of the passenger window of the pursuit vehicle. The guy was clutching a weapon and opened fire. Schwarz heard slugs clang against the rear of the 4x4. He turned and leaned across to drag Jacobi off the seat, pushing the man onto the floor.

"Just keep her steady," Schwarz called.

He climbed over the seat into the rear section of the 4x4, reaching to power down the window. Bracing himself against the sway of the vehicle, Schwarz steadied his Beretta in both hands and triggered a shot at the oncoming vehicle. He knew he'd missed. He adjusted his aim and fired again. His second shot scored a burn across the hood, glancing off the windshield.

The side window shooter, having a difficult time

maintaining his position, swung his weapon around and loosed off a burst. His weapon, rising and falling with the wild motion of the vehicle, sent his volley over the roof of the 4x4. The shooter turned to look across at his driver, mouth moving as he spoke. Schwarz took the brief respite to level his Beretta and aim again.

"Jack, you remember Arizona?"

"I remember."

"Same again, buddy. Do it now."

Grimaldi took his foot off the gas and applied pressure to the brake, slowing the 4x4 as smoothly as he could.

The pursuit vehicle loomed large in Schwarz's vision. The driver reacted and slammed on his brakes. The SUV dipped, then slid as the wheels lost their grip. As the enemy vehicle came around, Schwarz had a full-on shot at the gunner and he took it. He laid three rapid shots at the struggling figure. Two of the 9 mm slugs hit, punching in through the shooter's upper chest and throwing him back inside the vehicle. He fell across the driver. Schwarz caught a glimpse of the driver's startled expression and moved the muzzle of the Beretta. He fired again, another three fast shots into the windshield, glass shattering and imploding. He saw the driver jerk and throw up a hand to clutch at his face.

"Go, Jack."

Grimaldi hit the gas pedal and the 4x4 powered up. Behind them the SUV had swung off the trail. As they took a curve, Schwarz's final image was of the enemy plowing into the thick foliage at the side of the trail, crashing through the undergrowth before it slammed head on into a thick tree trunk. He climbed back into his seat and slumped against the rest.

"How we doing?" Grimaldi asked.

"I'll let you know when I figure it out."

Ahead of them the trees were thinning even more. Grimaldi eased off the gas and let the 4x4 slow. He was studying the terrain ahead and around them, his eyes scanning foliage and shadow.

"Those boys are smart enough to have someone stationed down this end of the trail," he said.

"Thought struck me, too."

Ahead of them a thin shaft of sunlight winked as it touched metal. Grimaldi had seen the reflection. He maintained his speed, making no show he had spotted the hidden gunner until he was almost on the guy.

"Coming up. Gunner on my left just beside that thick stand of undergrowth."

Schwarz angled his head slightly.

"I see him."

"Hang tight," Grimaldi said.

He spun the wheel and stamped hard on the pedal, feeding full force to the vehicle's powerful engine. The big truck lurched forward, tires kicking up sprays of leaf mold. Grimaldi held the 4x4 on a straight course, the front end crashing in through the undergrowth. He caught a glimpse of the shooter's startled face a second before the 4x4 hit him. The impact lifted him off his feet, the guy's scream cut off as his broken body described a lazy curve. He landed hard, bouncing as he struck the ground. Grimaldi wrenched the wheel around and took the 4x4 back to the trail.

Schwarz was pulling Jacobi back onto the rear seat. The soldier was coming around, his face ashen. He stared at Schwarz, panic in his eyes before he recognized the Stony Man warrior.

"You timed that right," Schwarz said. "We're just hitting town."

"We hit something," Grimaldi said under his breath.

He swung the truck off the forest trail and onto the tarmac strip that led to the single-span bridge over the river. Grimaldi drove slowly, watching the bridge. It would be a nasty spot to be ambushed. He checked out the underside of the bridge in case any shooters were concealed there but saw nothing, so he drove on across the rumbling boards and they cleared the far side without incident.

"Local doctor?" Schwarz asked.

"Take a left. Just after the diner, another left. The doc's place is along that road on the right. That's where it used to be. I've been a long time away."

They cleared main street and made a left after the diner. Grimaldi drove along the narrow road until he spotted the doctor's house. There was a dark-colored Ford parked outside.

"That's the place," Jacobi said.

Grimaldi pulled up outside the house.

"What do you think?" he asked, studying the place.

"If that chopper pilot radioed in that Jacobi got hit…" Schwarz said.

"Yeah. They might figure we'd make for the local quack."

"Jesus, you guys always this suspicious?" Jacobi asked.

"It's why we're so old and still alive," Grimaldi said.

Despite himself Jacobi had to smile.

"What do we do?" Grimaldi asked.

"Whatever you decide do it before I bleed out," Jacobi suggested.

Schwarz glanced at his shoulder and saw it was bleeding heavily now.

His cell phone rang. "Yeah?"

"ETA, any minute," Lyons said. "Where are you?"

"Back in Lansing. Off the main drag. Side road just after the diner. Parked outside the local doctor's house. We need to get Jacobi medical attention."

"Hey, ask him who's piloting?" Grimaldi asked.

Schwarz asked the question and relayed Lyons's reply.

"Charlie."

Charlie Mott was Stony Man's backup pilot. Though he had combat experience Mott preferred to stay out of the action. He was an excellent pilot and one of the few men Grimaldi would have been happy with handling *Dragon Slayer.*

"Coming in over the town now," Lyons said tersely.

It was Grimaldi who picked up the whack of rotors. He powered down his window and leaned out.

"There she is," he said. "Come to Poppa, baby."

He was referring to *Dragon Slayer,* the one-off combat helicopter belonging to Stony Man. If he was honest, Grimaldi considered the chopper to be his, only on loan to the Farm. He had worked on the original concept and the building of the unique machine, over the years supervising and helping to install updated electronics, weaponry and security modes. Grimaldi knew *Dragon Slayer* inside out. He could fly her with both eyes closed and make the chopper do things that weren't even in the original specifications.

The matte-black configuration swept into view across the rooftops of Lansing.

"Now that is a beautiful sight," Grimaldi said.

"Looks even more beautiful from inside the cabin," Schwarz said. "Damn sight safer, as well."

"Ah, you don't got no romance," Grimaldi rasped.

"Right now romance isn't going to get us out of this mess," Schwarz said as another black SUV burst from cover farther along the road. It crashed its way out of thick foliage and hit the tarmac, bouncing as the driver put his foot down.

"Don't these guys ever give up?" Grimaldi asked.

"Little assistance here," Schwarz said into his cell phone.

Dragon Slayer swept in over their heads, angling down to place itself between them and the advancing SUV. An errant gunner leaned out of the side window and opened fire with an autoweapon.

"Big mistake," Grimaldi whispered a second before *Dragon Slayer*'s underslung chain gun opened up. "Go, Charlie," he murmured under his breath.

The shattering burst from the 30 mm weapon hit the SUV with terrible, destructive power. The SUV's bodywork disintegrated under the relentless impact of the sustained firepower. Metal and glass ripped apart, tires exploded. The SUV shuddered and blew apart, spewing debris and human remains across the tarmac.

It was over as quickly as it began.

Schwarz stepped out of the 4x4, his Beretta in his hand as he surveyed the aftermath of *Dragon Slayer*'s assault. Behind him he heard Jacobi moving.

"Stay put, Luke."

"I wanted to give you this," Jacobi said. "I think you might find it useful."

He passed the cassette in his hand to Schwarz.

"This what I think it is?"

"Unless I picked up my vacation tape," Jacobi managed to joke. "Listen, I don't feel so good. You mind calling the doc out here?"

"Jack, go get the man," Schwarz said.

Grimaldi nodded. "You got it."

Schwarz studied the cassette in his hand. He just hoped it had all been worth it.

Dragon Slayer had swung down ahead of them, the rotor wash swirling the smoke rising from the damaged SUV. It touched down, the side hatch releasing and swinging open. Carl "Ironman" Lyons and Rosario Blancanales climbed out. They were armed but quickly realized the weapons were superfluous.

"And they say I'm the one who pisses people off," Lyons remarked, glancing at the wrecked SUV.

"You do," Schwarz said. "Just because you helped out here doesn't make you a better person."

Behind Lyons, Blancanales grinned.

"I know what you're doing," Lyons said.

"Hey, it's nice to be back together again," Blancanales said.

Grimaldi had emerged from the house with the doctor. The Stony Man pilot led him to where Jacobi had slumped on the rear seat of the 4x4. He helped the doctor ease the unconscious Jacobi out of the vehicle and take him inside.

Schwarz held up the cassette.

"That what this is all about?" Blancanales asked.

"So Jacobi says."

Lyons took a slow look around. "Soon as the doc gets him sorted, we get out of here."

"Best suggestion I've heard today." Schwarz headed for *Dragon Slayer*. "I'd better call home. Give them an update."

CHAPTER SIX

Chechnya

The HALO drop put Phoenix Force down five miles from the camp. McCarter consulted his GPS unit and checked their position as the rest of the team broke out equipment from their war bags. Before the Stony Man team had touched down, the C-130 had turned for its return to Turkey.

They were armed with M-16 A-2 auto rifles, fitted with 30-round magazines, each man carrying additional loads in the webbing over their camou fatigues. James had a grenade launcher fixed to his assault rifle. Apart from McCarter, who had his beloved Browning Hi-Power, the team carried 9 mm Beretta M-9 pistols, loaded with 15-round magazines. For communication they had tac com units in their small backpacks. Gary Manning was equipped with a pack somewhat larger than his teammates.

"Nice little stroll should get us there without even losing breath," McCarter announced with his usual breeziness.

"That's what we've been missing, T.J.," James said. "Mr. Congeniality."

"Who said *I* missed it?"

"Yes. Very amusing, ladies," McCarter muttered. "So cut it out."

James, checking his M-16/M-20 combo, nudged Hawkins. "He missed us."

Phoenix Force was sheltering behind a dark, wet outcropping. The chill wind, bringing cold rain across the rugged terrain, stung their exposed skin.

"At least we had warm weather in Israel," Hawkins said. "Hey, boss, can't we get a transfer?"

"Don't bloody well tempt me."

McCarter leaned back against the largest rock, facing the assembled team. "We all know what we're looking for?"

"Nukes. Khariza. Any of his cronies," Hawkins said.

"So you *were* awake at the briefing."

"Don't forget this Biriyenko character," Encizo said.

McCarter nodded. "Gary, you okay with those demolition packs?"

"Fine."

"Be one hell of bang if you take a bullet in that backpack," James commented.

"Thanks for reminding me."

"That's what buddies are for."

"You're a funny guy, Calvin."

"Rafe, take point," the Briton ordered. "Everyone, keep your eyes skinned. We can't be sure if this Dushinov character is sharp enough to have patrols out. Let's assume the worst. Time isn't on our side. We don't have the privilege of being able to wait until dark. So let's make sure we don't walk into anything we can't get out of."

They moved out, keeping distance between one another, every man constantly checking the surrounding landscape. The drifting rain lowered the light availability, reducing the range of vision. The only comfort was the fact it would be the same for anyone else.

The landscape was hilly, slopes studded with trees. Higher up, the foothills were well timbered. Their line of travel was taking them east. The Briton maintained a constant check on the GPS unit, using it with the small map encased in a plastic laminate. On the reverse was the satellite image of Dushinov's camp, showing the layout of the stone buildings. At the time of taking there had been a truck parked near one of the buildings. The image was a day and a half old, so the imaged vehicles could have gone by now. Taking that forward, McCarter accepted that the camp itself might be deserted by now. It was the way of these locations. They were often abandoned, the groups upping stakes and moving to a new spot, for no other reason than security.

Up ahead Encizo raised an arm, then indicated they should take cover. Phoenix Force vanished behind the closest cover, staying low until they received the all-clear from the Cuban. McCarter moved ahead and closed up with his point man.

"You see something?"

"I thought I did. When I checked again I realized it was a rock formation. The rain plays tricks with your eyes sometimes."

"No problem, mate. Rather a dodgy rock than a bloke with a gun."

McCarter dropped back to rejoin the others and told them what Encizo had reported.

"Easily done," Hawkins said. He sleeved rain from his face, taking a slow look around. "I keep imagining I can see a burger joint."

"That's just wishful thinking, my son."

"Ain't it just."

They lined out again and moved on. Their steady pace brought them along the narrow, rocky valley where Dushinov's camp was located. In the time it took them to reach this point, the weather had gotten worse. The rain was heavier, the increased wind sweeping it along the valley floor in chilled curtains.

"Worse than Manchester on a Friday night," McCarter muttered.

"I won't bother asking what that meant," James said.

"British folklore," McCarter said.

They huddled in the lee of a jagged rock, only partially sheltered from the weather. They had pulled the hoods of their combat jackets over their heads way back, covering the black knit caps they wore. They kept their weapons tight against their bodies.

McCarter pulled a pair of binoculars from his backpack and found himself a spot where he was able to look across the spread of the valley. He adjusted the settings and started a check of the area.

He found himself looking at the camp after his first sweep. The collection of stone buildings, a number of them in a poor condition, stood in an open area. There were stands of trees on the fringes of the village. He saw thin spirals of smoke rising from a couple of the buildings. The trails were dispersed by the wind as soon as they emerged. McCarter spotted vehicles parked in among the buildings, a battered truck and an open Toyota pickup. McCarter pulled back, widening his coverage. He picked up a solitary figure crossing the center of the camp, huddled in thick clothing against the rain. It was impossible to tell whether the figure was that of a man or a woman. The figure reached a building on the far side of the camp and vanished inside.

Beyond one of the most distant buildings McCarter saw the machine-gun emplacement fronting the dugout the satellite imagery had picked up. There were two of Dushinov's rebels huddled behind the Russian-made 7.62 mm belt-fed PK machine gun.

McCarter spent some time observing. After the figure crossing the camp he saw no one else. That meant little in itself. With the poor weather, the occupants were most probably sheltering inside. There wasn't much else they could do under the circumstances. The rebels were showing better sense than Phoenix Force.

Gary Manning joined the Briton.

"What do we know?"

"They're inside, relatively comfortable. We're outside. It's cold and it's wet. Who has the best deal?"

"Not showing their faces?"

"I've only seen one so far. Crossing from one building to another. Since then nothing."

Manning put his back against the rock. "Your call."

McCarter nodded in agreement.

"Sitting around like a bunch of wet rags isn't going to get this done. Let's get to it."

McCarter gathered the others around him. "Gary, I want you to tackle that dugout. Let Cal deal with the machine gun, and then you get in there and plant those charges."

"If we locate the nukes in there?" James asked. "It's unlikely, but just in case we do?"

"We can't go blowing them up in case it releases radioactive debris," McCarter agreed. "Assuming we do find them, we'll need to move them first."

"We're not going to carry them out," Manning said.

"These devices can be bulky packages. Not the easiest thing to slip into a backpack."

"If we need to, we'll have to call in some kind of help."

"All the way out here?" James asked. "I mean, it's not like dialing up the local branch of a courier service and saying come get this package."

"There's a backup plan in the system," McCarter said.

"Serves me right for asking." James grinned.

"Look, until we know one way or another, we can't afford to be in the middle of a firefight at this time," Manning pointed out.

McCarter nodded. "Okay. Cal, deal with the machine gun and get Gary inside that dugout. You can run your checks on what's in there and report. If it's only conventional weapons set your charges and move on. If it's the other possibility, we need to clear the place first so we can get the nukes out."

James and Manning moved to a point where they could observe the dugout.

"While we're on the subject of communication, get your tac com sets on, checked and working," McCarter added.

They donned the communications units, clipped the power packs to their belts and ran quick voice checks.

"T.J., you take the building directly ahead. I'll go for the larger one to the right. Rafe, I want you as backup, covering everyone from a distance. Last thing we need is some joker sneaking out by the back door. Those two buildings look to be the only ones in decent condition. Just in case, though, Rafe will watch the others while he covers our backs."

"You got it," Encizo said.

"Final check on weapons. Okay? Tac com units functioning? Let's move out, ladies, and make sure the same number come back. No excuses. We all go home."

Phoenix Force cleared their cover, each man moving toward his assigned target, senses on full alert, weapons cocked and held ready.

IT COULD HAVE BEEN bad timing, ill-luck, or just the way the cards fell. More likely it was Fate delivering the finger, but just as the SOG commandos broke from cover and began their move, the door to the largest building opened and the French mercenary, Bertran, stepped outside. He needed a breath of fresh air. The interior of the stone building, with a blazing log fire throwing heat across the crowded room, had become oppressive. Khariza's latest batch of volunteers had gathered for a briefing. The combination of damp clothing, sweat and cigarette smoke had become overwhelming. The mercenary had decided to clear his head.

As he stood on the threshold, taking a breath of air and ignoring the shouts and protests behind him about allowing cold air inside the building, Bertran looked across the village and saw the five armed intruders, already moving into the open and closing in fast.

He turned back inside the building, snatching up his AK from against the wall just inside the door. As he cocked the weapon he threw a command to the gathered volunteers and their instructors.

"We have hostiles in the area. Move now. Let's go."

Armed figures began to tumble out of the building. They lacked coordination, almost as if they weren't sure how to go on now they had committed themselves. None of them was fully protected from the weather. One of two were struggling to pull on heavy coats. Behind came an additional trio—Bertran's instructors. They began to move among the earlier group, pointing, yelling orders. They were also the first to open fire, targeting the incoming Phoenix Force.

THE TEAM MANNING the machine gun snapped into action at the sound of gunfire. They stared around them at Bertran's yell, searching and quickly locating Calvin James. He had broken away from the rest of the team, targeting the machine-gun emplacement. The Phoenix Force commando saw the crew start to pull the barrel of the machine gun in his direction. He triggered a burst from his M-16, the slugs bouncing off the stone wall surrounding the machine gun.

The gunner returned fire before the weapon was fully lined up on James's weaving figure. The burst of

7.62 mm fire went wild. The machine-gun team hauled the weapon around, the gunner bringing down the muzzle. He caught James in his sights and allowed himself a brief smile as he pulled the trigger. The machine gun fired two rounds—then jammed, locking solid. The gunner wasted precious seconds trying to fire again, his loader tugging at the ammunition belt in a vain attempt to free the jam.

James realized what had happened and increased his speed, going for the machine-gun team as they struggled. The tall black warrior took a hurdling leap over a pile of chopped logs lying in his path, landing lightly, turning as he sensed movement to his left. He caught a glimpse of a hooded figure wielding an AK, exiting the dugout behind the machine gun. James triggered as he brought his M-16 around with him, his triburst clouting the target high in the chest. The force kicked the man backward, arms thrown wide, the AK spilling from his fingers. Without breaking stride James kept on, driving toward his main target—the machine gun. The gunners abandoned their efforts to clear the jam, diving across their bunker to snatch up the weapons they had leaned against the wall. Still turning, the first man caught it from James as he breached the low wall of the bunker. He put his 3-round burst into the gunner's chest, the shots angling down. They cleaved through his body and drove him to the ground. As the second gunner came around, his AK picking up on James's moving figure, the Stony Man commando dropped into the bunker, and swung the butt of his M-16 in a short, sharp blow that cracked the gunner's left jaw, snapping his head around. The dazed gunner dropped backward, blood welling up from the side of his mouth. Not giving the guy time to recover and to use his AK again, James brought his M-16 into play and triggered a burst into the man's body. The close range drilled the 5.56 mm slugs into and through the gunner. He fell back, colliding with the machine gun, toppling it as he went down.

McCARTER SAW the group exit the largest building and cut across the uneven ground, his M-16 up and firing, returning the volleys that suddenly zipped his way. He barely heard the slugs whining off the rocky ground as he ran, concentrating on the men in front of him. He saw one go down, falling and staying on the ground. Another took a burst in the left shoulder, dropping his weapon to clutch at his ravaged flesh, shock registering when he felt the bloody wound and the shards of splintered bone sticking out from the lacerated flesh. The main group began to disperse. McCarter yanked a fragmentation grenade from his harness, pulling the pin with his teeth and letting the lever spring free. He took a silent count before launching the bomb at the group, then dropped to the ground a fraction of a second before the grenade detonated with a sharp crack. As the detonation faded, McCarter could hear someone screaming.

He rolled to his feet and plunged forward, eyes seeking moving figures as the smoke vanished, quickly dispersed by the wind and the falling rain. He picked up two men, moving around the blast area. They were staggering, one gripping his side. The other was staring at the mangled remains of his left arm. He had lost his hand. He stared around frantically as McCarter came barreling in his direction. The man's face was bloody, flesh torn, slivers of shrapnel embedded in his cheek. He had a pistol in his right hand, and he raised it at McCarter. The Briton triggered his M-16, jacking out a 3-round burst that hammered the man to the ground. Still moving, the Phoenix Force leader hit the other survivor, putting tribursts into the man's chest.

Behind McCarter, Rafael Encizo angled to one side and took on more of the armed figures leaving the building. His M-16 crackled sharply, the little Cuban picking his targets with unerring accuracy. He saw them tumble to the ground, most of them not even firing a shot. The numbers depleted rapidly. Encizo saw some of them turn aside and fall back, running around the end of the building to find cover.

"Don't let up," McCarter yelled into his tac com microphone. "Keep them on the run."

The Briton barely slowed his pace as he reached the building and charged inside, driven by adrenaline that boosted his energy and determination to end this attack as soon as he possibly could.

The main room had obviously been living quarters. There was an open fire with blazing logs throwing heat across the room. The place was littered with clothing, equipment and some crude wood furniture. McCarter came face-to-face with a rebel framed in a doorway on the far side of the room. The man raised a handgun and triggered a wild shot at him. The slug thudded into the door frame inches from McCarter's head. The Briton ducked, moving quickly to one side, then triggered a burst from waist level that hit the rebel in the lower body and threw him off balance. The man stumbled, still trying to return fire. He didn't get the chance to complete his move. McCarter hit him again, this burst delivered with precision. The 5.56 mm slugs hammered the man in the chest and he went down like a sack of grain, hitting the hard floor with a solid thump.

McCarter strode over to the body and went through the door. He found himself in a narrow, featureless passage with a couple of doors leading off. He kicked open the first. The room was bare except for a number of AKs stacked against one wall. As he booted open the second door, staying to one side as it swung wide, he was greeted by a rattle of shots. Slugs thumped the opposite wall, dusting the passage and sending stone chips flying. McCarter didn't deliberate. He used one of his grenades to clear the room. He flattened against the outer wall as he tossed the projectile through the door, feeling it shake as the grenade went off, immediately after a man had screamed in terror. The smoke and noise that erupted from the room was followed by the rattle of debris falling to the floor.

The Briton gave it a few seconds before he peered into the room and spotted the two bodies. In the confines of the small room they had taken the full brunt of the blast. One lay on his back, his lower torso ripped open by the detonation. The other had turned his back to the grenade, pushing himself into a corner in an attempt to escape. The blast had shredded his clothing and flesh, opening him up so that his spine and ribs lay exposed and bloody. As well as the usual debris, the room was littered by shreds of what looked like green paper. It took a moment before McCarter realized he was looking at the remnants of U.S. currency that had been caught in the explosion. A splintered table lay on its side with more dollar bills scattered around it, much of the currency scorched and smoking.

McCarter recognized one of the men as Abdul Wafiq from the identity photographs provided by Stony Man. When he turned over the second body he saw that it was Saeed Hassan.

T. J. HAWKINS MET resistance as he crossed open ground, his target the outer wall of the building in front of him. The stuttering crackle of autofire reached his ears, and he saw the bullet packs on the ground just ahead of him. An armed figure showed himself just above a crumbling wall section at the end of the building. The rebel swung the AK in Hawkins's direction, settling for a second burst.

Aware he was in the open with nowhere to go, the Phoenix Force commando did the only thing he could. He threw himself facedown on the ground, taking him below the shooter's weapon. Hawkins slid across the wet, muddy surface and came to a hard stop against the base of the wall. He kept a tight grip on his M-16, knowing that the rebel on the other side of the wall wasn't going to wait until his opponent got to his feet. Hawkins heard the man's rush of breath as he scrambled over the rubble, stones clattering underfoot. Twisting over onto his back and hauling himself into a sitting position, Hawkins picked up the rebel's shadow an instant before the man jumped the lowest section of the wall and lunged forward, the barrel of his AK swinging around to track its target. Hawkins fired first, a 3-round burst that punched into his adversary's chest and kicked him backward. The man's feet went from under him and he slammed down on his back. His AK swung out of control, the muzzle aiming skyward. As his body went into shock from the bullet hits, the rebel's finger closed against the trigger and the AK jacked out a sharp, noisy burst. The sound galvanized Hawkins and he fired again into the downed rebel, his second burst going in under the man's jaw, ripping up through his head and blowing off a sizable chunk of skull.

Hawkins climbed to his feet, bracing himself against the wall, shaking his head in surprise. It had come that close. Too damn close, he thought.

And then the world came back at him with a snap. The harsh crackle of autofire, bullets thumping into stone. The whine of ricochets. He was back in the combat zone with a vengeance.

RAFAEL ENCIZO, CROUCHED, caught a glimpse of an armed figure, autorifle at his shoulder, leaning through an open window. The guy was turning in Encino's general direction. The Cuban dropped to one knee, shouldered his M-16 and aimed and fired in a single, fluid moment. He saw the figure jerk back, dark flecks bursting from his right shoulder. Encizo fired again before the man disappeared completely, his follow-up triburst coring in through the man's upper chest. He went down this time, falling away from the window and Encizo made directly for it. Flat against the rain-slick wall he took a quick look inside. The man he'd shot lay sprawled on his back, chest and face bloody, eyes staring sightlessly at the ceiling. The room itself was bare, the hard earth floor littered with debris.

The thudding of running feet reached Encizo. He turned to see a team of gunners coming his way, their outlines hazy in the falling rain. Without hesitation Encizo pulled himself up onto the sill of the window and dropped inside, turning back to the rectangle of light as a face appeared, pushing the barrel of a rifle ahead of him. He brought up his M-16 and triggered into the face, saw it explode into a bloody mask. The man uttered a harsh scream and fell out of sight. Encizo primed a grenade and lobbed it through the window. The detonation was hard and sharp, followed by groans that faded as quickly as the sound of the explosion.

The Cuban sprinted across the room and turned in the direction of the door as he picked up movement on the other side. The door was kicked in, someone yelling in Arabic as he leaned inside, spraying the room with autofire. The Phoenix Force warrior had dropped to the floor the moment the door opened. He felt the vicious snap of the slugs as they laced the room, punching into the wall behind him. Still prone, Encizo tracked with his M-16, laying down a sustained burst. His low-level shots took the shooter in the legs, shattering bone and dropping the wounded man to his knees. Without pause Encizo rolled to his feet, turning to face the leg-shot man and put his last rounds into the guy's head, driving him to the floor.

Encizo flattened against the inner wall, reloading his M-16 before he moved. Crouching he checked beyond the door. A bare passage ended with a single door. There was a rusty bolt on the outside, locked. Intrigued, Encizo moved along the passage and eased the bolt free. Then he stepped to the side and pushed the door open with the muzzle of his M-16. It swung back. At first Encizo thought the room was empty. Then his nostrils picked up a stale odor emanating from the room. He checked inside and, despite the gloom, he was able to see the ragged, bloody figure of a man, upright and tethered to a ring in the wall.

Moving into the room Encizo saw that the man had been savagely beaten. He was barefoot and his feet were bloody and swollen. The hanging head glistened with blood. Heavy bruises covered every inch of skin. The ripped shirt exposed massive purple bruises on the chest and torso. Encizo pulled his Tanto knife and cut the ropes holding the captive to the wall ring. He caught the figure as it slumped, lowering the man to the cold floor of the room. As he did, the man groaned against being moved.

"Easy," Encizo said. "I'm trying not to hurt you."

"American," the man mumbled through a dislocated jaw. "I'm American. CIA. Did McAdam send you? McAdam?"

The name rang bells in Encizo's head.

Rod McAdam?

The CIA man whose name had come up in association with Gardener and Justin.

"Yes," Encizo said. "Rod McAdam. He needs your report." A brief hesitation and then Encizo said, "He needs to know for Gardener and Justin."

The man took a long, painful breath, clutching at his chest. "That son of a bitch, Khariza. He let them do this to me."

"We'll find him. What do I need to tell McAdam?"

"He has to warn Gardener his man Khalli is in danger. I think Khariza is going to use his nukes in Iraq. Crazy bastard wants to radiate the country…if he doesn't get what he wants."

"Control?"

"More. Khariza wants to be the man. Head honcho now Hussein has been ousted."

Who, Encizo wondered, was Khalli?

BERTRAN HAD SEEN the black man and his companion going for the dugout. They seemed to know exactly where the weapons were stored. They plainly had good intelligence. He wondered if they had anything to do with the American Dushinov had brought to the camp. Perhaps a search-and-retrieve team. On the other hand they might have come looking for Khariza. If that was the case, they would be disappointed. The Iraqi had already moved on to the next phase of his operation. Bertran was supposed to follow shortly. The French mercenary realized that if he didn't extricate himself from this mess he wouldn't be going anywhere.

As the newly trained volunteers fell at the guns of the attack force, Bertran turned around, ducking for cover behind the partly collapsed wall of an old well that had run dry years before. He sprawled on the wet and muddy ground, staying low as the sharp blast of a fragmentation grenade drowned out gunfire for a few seconds. He heard debris patter back to earth and heard, too, the moans of the fatally injured. No amount of training prepared a man for the time when he was the victim of such an attack. Personal injury couldn't be covered by any amount of instruction. Pain was something each man had to take on board and handle in his own way.

Out the corner of his eye Bertran spotted Dushinov. The Chechen was on his knees behind a wheel of the truck, a bright splash of fresh blood marking the shoulder of his coat. It was hard to tell if he had been injured or if it was simply blood from someone else. The rebel leader looked across at Bertran and indicated the dugout, pointing with the AK he was brandishing.

"Cover me," Dushinov yelled over the rattle of gunfire.

He didn't wait for the Frenchman's response. Dushinov pushed to his feet and struck out in the direction of the dugout, his assault rifle thrust in front of him. For his size Dushinov showed great agility. He moved quickly, covering the distance in a short time. Bertran saw him leap over the wall surrounding the machinegun emplacement and hurl himself inside the dugout.

MANNING HAD ALREADY established that the dugout held nothing more than conventional weapons—rifles, ammunition, grenades and a good supply of handheld rocket launchers. There were some crates bearing Korean markings, already open, that contained blocks of explosive compound. The Canadian keyed his headset and contacted McCarter.

"No nukes here. Just conventional ordnance."

"Check. You know what to do," the Briton said.

"Looks like our friends here are planning for a busy time," James said, examining the cache of weapons.

"Could be—" Manning began.

His words were cut off as a dark figure burst in through the dugout opening, an AK in his hands. It was Dushinov. The Chechen rebel swung the assault rifle around, clouting Manning across the side of the head, the blow toppling the Canadian into the stack of boxes. Dushinov gave a wild yell, striking out again at Manning, his second blow opening a bloody gash in Manning's jaw.

Calvin James, to one side, avoided the Chechen's initial assault and braced himself as the broad figure swung in his direction. Dushinov's bearded face was dark with rage. He launched himself at James and walked straight into the Stony Man commando's powerful kick. It caught the man in the ribs, knocking him against the wall of the dugout, stumbling to one knee, his AK slipping from his grasp. It was only the hard bulk of his body that prevented Dushinov from going fully down as he absorbed the power of the blow. James hadn't waited to see the result of his kick. He immediately delivered a follow-up, this time snapping a vicious blow that connected with Dushinov's left cheek. The impact turned Dushinov's head, cracking it against the wall of the dugout. James's kick had split his cheek wide open.

Blood began to stream down Dushinov's face, soaking into his beard. He lowered his body and pushed himself away from the wall, his hands reaching out to grab hold of James's clothing. Shoving hard with his legs Dushinov catapulted himself into the American, propelling them both across the dirt floor. James felt himself backpedaling, trying to stay on his feet, but the sheer weight of his adversary was too much and he fell. The impact might have winded him if he hadn't been prepared for it. Even so, James was momentarily stunned. He felt Dushinov's massive hands clawing for his throat and dropped his chin against his chest. Thick fingers dug into his flesh. Dushinov was grunting with the effort. The kick to his head had left him in pain and it was affecting him to a degree. Despite that, the Chechen still had strength in reserve and he used it to overwhelm his opponent.

Dushinov's heavy bulk had trapped the Phoenix Force commando's M-16 against his chest and he was unable to free the weapon. He brought his own legs up, scissoring them against Dushinov's body, attempting to put pressure on the man's ribs. Again Dushinov's heavy bulk and his thick clothing reduced the effect. There was enough pressure to make him pause. James squeezed harder. The Chechen rebel reared up, sucking breath into his lungs, allowing the American to pull his arms from under his body. The Stony Man warrior hauled his right fist back and drove it hard into Dushinov's face, directly over his nose. The blow crushed it, blood spurting. Dushinov roared in pain and anger. James hit him repeatedly. Dushinov rocked back and James pulled himself up off the ground, thrusting both arms out. He clamped his hands either side of his adversary's head and jabbed his thumbs deep into the man's eye sockets. Dushinov's roar of pain dissolved into howls as James's thumbs tore into his eyes. He stumbled to his feet, clutching his hands to his face.

Gary Manning had pushed to his feet and was directly in line with the dugout entrance when Bertran raced inside. The French mercenary had hesitated for only a short time before following Dushinov.

Bertran saw Dushinov, hands clutched to his bleeding face, stumble away from the black intruder, who was down on the ground. Bertran began to line up his assault rifle when he became aware of another figure in the dugout. It was Manning. The Canadian brought up his M-16 and fired before Bertran could react. The triburst drilled into the Frenchman's chest, kicking him back against the dugout wall. The impact pulled Bertran around in a half circle, his finger clamping against the AK's trigger, the reflex causing the weapon to emit a short burst that punched a group of 7.62 mm slugs into Dushinov's lower back. The rebel leader catapulted forward, clearing James as he rolled aside, and hit the hard ground on his face.

James pushed to his feet, retrieving his M-16.

"That was close," he said.

Manning dabbed at the bleeding gash on his face, staring at the blood. "Tell me about it, Cal."

James turned to watch the entrance of the dugout while Manning dropped to his knees and swung his backpack off his shoulders. He moved quickly, pulling out a couple of the explosive packs and placing them in among the weapons cache and setting the timers.

"Shall we go?" he suggested to James.

They left the dugout and cleared the emplacement wall. Manning keyed his headset and gave the rest of the team the warning about the coming blast.

"Main building," McCarter's voice came back. "I think we cleared the way. Keep your eyes open in case we missed any of the buggers."

James and Manning crossed the village, heading for the main building. McCarter came out to meet them. The big Canadian waved him back under cover and as they moved around the end of the building his explosives detonated. The ground shook as the blast leveled the dugout. The added power of the stored munitions kicked a thick cloud of fire, dust and debris into the air. Smoke curled up from the heart of the explosion, and clods of earth and shattered weapons were deposited across the area.

"Happy now?" McCarter asked.

Manning smiled. "It's called job satisfaction."

"No bloody way. You just like blowing things up."

McCarter led the way inside the building. He took Manning and James to the room he had hit with the grenade.

"Couple of Khariza's mates," he said.

James examined the bodies, glancing at the littered currency the grenade had scattered across the room.

"Looks like they were playing paymasters. If Khariza got into those money accounts he can buy just what he wants," Manning said.

McCarter picked up an incoming message over his tac com headset.

"Go ahead, Rafe. Okay, I'm on my way." McCarter caught James's eye. "With me, Cal. Gary, check this room and the rest of the building in case there's anything we can use."

With James in tow McCarter made his way across the village to Encizo.

"Rafe found a prisoner. Seems he's CIA and works for Rod McAdam."

"Could be interesting."

"I love your understatement, mate."

When they reached the interrogation room, James immediately opened his med pack and knelt over the CIA man.

"Rafe, he say anything. What's his story?"

"His name's Lane. He didn't give me too much. Mainly that McAdam needs to tell Gardener some guy called Khalli is in danger. Khariza is threatening to use those nukes inside Iraq. Not much else. The man is in a bad way, David. They worked on him pretty hard."

McCarter turned to watch as James did what he could for the injured man. He could hear Lane groaning. The Briton moved in to crouch beside his Phoenix Force partner. James's face was taut with his efforts, his body bent over the CIA agent, as he struggled to keep life going in the man's tortured body. McCarter didn't speak. He was aware how strongly James felt about keeping his patients alive. He took each one personally, giving everything he could under difficult circumstances. That was the problem. Battlefield casualties could be the most traumatic, needed the expertise and the equipment not normally available in the middle of a fire zone. Internal injuries called for instant attention, while external damage had problems all their own. And always time was the vital factor. There was never enough of that.

Lane died a few minutes later. He didn't speak. He just slipped away as his body became unable to deal with the damage inflicted by Khariza's henchmen.

James sat over the body, staring at his bloody hands.

"Sorry, man, I couldn't hold on to you."

"Cal, let's move on," Encizo said quietly, leaning over to place a hand on James's shoulder.

McCarter walked back through the building, checking rooms as he went. He glanced up as Hawkins appeared.

"Hey, boss, we done here?"

"We're done," the Briton replied.

"You okay?"

"Rafe found a prisoner. American. Looks like he could have been one of McAdam's CIA operatives."

"Could have?"

"He didn't make it."

"He give anything useful?"

"Confirmation Khariza intends using those stolen nukes."

"Not the best news I've heard lately."

McCarter keyed his tac com and spoke to the team.

"Before we leave this place I want it checked inch by inch. Every bloody room. Every rock and stone. Let's see if we can pick up anything that might give us a pointer where Khariza might have gone with those bombs. Let's spread out and get it done. I'll put in a call to Stony Man and have them fix our extraction."

Stony Man Farm, Virginia

"A RUSSIAN MILITARY TEAM is en route to lift you out," Price said. "It seems the Russian president is willing to overlook our unsanctioned strike seeing that you've done them a favor by removing Dushinov. Our President made it clear we're not in the habit of doing another nation's dirty work for them, but Dushinov was aiding a known enemy of the U.S. and giving him sanctuary. It also appears that those three nukes were part of a number stolen and sold by Russian ex-military, so the Russian president is caught between a rock and a hard place. He wants to smooth things over."

"My heart bleeds for him," McCarter said. "My main concern is where those bloody bombs are *now*. I don't give a damn where they came from."

"Okay, listen up," Price continued. "This is where we get the good news. The three nukes are in Syria. Mossad's inside man came through with the information. He passed a message to his home base. There's a base near the Syria-Iraq border where Khariza has been allowed to set up shop. The Mossad agent has Khariza and Barak there. The nukes were delivered from Dushinov's camp. Fedor Biriyenko is on site, showing Khariza and his team how to arm and set the nukes."

"Bloody, hell," McCarter said. "Can you confirm all this?"

"Bear's running satellite sweeps as we speak, based on the location the Mossad man sent through. We'll try to have everything ready when you relocate. Hal is talking to the President. They're liaising with U.S. Military Command in Iraq. You'll be given all the backup you need. The military will chopper you in and extract you when you call. There'll be a Nuclear Energy Search Team on hand to deal with the nukes if you locate them."

"About time we got a break on this."

"We'll send through photos of the Mossad agent and make sure you have current ID on all the other players."

"For now just get us out of this place," McCarter said. "It's cold, it's wet, and the locals aren't very friendly."

CHAPTER SEVEN

Syria-Iraq Border

Phoenix Force gathered in the chill shadows of dawn. A thin wind was blowing across the dusty terrain. The paling sky showed cloudless, cold, which would change swiftly enough as the day emerged from the darkness. Phoenix Force was established, close to its target.

Below them, nestled against the backdrop of low, stony hills, was the complex of buildings that was Razan Khariza's jump-off point for his move back into Iraq. From here he would make his strike for Baghdad, and the information Stony Man was working from indicated he would be carrying his nuclear devices with him. Phoenix Force had priorities—stopping Khariza and neutralizing the threat from the nuclear devices. In essence they had to succeed with one to stop the other, but Phoenix Force was aware that life didn't run along those fixed lines. Razan Khariza was no novice. He planned and made the best of every situation. He had three nuclear devices. Common sense dictated that he wasn't going to use them all in a single location. With nuclear weapons one was enough in any given spot. Khariza was canny enough to spread his options, which meant the possibility of three separate locations, each with its own device. So Phoenix Force had to go for the Syrian base in the hope they could find out where Khariza was planning to distribute his weapons.

Ben Sharon's inside man had passed along vital information pinpointing the location of the base. His time posing as a member of Khariza's group had finally paid off, but the information appeared to have come with a high price. There had been no further contact with him since he had passed along the location.

The men of Phoenix Force studied the base, scanning the layout as they ran final checks on their equipment and weapons. Fully armed with sidearms, M-16s and grenades, the commandos wore their tac com units to maintain contact. James had his M-16 fitted with an M-203 grenade launcher. Each man also carried a sheathed combat knife.

McCarter patted down his camou fatigues, making sure pockets and webbing were secure. He pulled down the peak of his cap, turning to face the team.

"Everybody set?" He received four nods. "Time to go then."

They eased away from cover, each man aware of his own responsibility in the upcoming strike. They all knew the importance of what was about to take place and the need to shut down Khariza's operation before it reached a critical stage. The man was intent on creating a major event within Iraq. He hadn't gone to all the expense and trouble to obtain three nuclear devices without having some definite use for them. And detonating the bombs within Iraq itself, on top of the long-term effects, would kill a lot of people. That included Iraqi citizens, members of the coalition forces and any number of international individuals resident in the country for diverse reasons.

No one had come up with any logic to Khariza's intentions. In his mind he might have come to the conclusion that if Iraq was beyond his grasp, then the country had to be denied to what he termed as its invaders, the corrupt and devious Westerners who had come in and stolen his nation.

David McCarter, for one, didn't look too deeply at that part of the problem. The reason why didn't concern him. His job was to prevent Khariza going through with his plans. He would let others figure out why at a later date. Razan Khariza had created enough mayhem already and his influence had spread out as far as the U.K. and into America. The twisted logic of a man who could order the detonation of a bomb that had wiped out a community in Texas wasn't something to be discussed over a cup of coffee. It had to be faced down and ended, period.

The Briton heard a low voice over his tac com unit. Hawkins.

"Perimeter guard. North section. There may be more, so watch yourselves."

"Thanks, T.J.," McCarter acknowledged.

HAWKINS'S WARNING was fresh in Rafael Encizo's mind. The Cuban, coming in from the east of the base, had unsheathed his Cold Steel Tanto knife long before the warning had been transmitted. He held the keen-edged blade against his thigh as he trod the hard ground, his M-16 in his left hand.

Rounding a jagged outcropping, Encizo held back on impulse. Something, maybe a slight sound, a faint shadow, even an odor, warned him he wasn't alone. His pause gave him the advantage, the split-second moment that divided life from death. In combat situations instinct and an ability to sense approaching danger had saved many lives. This time it paid off for Encizo.

A man in combat fatigues, carrying an AK-74, a scarf looped across the lower part of his face, swung around the rock and came face-to-face with him.

The sentry opted for his weapon, bringing the AK into target acquisition.

Encizo had little to slow him down. He held the combat knife in his right hand. His arm swept up, the blade flashing slightly in the early light. It cut back and forth, the chill steel slicing in through the folds of the scarf to sever the flesh below. The sentry tried to draw breath. Instead he uttered a strange, gurgling sound, unable to suck air into his lungs. He barely saw the moving figure in front of him draw closer, was barely aware of Encizo leaning in to thrust the blade between his ribs and into his heart. The little Cuban turned the knife, feeling it cut deep. The sentry fell back against the rock. He struggled against the enveloping sensation that was, in fact, his body starting to close down. Encizo held him, his shoulder wedged against the man's chest until he became a loose deadweight. He lowered the man to the ground, easing the knife from his chest. He wiped the blade along the leg of his fatigue pants before slipping it back in the sheath. Crouching beside the rock, Encizo activated his tac com.

"One sentry down."

As PHOENIX FORCE CLOSED on the base, the approach was slowed by the presence of the patrolling sentries. Two more were silenced before the Stony Man commandos reached the exterior wall.

Hawkins was the first to reach his position. He took the opportunity to check inside the area. The place was silent; no one was up and about yet. The huddle of stone buildings might have been deserted if it hadn't been for the vehicles parked in a central section. Hawkins counted four, three dusty, well-used Toyota pickups and a newer German 4x4.

He was about to pass along the information when he spotted movement, a man stepping out of an open door, a steaming mug in one hand.

"We have an early riser," Hawkins warned. He watched the man stare around him, taking gulps from the mug. After a few seconds the man turned and went back inside, closing the door behind him. "All clear," he reported.

MCCARTER WAS AWARE that their time on Syrian soil might be short. He kept in mind that Syrian forces could be in the area and once any hostilities commenced they might show their faces in defense of their guests. He had to try to keep their strike at Khariza's base short and sharp. Make the best of the opportunity they had and gain whatever they could before moving out.

With that in mind he made his final check, confirming his people were in position before giving the operation the go-ahead.

"Short and sweet, mates. No time for sightseeing on this trip. We know what we've come for. Let's do it and go home. Cal, hit those vehicles. That should wake up the rest of our friends in there."

Calvin James wasted no time. He had already loaded a high-explosive grenade in the M-203. Now he aimed and fired, taking out the SUV first. The detonation shook the ground. The hefty 4x4 blew apart in a ball of fire, scattering metal debris in all directions. Before most had rained back to earth James fired off a second grenade into one of the pickups, following with a third that wrote off another vehicle. The calm of the early morning was shattered as the grouped vehicles were turned into a fiery tangle of twisted metal and smoking rubber, blazing fuel spraying across the immediate area. The roar of the flames, sucking greedily at the air, was accompanied by the thump of broken parts crashing back on the ground.

"As they say in the best B-movies," McCarter told them, "it's time to rock and roll."

ARMED MEN RACED from open doors, weapons up and tracking for targets. In the pale light of the dawn they hit the ground running, eyes blinking against the new day, slow to come to terms with the sudden appearance of armed intruders and the destruction of their vehicles.

The crackle of gunfire broke through the hissing sound of burning vehicles. Khariza's people were firing as they moved, some uncertain of their targets, others slightly more aware as they took aim at the fleeting figures of the attacking force. Bullets crisscrossed, thumping into walls and filling the air with dust and stone chips.

Phoenix Force closed in, already in combat mode, their senses fine-tuned to the task ahead. They returned fire with harsh precision, knowing what lay behind the presence of these Khariza followers. The hard-liners from the former regime were intent on prolonging the effects of the old administration, and despite the capture and incarceration of Saddam Hussein, these people were unwilling to relinquish the way of life that had kept them in luxury that had been denied the rest of the Iraqi people. They were refusing to lay down their arms, forgo the hatred that had been engendered through the years, and were determined to cause as much hardship and misery as they could.

Hawkins had targeted the doorway where he had seen the first early riser. He raised a booted foot and kicked the door wide, ducking as he passed through. He was in a kitchen and the guy he had seen with the mug was still there. By the time Hawkins appeared, the man had dropped his mug, reaching for the pistol he had on the cluttered table. He spun in Hawkins's direction, half crouching as he searched for his target. The American commando was low, hidden by the table, but he was able to see the other man's lower body. Hawkins leveled his M-16 and fired a burst that cored in through the man's thighs. The man screamed, falling forward, bracing himself with one hand on the table as he started to fire the pistol. His shots burst through the wooden top, impacting against the floor, inches from Hawkins. The Phoenix Force commando triggered his rifle a second time, angling the muzzle up a fraction so that his burst took the man in the chest. The guy dropped to the floor, the pistol spinning from his lax fingers.

Hawkins pushed to his feet and crossed the kitchen, making for the door that would take him farther into the building. He could hear yelling and the rattle of gunfire coming from both inside and outside the building.

MANNING SKIRTED the wrecked and burning vehicles and ran for the cover of a doorway. He could hear the zip and whack of slugs pounding the ground in his wake. The door in front of him was closed. The burly Canadian assessed the bleached wood as he neared the door, then hit it with his left shoulder, feeling the wood splinter. It caved in under his bulk and he followed it inside the room. As he went through he turned aside, clearing the open frame where he would have been silhouetted. The thud of slugs hitting the stone and the wooden frame reached his ears. Manning dropped to one knee, lowering his frame. One of the shooters followed him into the room, pausing because he failed to see the intruder. The Phoenix Force pro tilted the M-16 and triggered a burst that took the shooter in the chest, spinning him away from the door.

Pushing to his feet, Manning moved to the far side of the empty, dusty room and hauled open the door leading through into the main building. Checking the passage stretched in front of him, he picked up the sound of movement ahead and plucked a stun grenade from his webbing. He pulled the pin, holding the grenade in his right hand as he neared the end of the passage. Peering around the corner, he saw a group of gunners engaged in some kind of discussion. They seemed in doubt as to what to do. Manning made a decision for them. He released the lever on the stun grenade, then tossed the bomb in their direction. It hit the floor, bouncing a couple of times before it detonated. Manning had withdrawn around the corner, turning away, his hands clasped to his ears. The grenade exploded with a sharp crack and a burst of blinding light that left the victims deafened and barely able to see. When Manning showed himself, they were stumbling around in confusion.

One still held his rifle and he opened fire, spraying the passage with bullets that bounced off the walls and ceiling, causing more damage to the structure than anything else. Manning crouched, returned fire and put the shooter down with a 3-round burst from his M-16.

One of the other fedayeen clawed a grenade from his belt and fumbled with the pin. He pulled it before Manning could prevent him and threw it blindly. The grenade hit one of the walls and rolled across the floor. It detonated with a loud crack, filling the passage with hot fragments that cut into any human flesh it found. The fedayeen themselves were caught in the blast, bodies receiving fatal wounds from the shrapnel. Manning had pulled back around the corner when he spotted the grenade. He wasn't quite fast enough and felt the tearing snatch of something gouging his left arm just above the elbow. He didn't experience any immediate pain. Manning knew that would come later. Glancing at his arm, he saw the tear in his sleeve and blood starting to soak the material. He pushed around the corner and started along the passage, now strewed with bodies and debris from the grenade burst.

The door near the fedayeen had been pushed partway open by the blast. The room beyond looked to have been some kind of operations center. It was deserted now, chairs pushed back from tables, monitor screens on two laptop still functioning. Manning crossed to check them out. The first showed a schematic of some kind of mechanism and after staring at it Manning realized he was looking at a diagram of a bomb. More importantly, a nuclear device. Manning was Phoenix Force's explosive specialist. Being a perfectionist, the Canadian had immersed himself in explosives theory and the construction of devices, including nuclear. Manning might not have been able to construct a nuclear device, but his background allowed him to recognize what he was seeing on the monitor.

This would be one of the nuclear devices supplied by the North Korean, Sun Yang Ho. And Fedor Biriyenko, the Russian, was showing the Iraqis how to arm and detonate the devices.

Manning moved to the second screen. It was a map

of Iraq. He recognized the configuration immediately, and its border with Syria, Turkey and Kuwait. Manning's attention was drawn to specific areas. Three in total, marked with red circles: Baghdad, the Kurdish-held area close to the Turkish border and the Western Hijara Desert—specifically Rumayla—where one of the country's richest oilfields lay.

He stared at the map.

Three locations.

Three nuclear devices.

Each important in its own right.

Detonating a nuclear device in any of those spots would create devastation. The resultant radiation would also isolate the locations for an indeterminate length of time, rendering them inhospitable. If Khariza was serious in his intent, he would leave Iraq a deadly legacy.

The chilling truth, as far as Manning was concerned, was that Khariza could do exactly that. The man would deny Iraq part of its future to satisfy his own whim.

Manning checked out the table, noting a printer next to the laptop showing the Iraq map. Reaching for the mouse, he opened the print function and clicked on the map. Seconds later the printer began to operate, the sheet emerging from the machine. Manning checked it, then folded it and placed the sheet in one of his pockets. It was insurance in case the laptop was damaged and the map lost from its memory.

He clicked on his tac com.

"I think I have one of the things we came for. Locations Khariza could be going for with his nukes."

"Bloody great," McCarter enthused. "Don't lose it, mate."

"Trust me. I do this for a living."

ENCIZO HAD FOUND Fedor Biriyenko. The Russian was in one of the rooms being used as sleeping quarters. The man lay across the sagging bed, with its thin mattress and grubby sheets. His throat had been cut, deeply and from ear to ear, so that blood had surged from the severed arteries, soaking into the bedding beneath him. Encizo had been attracted to the room by the incessant buzzing sound, which had come from the dark mass of flies settled on or hovering above the gaping wound. There was already a smell coming from the body. Encizo stood just inside the door, studying the corpse. Biriyenko had plainly served his purpose. Khariza had rewarded him by having him killed, guaranteeing that the Russian wouldn't be able to betray his former employer.

"Biriyenko accounted for. He isn't going to tell us much. Not in his condition."

"I get you. Let's get together, people. If we have what we came for, it's time to call our ride out of here."

THE THREE ARMED MEN were determined to prevent Calvin James from securing the room behind them. He had fought his way through the building only to be confronted by the trio. There was something in their hard resistance that brought him to the conclusion they had something to hide.

They had formed a barricade of wooden packing cases and some steel barrels and were using this to prevent access to the room. James had come on the obstacle when he had descended stone steps to the cellar of the building. The opening volley of shots peppered his face with dust from the stone wall and James had dropped, crawling for cover behind a pillar. He hunkered down, peering around the edge of the pillar to assess the odds.

One barricade.

Three armed men wielding AK-74s.

James was under no illusions. These men were guarding something with their lives. Nothing less. With the knowledge of Khariza's three nuclear devices, James began to get the feeling he might have walked in on the location of the main prize without even being aware of it, which meant sweet nothing if he couldn't get the three guards away from that door. He debated about using one of his grenades, dismissing the thought almost in the same breath. He didn't want to use anything that might damage whatever lay behind the door. Nuclear devices weren't liable to actually detonate if he used a grenade. They didn't work that way. But damage to any casing might release harmful radiation, and he had no desire to do that, either. So he was going to have to remove the three men by more conventional means.

James fisted a stun grenade, pulled the pin and let the lever spring free. He held the canister for counted seconds before lobbing it in the direction of the barricade, then swung back out of the blast area, sheltering behind the rise of the stone steps. He heard someone yell, picked up the scrape of boots on the cellar floor as the men behind the barricade tried to avoid the grenade. Time ran out for them and the hard crack of the blast, followed by the intense flash, confirmed the fact.

The moment the brilliant glare faded James pushed to his feet and advanced on the barricade. He saw one of the trio, stagger in front of him. The fedayeen squinted through tear-filled eyes, locating James through a watery haze and tried to bring his weapon on line. James fired first, the 3-round burst catching the guy in the chest. The impact of the shots pushed the gunner back against the barricade. He made an attempt to regain his balance but James's second burst put him down for good.

The click of a weapon being cocked told James at least one of the remaining pair was still capable of handling his weapon. A shadow on the cellar floor warned the Phoenix Force commando that he was about to be faced by another hostile. There was no gain in delaying the inevitable. James made the play, sweeping wide around the edge of the barricade and the moment he locked onto the would-be shooter he opened up with his M-16. The burst cored in through the guy's upper chest and neck. He skidded back from the barricade, half falling against the wall, still maintaining his grip on his AK. James fired again, placing his burst over the man's heart. The fedayeen slithered along the wall, slumping in a kneeling position, head down on his chest.

The surviving member of the group, frantically blinking his eyes and mouthing unintelligible words, erupted out of the far corner of the barricade, thrusting his right arm forward. He held a pistol in his fist and started firing the moment he turned around. James felt the burn of one slug across the back of his left hand. He turned away, then cut loose with a return volley from his M-16. The assault rifle jacked out its rapid burst, the 5.56 mm slugs tearing away the target's lower jaw. James lowered the muzzle and triggered a second burst, the slugs driving the guy to the cellar floor.

James stepped around the bodies and stood in front of the door, which was secured by sturdy bolts. He yanked them across and hauled the heavy door wide open. Spotting a light switch set in the exterior wall close to the door, he flicked it and the room was flooded with light.

The first thing he saw was the pair of identical packs on a small wood bench. Crossing to stand in front of it, James examined the packs. He knew he was looking at two of Razan Khariza's nuclear devices. In their current location they didn't look all that threatening. Just a couple of large, square, boxlike units that might have been many things. James knew better. Phoenix Force had been confronted by nuclear devices on more than one occasion, and it needed only a closer look for James to identify the configuration of the bombs.

He took a look around the cell-like room. Other than the bench, it was devoid of anything else, except for a discarded pile of crumpled blankets in one corner.

There were only two nuclear devices in the room, which meant one of them had been removed.

James experienced a moment of dread as he assimilated the fact. Unless the missing device was somewhere within the base, it could have already been sent on its way.

To where?

A fleeting thought flashed around inside his head. If Razan Khariza wasn't among the fedayeen hostiles at the base, the most likely destination for the third device would be Baghdad. It was the only place for Khariza to go. If he wanted to make some grand gesture, he would need to do it high-profile. His ultimate goal was to try to seize power, and Khariza would have to grandstand his ambition.

James called in his find and expressed his feelings to McCarter. There was a long pause as the Briton considered the suggestion. Then his voice came back through the tac com unit.

"We haven't any sign of Khariza or that bloody Barak bloke up here. We did find Biriyenko dead, so Khariza must have got what he needed from him. Cal, we'll have those two nukes airlifted out of here. I'll call for our ride back to Iraq."

"You calling in NEST?"

"Too bloody right. I don't want us lugging those things around and accidentally pressing some button."

James took a second turn around the room, just in case he had missed anything. He was moving by the pile of blankets when his boot nudged something solid. He glanced down and saw a bloody, naked human foot protruding from the mass of stained, crumpled cloth.

On his knees, James dragged the mass of material aside and found himself staring down at a battered, bloody human form. The face was turned so he could see it and James made recognition.

The man lying on the floor was the Mossad deep-cover agent, the man who had passed along the information that had brought Phoenix Force into Syria.

Stony Man Farm, Virginia

"TWO DOWN, ONE TO GO," Barbara Price said. "But no Khariza?"

"That bloke seems to stay one step ahead of us every time we manage to get close," McCarter grumbled. "He's got a lucky streak. That, or a bloody effective crystal ball."

"At least you've got an indication where he intends to deliver those nukes. Taking a wild guess, I'd go for Khariza handling the Baghdad location."

"That's what we decided. He'll want the big stage. So we're heading there now. The military is sending teams to the other locations. Ground forces and airborne recon. They'll see if they can pick anything up. We couldn't cover big areas like those so it's best we go for the city option."

"Still a big place to cover."

"There *are* five of us," McCarter said with mock severity.

Price chuckled. "We're monitoring all message sources. Phone. Radio. E-mail. Aaron has a tap into Echelon and all the other security agencies. One way or another these people have to keep in communication. They can't do it via snail mail or message carriers. There's been an increase in message transmissions ever since Bucklow. You'd be surprised at the claims for that. Every fringe group has claimed responsibility. They all want to jump on the bandwagon. You read some of the stuff that came in, and it makes you realize we don't need enemies overseas. There are plenty here on the mainland."

"It's a weird world we live in, Barb. Don't let it worry you. Long as I'm around, you're safe."

"What a smoothie. I feel better already."

"If Mr. Grumpy Bear comes up with anything, pass it down the line."

"Will do."

"How is Able doing?"

"You think your life is complicated? Think along the lines of opened, worms, can. That give you a hint?"

"I get the message."

CHAPTER EIGHT

Iraq, East of Baghdad

It was midafternoon when the Hummer came into sight along the rough track, dust billowing into the air behind the spinning wheels. As it rounded the final bend before it reached the shallow stream that crossed the track, the driver braked, slowing the vehicle. It rolled to a stop a couple yards short of the water, the V8 diesel engine ticking over.

"What do you think, Sarge?" the driver asked. He was staring at the two huddled figures on the ground just short of the water. It looked like an old couple, an elderly man bending over the sagging figure of an equally old woman. Battered packs were scattered around them, spilled clothing and personal belongings strewed across the earth. The old man had turned to stare at them, lifting his bony hands in a gesture of helplessness.

"They genuine or what?"

"How the hell do I know?"

Sergeant Mace Horton reached for his M-16, checking that the safety was off before he swung his legs outside the vehicle. He stood for a moment and scanned the immediate area. It was a fairly flat stretch of desert. Only a few shallow humps marred the terrain a hundred yards away. A low wind was blowing in and out of the wasteland, stirring up gritty dust. Horton hated that. It seemed to be an almost permanent feature of the damn country. Hot, dry wind that carried dust with it that got into everything. He squared his helmet, turned and spoke to Ruggello, the crewman on the swivel-mounted .50-caliber machine gun.

"You keep your finger on that trigger, Ruggello. And keep your eyes open."

Ruggello nodded. He was a big man, broad across the shoulders and chest.

"You got it."

"You want me with you?" the driver asked.

His name was Denny, and he had just turned twenty that week. As he spoke, Denny was stepping out of the Hummer, his M-16 already in his hands.

"You stay inside. Keep the engine running. And call this in to HQ."

Denny nodded.

It was the last thing he did before his head blew apart. He spun, banging up against the side of the Hummer before he went down, his blood soaking into the greedy, dry Iraqi dust. The distant crack of the shot followed.

Ruggello began to swing around the .50-caliber gun. He was still traversing when a bullet struck him just above his left eye. It flipped him backward, his legs catching the edge of the Hummer's frame. He fell outside the vehicle.

Horton moved to cover behind the vehicle's solid bulk. He stared out across the empty terrain and realized there was only one place the shots could have come from.

The slight humps off to the left. Had to be there. Unless they were being covered by some sniper buried under the surface of the ground. Horton leaned inside the Hummer and picked up the binoculars resting on the seat. He raised the glasses to his eyes and focused them through the interior of the vehicle, sharpening the image as he picked up the humps. He paned left to right and back again. On his second pass he picked up a shape that was alien to the natural formation of the terrain.

It was the motionless outline of a man's head and shoulders. Horton increased the focus.

Got you, you son of a bitch, he murmured to himself. Shoot my boys, bastard? You want to try me?

He put down the glasses and bent to make a final check of his M-16, his mind working on his next move.

He knew he should radio in and advise HQ. That was the thing to do. But the bastard sniper out there wasn't about to sit and wait for Horton to go through the motions. The sergeant was angry. He felt personally responsible for the deaths of his men. They should have kept going, ignored the pair down by the water…for the first time since the shooting he remembered the reason they had stopped, and also acknowledge they had been well and truly suckered. The old couple had been nothing more than decoys.

Which meant they'd known what was going to happen. Which put them in the same bed as the bastard doing the shooting. Horton gripped his rifle tightly.

Okay, you miserable fucks. You play the game, you pay the price.

He turned his head toward the stream and heard the whisper of soft footfalls on the dusty ground, saw the shadow fall over the Hummer just short of where he crouched.

Horton had a fraction of a second left to him. He recognized the outline of an automatic pistol in the wrinkled hand before the old man pulled the trigger and fired, and kept firing, following him down to the ground.

RAZAN KHARIZA, FULLY OUTFITTED in a U.S. combat uniform, complete with helmet and weapons, emerged from cover, with Barak close behind him. Barak was also dressed in U.S. gear and carried an SSG-550 sniper rifle. The Swiss-manufactured weapon had everything a marksman would need to gain advantage. Two-stage trigger that could be adjusted to the shooter's preference, the same as the telescopic sight. Buttstock and pistol grip were able to be set to the shooter's liking, allowing him to customize the weapon. There was even an antireflective screen over the barrel, positioned to disperse any hot-air disturbance that might interfere with the sight line. Chambered for 5.56 mm loads, the rifle had the option for a 20- or 30-round magazine. Barak had used the 550 on a number of occasions and had never once used even a quarter of a magazine during any strike. The true assassin made his hit quickly and cleanly, and in any given situation there were never more than two, three at the most, targets to put down. His job was to make a clean, efficient kill, then leave, not stay around spraying the area with a full magazine of bullets.

Behind Barak were two more of Khariza's fedayeen faithful. In full U.S. uniforms they carried the third nuclear device between them. It was contained within a canvas equipment cover of U.S. make, showing American military markings. The four men made their way across the open ground to where the Hummer stood.

The nuclear device was placed in the back of the vehicle, and Khariza's two Fedayeen climbed in to stay with it.

Barak went from body to body, removing weapons and ammunition. He placed the items in the Hummer, along with his sniper rifle. The elderly couple had uncovered a hole that had been prepared earlier. The dead soldiers were rolled into the hole and the old couple set to refilling it. Khariza spoke to them when they had finished, embracing them both and sending them on their way. He returned to the waiting vehicle where Barak had finished removing any blood traces.

"We should reach Baghdad by dark," Khariza said.

Barak climbed in behind the wheel, Khariza taking the passenger seat beside him.

"Take us home."

Barak dropped the Hummer into gear and swung it toward Baghdad.

Khariza settled in the seat, fixing his gaze on the wide, empty spread of the land. He was well aware that this journey might end with his death. If his plan didn't go the way he had envisioned, that was one option. But if he did have to die, he would leave behind something that would be talked of in years to come. The Americans wouldn't be left with an unspoiled Iraq. What they had destroyed would pale to insignificance against Khariza's legacy.

Before he had departed from the Syrian base Khariza had been informed of the strike at Zehlivic's Chechen camp. He had also learned of the death of Zoltan Dushinov and the recruits who had been training alongside Bertran. The Frenchman was also dead.

The news had been disheartening. Not enough to dissuade Khariza from his plan of action. Setbacks were simply that. They didn't mean the end of everything. Khariza still had plenty of faithful followers in and around Iraq, ready to come to his aid. And he still had his nuclear devices. Once they were in position he would have bargaining power not even the Americans would be able to ignore.

If Khariza failed to achieve his goal, he *would* detonate the nuclear devices. His followers would be left with a nation blown back into the Stone Age. The insurgents would have free rein to do what they wanted with the ravaged land and it would be a long time before the region became a stable, safe place once again.

Khariza wanted to emerge from this intended standoff with his demands met and himself in a position of power. He knew the risks. He understood the price of failure. Already he had delivered a blow to America on their own ground and his followers had, and were still creating unrest around the Middle East region. That would go on even if he was no longer around. The money deposits back under fedayeen control would insure there would be available funds for years to come. Whatever else took place, Khariza's people would be able to continue their war against the common enemy. He had hoped, with his emergence from the shadows, that he might step back center stage and lead the resistance against the Americans. He was, however, aware

that Fate might have other plans for him. Khariza was
prepared to allow that to happen. His death, as a mar-
tyr to the cause, would be long remembered. His name
would stay on the lips of Iraqis for generations. He
would be remembered as the man who defied the Americans and their scurrying allies. He would go down
fighting. Razan Khariza wouldn't be found in a hole in
the ground. He would fight to the last drop of his blood
and he would take many of his enemies with him before they took him down.

BARAK KNEW the terrain well. Like Khariza, he was on
home ground. He was able to approach the city by cutting back and forth, using back roads and trails off the
main. More than once they saw American military vehicles in the distance. A couple of times they passed
close to these vehicles. Barak drove steadily, even raising a hand in greeting as they drove by the Americans.
They received answering waves. Dusk was already
gathering as they came within sight of the city out-
skirts.

During the trip, the radio had been activated by a
voice from the HQ of the crew they had replaced.
Khariza had made a pretence of replying, his voice
muffled as he reported a problem with the communication equipment. He had shut down the radio after that.
It was a risky maneuver, but there was nothing else they
could do. He hoped it would take some time before the

Americans realized there was something suspicious taking place. By the time this happened, Khariza and his people would be in Baghdad. A calculated risk certainly, but any military endeavor carried an element of risk. It was part of the strategy. No military plan carried with it a hundred-percent trouble-free guarantee.

Barak drove them through the back streets until their destination came into view—a television and radio studio, one of the smaller facilities. He pulled the Hummer to a stop and reversed into a dark alley, cut the lights and the engine.

Khariza took a cell phone from one of his pockets. He had carried the phone since leaving Syria, and it had a single purpose: to alert waiting followers that Khariza was about to put his operation into action. The one-off message, to the man responsible for coordinating the Baghdad response, would bring a force of armed fedayeen to the studio location where they would form a protective shield around the building. Their presence would make a show of defiance. Resistance to anyone trying to penetrate the studio building and prevent Khariza carrying through his plan.

They waited until Khariza received the word that the call had started the force moving. Then he ordered Barak to drive them the final stretch of their journey to the studio.

"Are we prepared for this, brothers?" Khariza asked.

The two fedayeen, named Tariq and Omar, in the rear

of the Hummer nodded. They, along with Khariza and
Barak, had been instructed by Fedor Biriyenko, how to
program in the arming instructions and code that would
activate the nuclear device.

"We are, Colonel."

"Barak?"

The lean figure turned in his seat.

"Do you need to ask?"

Khariza smiled.

"I should have known better."

"Yes."

"We know what to do once we are inside? What we
might have to sacrifice?"

"Everything is clear, Colonel."

"Barak, time to go."

Barak rolled the Hummer into the studio parking
lot, brought it to a stop and cut the engine. He checked
the open area. There were no more than a half dozen
vehicles in the parking lot. At this time of night there
were only a few employees on duty. The studio building itself was well lit and he was able to see through the
main entrance door into the lobby. There was a reception desk with a lone female on the telephone.

"Let me get inside, then follow quickly," Barak said.

He laid the SSG sniper rifle down and reached
inside his combat uniform. The pistol he carried was fitted with a bulky suppressor. Barak checked the magazine and worked the slide to place a bullet in the breech.

He stepped out of the vehicle and walked across the lot, up to the door, the pistol held behind his back. As soon as the doors slid open, Barak walked inside. He went up to the reception desk and waited patiently until the woman had completed her call. The moment she replaced the receiver and turned to speak to him, Barak pulled the pistol into view, raised it and shot her in the head. The woman was knocked from her seat and fell to the floor behind the desk. Barak turned and raised his hand, gesturing for the others to join him.

Khariza picked up his M-16 rifle and the SSG-550. Behind him the two fedayeen were already manhandling the large, packaged nuclear device out of the rear of the Hummer. With Khariza covering them from behind, they crossed the parking lot and made for the entrance. They stepped inside. Barak immediately crossed to the doors and cut the power from the small wall-mounted box. That would prevent anyone getting inside unless they forced the doors. Not impossible but time-consuming.

The elevator was directly in front of them. Barak hit the floor button and they waited until the elevator dropped to the lobby level. He covered the doors as they slid open. The interior was empty. They moved inside. Khariza chose the floor they wanted and the elevator began to rise. Khariza handed Barak his sniper rifle and he slung it from his shoulder by the strap. At their floor Barak stepped out first, checking the immediate area. A corridor led to the studio they wanted. He led the way.

As they reached the soundproof door, it swung open and a man reading a clipboard stepped out. He was so absorbed in his data he didn't even see them until the last moment. Which it literally became as Barak put a single, suppressed bullet in the man's skull. As the man dropped to the floor, Barak put his foot against the door, preventing it from closing. With Khariza's help, he dragged the door fully open so that Tariq and Omar could move inside the studio with their heavy package. As soon as they were all inside, Barak closed the door and locked it.

The studio was medium-size, used for news presentation and interviews. The simple set, with desk and chairs, had a plain backdrop. There were three cameras, plus the clutter of lights and cables snaking across the sound-reducing floor. At the far side of the studio, behind soundproof glass was the compact control room. The control room crew was on the studio floor, gathered around the floor manager, cameramen and crew.

There were two men standing a little way off. They tried to appear casual but the way they held themselves advertised who they were—bodyguards—to the robed figure who was the center of attention as he spoke with the studio personnel.

All eyes turned to Khariza and his team as they crossed the studio floor to confront them.

"What is this?" the studio manager asked. He took in the U.S. uniforms and the weapons. "You people have no right to just—"

Barak raised his pistol and fired. The manager was hit in the chest. He fell back and was caught by one of his assistants who lowered the dying man to the floor.

"That gives us the right," Barak said.

Khariza stepped forward, his own weapon trained on the bodyguards.

"I want to see empty hands."

The bodyguards raised their arms above their heads. Barak moved to where they stood, his pistol covering them. He removed their holstered handguns, then ordered them to lie facedown on the floor. The moment the two were down Barak stood over them. He brought his suppressed pistol on target and shot each man through the back of the skull.

Tariq and Omar carried the package to the desk that occupied the center of the set. They cleared the top and set the heavy package on the flat surface.

"I want you all on the floor," Khariza ordered. "Facedown with your hands on your heads. If anyone does not agree with that, say so and I will shoot them now."

There was no argument. The captives obeyed, except for the one clad in robes. He stood facing Khariza, who stared back at him, more curious than angry.

Recognition took a few seconds.

Khalli al-Basur broke the silence. "I had hoped you might be dead."

Khariza found the words almost comforting. "How many times did I try to rid myself of you and fail? Always before, you managed to elude me. Did you know how much I admired you for that?"

"And now? This time there is no one to stop you."

Khariza moved across the studio floor, his M-16 steady as he covered Basur. He searched the man, who wasn't armed.

"It must be a great disappointment to you. I presume you were ready to announce your triumphal return to Iraq, and it is about to be snatched away from you."

Basur attempted to maintain his composure under Khariza's taunting. It was difficult and it showed.

"Sit down, Basur. You may as well because we could be here for a long time."

Basur slumped on a chair. He watched Khariza as the man crossed to the gathered studio technicians and spoke to them. He was unable to hear what Khariza was saying, but the expressions on the faces of the technicians told him they were far from pleased.

He glanced across to where Tariq was standing in front of the bulky package on the desk. The cover was being removed. Basur had no idea what the package contained.

Khariza gestured to Omar, and the man joined him.

"Colonel?"

"Once Tariq has the device armed, I want you to escort those two into the control room and get me on air. If there is any kind of protest, or they try to trick you…do what needs to be done to make them understand."

"They will do what they are told, Colonel."

"Make them realize we are not here to play games. I don't care what you do as long as they remain capable of operating the equipment."

Tariq caught Khariza's attention.

"It's ready."

"Good. Omar, the technicians. Take them now."

Omar nodded and herded the controller and his assistant in the direction of the control room.

Tariq took up a position where he could watch the remaining hostages and the studio door.

Barak took a compact transceiver from one of his pockets. He handed it to Khariza.

"It is time I was on the roof keeping watch."

Khariza took the unit and switched it on. "You have yours? Silly question, Barak. You of all would not forget something like that."

Barak pointed to a door on the far side of the studio.

"From there I can reach the access to the roof. Make sure you lock it once I go through."

Khariza followed him to the door. Barak opened it, stepped into the narrow passage, then turned to face Khariza.

"Win or lose, Colonel, the game has been interesting."

Khariza closed the door behind him, making sure it was secured. He made his way back to the main studio.

He stepped up behind the desk and examined the nuclear device. The activation lights were lit, showing that the weapon had been armed. From the instructions they had been given by the late Fedor Biriyenko, he knew that all he had to do was move the single toggle switch and the bomb would detonate. There was an override button set in the panel. It would cut the power and make the device safe until it was rearmed by entering a code number via the small digital readout sequencer. All very straightforward and simple if you knew the rules.

Khariza studied the device. Within that package sat the potential to turn ninety percent of Baghdad into a smoking wasteland. Not only would it destroy everything within the initial blast area, it would contaminate the city with enough deadly radiation to eventually destroy every living creature. The lingering radiation would be spread by the wind and would be difficult to estimate how far it would travel.

Khariza thought about the other devices. The two teams charged with placing them had farther to travel than Khariza and their chances of discovery were greater. It had been a gamble, but nothing was ever achieved by playing safe. If one or both were stopped, then at least he had reached his target. He was aware of the dedication of his people and it wouldn't have surprised him if—given the chance they were apprehended—they attempted to detonate their devices before being taken prisoner. Nuclear bombs didn't have to be placed precisely on target. They could be detonated a distance away and still spread their destructive power over a wide area.

He looked up and saw that Khalli al-Basur was studying him closely.

Had the man guessed?

Did he even realize what was going on?

Not that it mattered. There was nothing he could do about it now. Khariza raised a hand and beckoned the man to join him. When Basur neared the desk Khariza gestured at the device.

"Do you know what this is?"

"I am beginning to suspect but indulge me and explain."

"This is a nuclear device. A bomb. Powerful enough to destroy most of the city and poison it with radiation for many years. It will destroy America's grip on this nation because they are responsible for it being here. They came to Iraq unasked, invaders who have laid their greedy eyes on Iraq's oil wealth and want it for themselves. They will not get it. I have other bombs to be detonated at other sites. Rather a dead Iraq than one overseen by American devils. When Iraq burns in the desert wind, let us see how long the Americans remain."

Basur started to reply but remained silent. He had to weigh his words with care. His past history with Razan Khariza cautioned him against any reckless retort.

Something in Basur's eyes attracted Khariza's close scrutiny. He leaned forward, a knowing smile edging his lips. He jabbed a finger in Basur's face.

"I suspect your motives, Khalli al-Basur. You were always sympathetic of America. Ha! Did you not expect me to know that? First you vanish when Iraq had need of you."

"What use would I have been dead? My leaving was because you made it clear my life would be forfeit if I stayed."

"But now the Americans have forced themselves in-to power, you come crawling back." Khariza waved his finger at Basur again. "The Americans are behind this. You have sold yourself to them. They will help you gain power and in return you will offer them what they really want. Our oil. Even the lowliest beggar on the street knows the Americans covet our oilfields. They would give anything to have control. It will feed their war machine so they remain all powerful. In the end they want it all."

Basur remained silent. He admired Khariza's insight. The man had a perceptive brain. His mind worked on a razor edge, paring away the outer layers until he was able to expose the reality underneath.

"No reply? Could it be I have uncovered your se-cret, Basur? Have I come closer to the truth than you would like?"

Basur maintained his silence. There *was* truth in

Khariza's reasoning but he wasn't about to openly admit it to the man. He was desperately trying to make some kind of sense out of the situation. A turn of events that had brought him face-to-face with an old enemy, and one who was the most dangerous man Basur had ever known. He only had to consider the implications of Khariza's scheme to realize the extent of the threat he posed. Khariza had ambitions. It was plain to see what they were. The man wanted more or less the same thing as Basur. Control over Iraq. The difference was in how they would individually attempt to gain that power.

Basur wanted to use his popularity. His ability to appeal to all factions of the diverse Iraqi makeup. It had been his reason for coming to the studio this night. An appeal put out over television that would plead his cause and open the way for his return to the country. His way had been paved by judicious manipulation of contacts within the Iraqi media, plus the financial clout that had come via Chase Gardener, who had done some manipulation of his own through his powerful influence. It had all been neatly orchestrated so that Basur would make his televised appearance as low-key as possible. His moderate speech would have brought home exactly what Basur intended. He had no intention of bludgeoning his countrymen with histrionics. He wanted people to hear his words in a mood of calm optimism, rather than have them raised to nationalistic fervor. Basur had intended to draw his listeners along with him, insuring their concerns would be heeded and their desires fulfilled.

Confronted by Razan Khariza, his armed people and the nuclear device he had just been shown, Basur saw sense and reason fading quickly, to be replaced by rant and unreasoning demands. Khariza had come to stake his own claim for Iraq, but he wanted to achieve that by terror and the implicit threat of destruction, death and a lingering aftermath.

Basur saw no reassuring outcome to the situation. He knew Khariza too well. The man knew only how to use force. How to wound and kill. It was how he had behaved during his time serving under Hussein. Nothing had changed, except that now Khariza was acting purely to his own agenda.

An agenda that was pure madness.

CHAPTER NINE

U.S. Military Base, Iraq, Earlier Same Day

The men of Phoenix Force assembled in the tent that had been assigned to them. They had their own communication setup, and McCarter was in contact with Stony Man. He was speaking to Barbara Price.

"The situation is this," Price said. "You're up to date with the military searches of the Kurdish and Rumayla locations. Land and air overviews have come up zero. I still think the missing bomb is heading for Baghdad."

"We're ready to go there now," McCarter said. "The Army is going to fly us in and we'll coordinate from there. It'll be dark by the time we arrive. Make things that much harder, but we don't have any choice."

"David, you sure you need to do this? If Khariza is in the city with a nuclear device it's one hell of a risk."

"Listen, Barbara, we've already been through this.

The team is determined to find this bloody maniac and stop his clock one way or another. If you even suggest they back off, I don't fancy your chances."

"Okay, I haven't said a thing. Listen, we'll keep monitoring every source we can while you're on your way in. See if we can pick up anything on Khariza's whereabouts. There is one thing we're working on. Akira came up with the opener. If Khariza wants to make a statement before he hits the red button, he might be looking at some kind of media message. Radio or television. He'll want to get whatever he has to say across to a wide audience. We're assuming he's going to try to work a deal first. He wants us out of Iraq, no question there. So he needs to let us know what he plans. He isn't going to waste the opportunity."

"Just come up with something we can work with."

Stony Man Farm, Virginia

"I JUST HAD THE WORD from Phoenix. If we don't pull something out of the hat, Baghdad could end up a second Bucklow. Only worse. So hit those keys, people. Nobody goes home until we have this tied down. Find me something. Anything."

Kurtzman was busy at his workstation. Data flashed across his monitor screen as he applied himself to his task. The signs were there for them all to see.

The Bear was at home and didn't want to be disturbed. It lasted for three-quarters of an hour. Up to the moment when Kurtzman wheeled his chair back from the workstation and caught Price's eye.

"Patch me through to Phoenix," he said.

When McCarter came on the link, Price passed him over to Kurtzman.

"You got something for me?"

"How about Khariza's current location?"

"For bloody certain?"

"Unless he's traded in for a new cell phone I feel sure enough to say yes."

"Go ahead."

"I'm going to send this through to the computer the military assigned you. You should be able to feed it into your GPS unit. Map references will pin it down pretty close."

"Send away, mate. So where is he?"

"Going on what you were saying earlier about Khariza wanting to make his big statement, we figured some kind of media setup. Radio or television. So a studio facility he can put out to as many as he wants to hear."

"Sounds right."

"If I've hit the right buttons, we have Khariza at a studio facility in Baghdad. Transmits radio and television news to the city and surrounding areas."

"How accurate is this?"

"Within five yards of the signal source. The source being Khariza's cell phone."

"How the hell do you do that?"

"Has to do with a constant signal sent from the phone

to the cell towers and satellite. The signal bounces around between towers, in part to do with locating the best source for keeping in range. It started out being called cell phone location monitoring a couple of years back. It's been in development ever since. Moved to a more sophisticated level now. I installed it some months back, been revamping it for our own use ever since. Had to put in some of my own refinements but tests have come up pretty positive. This is the first time I've used it in the field."

"So what do you need to use it?"

"Just the cell phone number."

"How do we know this one is Khariza's?"

"Part gamble, part running checks on every phone and calls we've picked up from the opposition during this mission. Ran comparison checks on all the stored cell phone numbers. One came out of every phone we had. So I ran a trace on that number. It gave me a location. I map-referenced that phone to a point in Syria, then on into Baghdad. I transposed the location over map grid references and tied it down to its present location."

"A transmitting studio?"

"You got it."

"Hold on. Data coming through."

Kurtzman turned his head to see his entire cyberteam watching him.

"I'll send each of you a system download," he said

to them. "No point until I had all the bugs worked out. Given we ever have a quiet moment, I'll run through the details with you."

Kurtzman checked his monitor. The indicator in the bottom-right corner told him there was still some time left before all the data reached McCarter's computer. He picked up his mug and went to get a refill.

Baghdad

THEY CLOSED IN SILENTLY, swiftly, knowing that every second clicking off the clock might be the one when Razan Khariza made his fatal move to detonate the nuclear device under his control.

Despite carrying that knowledge, they acted coolly, fully in control. Aware of the possibility of a detonation at any given moment, Phoenix Force approached the studio building with measured caution.

They were black-clad, equipped with an assortment of weapons that ranged from M-16s down through personal pistols and sheathed knives. They had grenades clipped to their combat webbing: fragmentation, stun and smoke canisters. Gary Manning had a Barnet crossbow slung over his shoulder and a pouch holding hardwood shafts filled with cyanide for swift, silent kills. As always, Calvin James's M-16 was fitted with an M-203 grenade launcher. The launcher had almost become James's personal weapon. He used it more than any of the team members. He carried a selection of loads for the weapon, including HE and incendiary. In addition to his M-16, Hawkins was carrying a Mossberg Double Action shotgun fitted with a 9-round capacity, plus a 6-load Side-Saddle attachment. They were all carrying night-vision goggles. For communication the team wore tac com units, and each man had a signal device clipped to his belt that could be used to give the all-clear to the U.S. military backup waiting two streets away.

With combat cosmetics covering faces and hands, plus black wool caps pulled low on their heads Phoenix Force would be able to move around in the shadows without being spotted.

Razan Khariza had come on air thirty minutes earlier. His image was being broadcast across Baghdad and beyond from the studio building. The television picture showed him seated at a desk in the news studio set, with the nuclear device in front of him. Khariza had made his demands known clearly and simply. If the U.S. military failed to remove itself from Baghdad within the time period he was going to give them he would detonate the bomb and lay waste to the city. Within minutes of his going on air, other stations picked up the transmission and Khariza's image started to filter in to other Middle East stations.

Phoenix Force, along with U.S. military experts, were able to identify that the bomb Khariza had in his possession was identical to the two devices they had airlifted out of Syria. And those bombs had been genuine. Not fakes. NEST, into whose care the two devices had been placed, were able to confirm the live status of the weapons.

From the televised pictures it had been established which of the station's studios the transmission was coming from. Knowing that pinned down Khariza's exact location within the building.

Khariza had spoken calmly, establishing the reasons for his actions and making it crystal-clear he had no intentions of allowing the U.S. to remain in Iraq. He spoke without pause, sometimes in English, but mostly in his own language as he explained to Iraqis the course of action he was determined to follow if his demands weren't met. He made no excuses for his prewar behavior, or for what he was threatening even now. There was nothing he had regrets over. In the end, he stated, Iraq belonged to the Iraqis. Not to the heavy hand of the oppressors who were changing the face of the nation to meet their own demands. Iraq had to stay in the hands of its people. As long as he had any kind of influence Khariza would maintain the insurgency. His attacks on the West would go on. America and its allies would pay an everlasting price for what they had done. The war they started had reached back as far as the American homeland. The strike against Bucklow wouldn't be the last. And what might happen here in Iraq was only a foretaste of what could happen in the U.S. If he, Khariza, died in Baghdad, it wouldn't be an end. There were others who would carry the fight on, who would bring the terror to America's shores in a struggle that would see no end.

"He likes to talk," Hawkins said. "That guy could put a body to sleep."

Before moving in, Phoenix Force had studied floor-by-floor layouts for the entire building, identifying all exits and stairs, as well as a detailed floor plan of the television studio Khariza was in control of.

"You know what I'd do if I was taking that place over?" Manning said.

McCarter turned to the Canadian. "What?"

"I'd have someone on the roof with a high-powered rifle keeping watch and ready to hit anyone trying to sneak in through the ground defense."

"The lad is being extra sharp today," McCarter said. "The answer would be for us to get someone in position who could deal with that problem. And as official sharpshooter I think you've just landed yourself that little job, Gary, me boy."

Manning went to study the photos and maps, looking for a building that might provide superior height access. He was disappointed to find there were no buildings within the immediate area that would present him with what he wanted. His only way to his target designation was going to be via the building itself. Manning would have to get on the roof without alerting whoever was up there.

Half an hour later Phoenix Force was on its way. As they reached the outer ring of U.S. military presence, the first thing they noted was the area of darkness surrounding the studio building.

"Not our doing," the Army major in charge told the Phoenix Force leader when he asked the question. "They cut the power for the street illumination about twenty minutes ago. Makes it hard for us to see them."

"Pity someone can't cut the power to the studio," Hawkins said.

"We already considered that," the major said. "It has its own generator in the basement. And you can bank on it Khariza will have it well guarded by now."

"Even if we did manage to cut the power it would just let Khariza know we were on to him," Encizo said. "He could just decide to say the hell with it and push the button on that bomb before we could reach him."

"Well, cutting the streetlights can work for us," the Briton said. "Should make it easier for us to get in closer."

The major scrubbed a hand over his cropped hair.

"Sounds easy when you say it, sir."

"Believe me, mate, I wasn't suggesting it's going to be easy. So, Major, any suggestions as to where we should go in? Any spots less covered than others?"

The major indicated a chart spread across the hood of his Hummer.

"Recon did ascertain they've placed the bulk of their

people along the front of the building, that's here. Facing south. There's a group along the west wall. One here, by the east section. And we did spot three at the rear. On the back wall there's a loading bay with a roll-up door so they can handle equipment coming in or going out of the studio. It has a smaller side door to the left of the roll-up for personnel access. There's also a roof-access steel ladder fixed to the wall at the rear."

"We saw that on our plans," McCarter said. He tapped the spot. "Could be our way in. It's on the far side of the building away from the studio Khariza's occupying, so a degree of noise probably wouldn't alert him."

"Remember that the studio will be soundproofed, so any external noise especially from that distance, isn't going to reach it."

"Khariza might have some of his force roaming around inside the building," James pointed out. "The bloke might be crazy but I can't say he's stupid."

"Have we established how many people are inside?" McCarter asked the major.

"No more than a dozen, excluding those in Khariza's studio. They were spread through the building. No one came out so we assume they're locked down somewhere. Probably being held by Khariza's people."

"Our priority is that studio where Khariza is. If we don't take him down and that bomb goes off, it won't matter how many are inside or outside that building."

"Say the word, sir, and I can get some of my guys to go in with you."

"No offence, Major, but we've worked together a long time. I wouldn't want to be responsible for new-comers at a time like this."

The major nodded. "Understood. My people are the same."

"Just keep your blokes ready. The minute you get a signal from us you hit those teams out there and come get us. Same time you can go look for any hostages."

One of the communication team pushed his way to McCarter's side.

"Call for you, sir."

McCarter took the phone the operator held out to him. It was Price.

"Aaron has been monitoring Khariza's cell phone. He had a call. I just got the translation. The word got through to his people that the Syrian base was taken out and the bombs removed."

"Not the kind of news to make him ready to down tools and go home."

"More likely to make him determined to hit that but-ton if things don't start going his way."

"We're on our way," McCarter said.

Watching as Phoenix Force left the command post, a lieutenant turned to the major.

"Just who are those guys, sir?"

"Ask me something I know, Wojtowicz. All I do

know is they were cleared from the top. And I mean *the top*. I was told to give them anything they wanted as fast as they wanted it."

TO REACH THE REAR of the studio building without being observed Phoenix Force had to make a wide looping approach, moving through the empty streets. They were passed from group to group of waiting U.S. military until they were able to crouch in the shell of a building showing damage from the original occupation of Baghdad at the height of the war.

A sergeant in charge of the small squad pointed the way ahead. He was young, solid built, with a wide jaw, pale blond hair and blue eyes.

"Three along the back wall. Roving patrol. You see 'em?"

McCarter nodded.

The sergeant flopped down in the dust, pushing his helmet to the back of his head.

"You guys going in quiet?"

"That's the idea, Sarge."

"I'd like to send in some armor and blow their asses away."

"Don't think I wouldn't. But we need to get inside and take out the head man without giving him a chance to hit that button."

Manning moved up to where McCarter crouched. The Canadian had his crossbow slung across his shoulder.

"You set?"

Manning nodded.

"Go."

Manning moved around the end of the crumbling wall, dropping into deep shadow. He vanished from McCarter's sight in seconds, pushing forward in the direction of the studio building. McCarter leaned his back against the wall, glancing at the sergeant.

"Now we wait."

The sergeant nodded.

"Ain't it the way?"

"Okay, Sergeant," McCarter said, "you know any good dirty jokes? Tell me yours and I'll tell you mine."

MANNING LAY PRONE, studying the way ahead. His night-vision goggles' green-tinged image shimmered slightly as he assessed the odds. He had already counted the three armed guards, dressed in dusty clothing, a mix of military uniforms and civilian garb. Their weapons were identical, ubiquitous Kalashnikov AK-74s. One also had a shoulder-slung rocket launcher.

Crouching behind a low wall, Manning keyed his tac com.

"In position. I have three armed guards in sight. All carrying AKs. One has a rocket launcher."

"You dealing with the situation?"

"Just about to. I'll call when I'm clear."

Manning propped his M-16 against the wall. He

cocked the crossbow, opened the container holding the hardwood shafts and removed one. He laid it in the slot and got on his knees.

He checked the position of the three guards. As he had hoped, they were moving, spread along the length of the rear wall. The Canadian waited until they were at the extreme point of separation, choosing the one who was farthest away. The guard was still moving away from his nearest companion. Manning raised the crossbow, settling his sights on the distant figure. He followed the target for long seconds, then eased back on the trigger. He heard the faint hum of the shaft as it cut the night air. It made barely a sound as it struck the target just below the right ear. As the shaft buried itself in the guard's neck the hardwood shattered and released the cyanide. The guard had no time to call out before the deadly poison spread through his body and killed him. He went down in a loose sprawl.

Manning had already cocked the crossbow again, picking up a second shaft. He tracked in on his second target, being presented with the guard's broad back. The shaft struck between the man's shoulders, to one side of his spine, pitching him facedown on the ground. As the guard fell, his AK slipped from his fingers and hit the ground with a clatter. The sound alerted guard three. He turned to see the downed man and moved toward him.

Manning calmly reloaded, coming up off his knees as the guard began to raise his assault rifle.

The guard had turned and was facing in Manning's direction when the third shaft left the crossbow. It buried itself in his throat, below his chin. The guard reached up with a clawing hand and made a futile grab at the shaft. Then the cyanide kicked in and there was no time left.

"Clear," Manning transmitted. "You want to join me?"

BY THE TIME the rest of Phoenix Force had joined him Manning had located the roof-access ladder. He indicated the small personnel door a few feet along the loading bay.

"All yours."

Without another word he secured his M-16 across his shoulder and started to climb the ladder.

McCarter led the team to the personnel door. He checked the handle and wasn't overly surprised to find it unlocked. Khariza's men, on guard at the rear of the building, would have needed instant access to the interior in case of an emergency and having to deal with a locked door would have wasted time. The Briton eased the door open. The moment the gap was wide enough, Encizo slipped inside, followed by James and Hawkins. McCarter brought up the rear. Once inside the Phoenix Force leader pulled the door shut and snapped the lock on, preventing anyone from entering unannounced.

The storage area was an untidy mess of equipment

and storage boxes. It was illuminated by a number of security lights mounted on the walls. The light allowed the men to remove their goggles.

Phoenix Force made its way across the floor, heading for the double doors that would allow them access to the main area of the building. James eased open one of the doors and peered into the lit passage beyond. It ran in both directions. The section to the left ended in a set of plain concrete steps with the doors to an elevator next to them. To the right he saw a number of closed doors before the passage terminated in blank wall.

"Left it is, guys," he announced.

Their rubber-soled combat boots made no sound on the floor as they made for the stairs.

THE STUDIO Khariza occupied was on the third floor.

From where he sat behind the news desk he could see directly into the control room where Omar had the two operators under his steady gaze. For the moment Khariza had fallen silent, having delivered his extended monologue to the camera in front of him. He had ended by warning that his demands should be rapidly met or the bomb sitting in front of him would be detonated.

In truth Khariza needed a time for reflection. The cell phone message, coming from one of his Syrian contacts, had informed him that the base had been hit and the two bombs there had fallen into American hands.

His threat had been reduced by two-thirds. Something told him the American team who had been at his heels almost from the start were behind this latest defeat. As the message had come through, Khariza had listened in silence, almost disbelieving the information.

How much bad luck could befall one man?

His thoughts had snapped back to the present. What had happened couldn't be reversed. All he could do was move forward, place his demands at the feet of the Americans and see what they intended. The choice was simple. They withdrew, or Baghdad was torn apart and laid waste by the nuclear device sitting in front of him. His death was a small price to pay. What he left behind would remain for many years: a powerful reminder to all those who followed America that meddling in another nation's destiny came with a high price.

Khariza sensed he was being watched. When he looked up he saw it was Basur.

"There has to be another way, Razan Khariza. A better way than this."

"Such as? Relinquish everything to the Americans? Allow them to rule our country and take away our pride and our heritage? Is this what you have agreed to with your American *friends?* Where is the honor in that, Basur? It may be your way. It will never be mine."

"You would rather turn Baghdad into a radioactive wasteland? Destroy it and many of your fellow countrymen just to defy the Americans? Where is the victory in that?"

"There are many who will die happy that they are serving God. Better that than bowing to America."

"Listen to yourself, Khariza. You talk foolishness. Wasteful death is as much a blasphemy as denying your faith. Ask yourself how many would disagree with what you intend. But you won't. You ignore them because your arrogance turns you from the fact. Their desires are cast aside because *you* make the decisions. *You* condemn the Americans for what you call their interference in the destiny of Iraq. Isn't that exactly what you are doing? We all deserve to have a say in the final choice but you are taking that choice away."

"The people are not capable of making such decisions. They see things only from a shallow vision. It has to be seen from afar. Looking into the future. When a man is only concerned with obtaining a loaf of bread for today, how can he decide on something that will affect us for years to come?"

Basur shook his head, a smile edging his lips.

"If I am going to die tonight, at least I will have been entertained," he said. "If nothing else, Khariza, you have proved yourself to be completely mad."

Khariza pushed to his feet, leaning both hands on the nuclear device.

"You think this is madness? Wait until I press the button that will send us both to Paradise. When you stand at the gates and see what God has prepared, you will understand."

"I understand you are forcing me to martyrdom. For that I have nothing but contempt. I would willingly die for my own beliefs. Not for those of a murdering madman."

"Keep your beliefs, Basur. Let it be my final gift to you."

Khariza snatched up the M-16 leaning against the desk. He turned it on Basur and hit him with a burst that drove the man from his chair. Basur hit the studio floor facedown, blood starting to soak through his robes.

PHOENIX FORCE HAD reached the second floor without encountering any opposition.

As they stepped onto the landing, moving toward the next flight of stairs, shadows on the wall ahead made them pause. They flattened against the wall at McCarter's signal. The Briton dropped to a crouch and peered around the corner.

An armed man was striding along the passage, no more than a few feet away and heading in their direction. There was no time for the team to retreat without being heard or seen.

McCarter passed his M-16 to James, eased his sheathed knife clear and waited until the guy stepped into sight. The motionless figures registered as the man cleared the edge of the wall. He grabbed for the AK slung from his shoulder. That was the moment Mc-Carter lunged up from his crouch, the blade of his knife cutting through the guy's thin shirt and in under his ribs. His left hand clamped over the stricken man's mouth, fingers digging in hard as he used the bulk of his body to force the other to the floor. The Briton worked the blade of the knife, ignoring the blood that started to pulse from the extended wound he had made. The guy thrashed in agony, feet drumming against the soft floor covering. McCarter maintained his grip until the man's struggles weakened and finally ceased. He pulled the knife clear and sat up.

Two more armed men came into view at the far end of the passage. They saw their man down, the spreading pool of blood on the floor, and McCarter holding his bloody knife. They ran forward, weapons coming up and into play.

McCarter—exposed—did the only thing he could. He grabbed the dead man and dragged him in front to cover himself in the split second before the advancing pair opened fire. He felt the corpse shudder as slugs punched into its flesh. He lost his balance and fell back, the dead man on top of him. As he went down, Mc-Carter felt a solid blow to his left hip.

Behind him the rest of the team stepped into the passage, weapons up and ready. They engaged the shooters and for long seconds the passage echoed to the clatter of autoweapons.

The lead shooter went down under a barrage of 5.56 mm slugs, his torso and upper thighs punctured. His partner survived slightly longer before a burst from Hawkins cored in through his chest, spinning him and dumping him on the floor.

"David, you okay?" James asked as the dead man was pulled off McCarter.

A great deal of blood covered McCarter's blacksuit.

"I'm always fine with a bloody 7.62 mm bullet in my hip," McCarter snapped.

"Always gracious, even under pressure," Encizo remarked as they pulled McCarter to the side of the passage.

The Cuban went to stand with Hawkins, covering the passage, while James checked McCarter's wound.

"Went through him first," McCarter said, nodding at the dead Iraqi. "Slowed it down a bit. I don't think it went in too deep."

"Okay, Doc, should I operate now or wait until later?" James replied. "I mean, I wouldn't want to do anything without your say-so."

"Bloody hell, aren't we all touchy today." McCarter clicked on his tac com. "Gary, we engaged down here. Things could start hotting up, so don't waste time."

"You sound a little edgy. Everything okay?"

"We're feeling a little sorry for ourselves 'cause we caught a bullet," James interrupted. "Gary, we're fine."

He ignored McCarter's glare.

Encizo looked around. "We should move in case they picked up the shooting on the next floor."

"Go ahead," James said. "I'll bring our beloved leader."

Hawkins gave a wide grin.

"I can see you, T.J.," McCarter said. "You wait, sonny."

Manning's voice, faint but distinct, came through the tac com.

"Top of the world, Ma," he said. "I don't think it's James Cagney, but I do have company up here…"

ENCIZO AND HAWKINS hit the stairs and went up fast. From the landing above, an autoweapon clattered, the sound reverberating off the close walls of the stairwell. Plaster dust misted the air, and spent cartridge cases dropped from the upper stair railing, bouncing off the steps. Hawkins raised his M-16 and fired up at the source. It gave Encizo time to free a grenade and throw it over the rail. The blast threw a cloud of smoke and debris down the stairwell. Even while the blast was still echoing around them Encizo and Hawkins went up the last flight of stairs and onto the landing.

Armed figures lurched out of the smoke. The Phoenix Force pair engaged and cut them down without breaking stride. The area was littered with debris from the walls that had contained and concentrated the blast. Chunks of plaster had fallen from the ceiling.

Somewhere a burst pipe sprayed cold water over the passage. At least four bodies, tattered and bloody from the grenade burst, sprawled on the floor.

James called over the tac com.

"You okay?"

"We cleared the third-floor landing," Encizo said. "We're going for the studio now."

"We're right behind you. We'll cover your backs from here."

Encizo and Hawkins made their way along the passage, taking the turn where it angled to the right and followed it along until they spotted the door they wanted at the far end.

"That's the studio," Hawkins said, reading the number on the door.

They reached the door. It was locked. Encizo peered in through the small window and could see the whole setup.

Razan Khariza behind a desk on which sat the nuclear device package, while an armed man covered the interior of the studio. People were stretched out on the floor, and two had bloody head wounds

A third man, dressed in traditional robes, was down, bullet exit wounds in his back. Blood had spread out from beneath his body.

There were also a couple of technicians, standing behind cameras that were trained on Khariza.

"Doesn't look like the grenade burst reached this

far. Good thing soundproofing works from both sides of the door. T.J., take a look."

Encizo stepped aside so that Hawkins could assess the setup.

"We need to go in fast once we breach this door. We're not going to have much time. Khariza could decide to hit that button if he figures the game is finished. We need to take him out first."

Hawkins studied the door. "It's only soundproof. It isn't a bank vault armored door. I can take out the lock with the shotgun. Soon as it's clear you go in and deal with the colonel. I'll handle the backup."

Hawkins unlimbered the Mossberg, checked the load and made sure the weapon was ready to fire.

"I want Khariza away from that desk," Encizo said. "We need a few seconds after you hit that door. If he stays where he is with his finger right by that button, we'll be seeing a mushroom cloud before we even step inside that studio."

Hawkins eyed the Cuban. "Now that's a mighty comforting thought."

Khariza turned to speak to his man with the autorifle. He glanced across the studio to a point Encizo was unable to see. Khariza raised a hand, beckoning to someone. Then he stepped away from the desk, to the edge of the raised area, still gesturing. Seconds later a man appeared. He was also armed. He joined Khariza and they fell into conversation.

"Third man," Encizo said.

Hawkins took a look. "Rafe, it isn't going to get any better than this."

"Let's do it."

Encizo stepped back, cradling his M-16.

The muzzle of the Mossberg centered on the lock area. Hawkins pulled the trigger and kept working it until he had expended all nine shells. The combined force of the charges tore into the thick wood construction of the heavy studio door, tearing the lock apart and leaving a ragged hole where it had been. Hawkins tossed the shotgun aside, reached out and grasped the edge of the hole, yanking the door open. The moment it cleared the frame Encizo went through, his eyes fixed on Khariza and the second armed man—Omar.

Hawkins was one step behind the Cuban, his M-16 tracking the man near the door—Tariq.

The crackle of Tariq's weapon filled the air as Hawkins took a long dive across the studio floor, twisting his body to keep himself on his belly. He pushed the M-16 forward, triggering triple bursts at Tariq as the Iraqi tried to pull his own weapon down to Hawkins's level.

The first 3-round burst clipped Tariq's left thigh, tearing out a chunk of muscle and flesh. The impact threw him off balance and he fell to one knee, bringing himself directly in line with Hawkins's second burst. This time the hit was solid, punching in through Tariq's torso and shattering three ribs before burning in deep. Splintered bone was driven into the wound, tearing at soft organs and extending the damage. By the time Tariq hit the floor he was in no state to offer further resistance.

The crackle of Hawkins's M-16 hammered in Encizo's ears as he powered himself across the studio, his own rifle coming to his shoulder. He was concentrating on Razan Khariza's moving figure as the Iraqi turned and made for the nuclear device sitting on the desk. Even at the distance he was from the man, Encizo could see the taut scowl on Khariza's face. The man had been pushed as far as he would allow, and he was determined to carry out his remaining act of total defiance. All his plans, his wide-reaching schemes, were coming apart and in his final moments he was about to perpetrate the ultimate obscenity.

Khariza was going to detonate his nuclear bomb and bring Baghdad down in a rain of radioactive fire.

Encizo saw Khariza reach the last few feet separating him from the desk. The Cuban forced himself to a stop, unwilling to fire on the move. He was only going to get one chance. If he missed, Khariza would reach the bomb and hit the switch that would end it for them all.

He sucked in a breath, lowered the M-16's muzzle and pulled the trigger. He felt the weapon push back against his shoulder as it jacked out a 3-round burst.

Khariza jerked to one side as the 5.56 mm slugs

punched in through his upper body. The Iraqi made a supreme effort and lunged in toward the desk, crashing down hard. Blood arced from the wounds in his chest. He used his left hand to brace himself, dragging his body over the desk, right hand sweeping toward the bomb.

Encizo fired again. The shots were on target, the slugs tearing into Khariza's hand. They blew out in a bloody shred of bone and flesh, taking off fingers and leaving behind a mangled stump. A shrill cry of agony burst from Khariza's lips. Even now he made yet another attempt to reach his goal, pushing back to regain his feet and drag himself around the desk.

As Khariza pushed himself upright, Encizo closed in. He pulled the muzzle of his rifle around, catching Khariza full in his sights and repeatedly pulled the trigger until he had exhausted the magazine. The multiple bursts blew holes in the Iraqi, driving him off the desk in a convulsive roll that dumped him hard on the floor. His body was cut to bloody ribbons as Encizo fired round after round.

"You're not running out this time, *cabrón*. This time you stay and you pay."

"Rafe."

Encizo looked round at Hawkins's warning yell. He saw Omar, his hand holding an autopistol, coming at him. The Cuban was aware *he* was holding an empty weapon. He reacted instinctively, dropping the rifle and launching himself over the desk.

He heard the crash of a shot, felt the dulling impact as the bullet struck his left arm. He fell across the desk, striking the nuclear device and feeling it slide across the desk along with him. As he dropped over the far side, the device followed him down. A heavy weight struck Encizo.

From a distance he heard the crackle of shots as Hawkins opened up. A second burst followed, then a third. The sound of a body hitting the floor.

Encizo moved, trying to sit up. His head was hurting where the falling bomb had struck him. He could feel blood trickling down the side of his face. A shadow fell across him and he looked up. It was Hawkins.

"You finished screwing around with the nuclear device, *amigo?*"

"Just get on the line and tell the others we're clear in here."

Hawkins smiled. He contacted the others, then hit the button on the signal device that would bring in the military units waiting in the streets below.

GARY MANNING REMOVED his goggles and laid his crossbow on the roof. Only a single shaft remained, and there were too many obstacles between him and the distant figure. He didn't want to restrict himself to a single shot in case of a miss. He unslung the M-16, taking off the safety.

As quiet as he was, Manning had to have alerted his

potential opponent. The sniper moved suddenly, turning away from the parapet, the long rifle in his hands lining up on the Phoenix Force commando. The crack of the shot sounded loud in the silence of the rooftop. Manning heard a clang against one of the many aerial support masts that were dotted across the roof. Ducking to a crouch, Manning moved for cover behind a ventilation duct. He picked up the sound of boots moving over the roof. He followed the sound. His man had moved off to Manning's right. He was trying to circle around to catch the big Canadian in an exposed position.

Holding his rifle close, Manning eased around the duct. It was fairly bulky, standing at least eight feet high, with five-foot-wide sides. He made his way to the far side, still low, and studied the spread of the roof. There was enough moonlight to cast pale illumination at this height. Manning kept his position, scanning the distant section of the roof. His patience was rewarded after a couple of minutes when a long shadow broke from cover and moved swiftly across an open section, merging with the dark outline of another duct.

"This could go on all damn night," Manning muttered. "The hell with it."

He freed two fragmentation grenades and pulled the pin on the first one. He lobbed the bomb in the direction of the distant vent duct. The blast ripped away a section of the duct. Manning tossed his second grenade, laying it closer this time. The second blast took away the lower section of the duct, sheered metal flying through the air. As the smoke drifted away, Manning caught a glimpse of the exposed sniper.

There was enough moonlight for him to identify Barak—Khariza's personal assassin. The man who had taken Haruni el Sharii captive. Manning had heard about her ordeal on board the *Petra*. He had most likely had a hand in the death of Fedor Biriyenko once the Russian had passed along his advice on the use of the nuclear devices.

Barak had caught part of the grenade blast down his right side, leaving him bloody and dazed. He was trying to raise the rifle in his left hand.

"Good to put a face to the name," Manning said.

He leveled the M-16 and put a couple of tribursts into Barak. The impact kicked the assassin backward. He caught the back of his legs on the parapet that edged the roof and uttered a brief scream as he toppled out of sight.

Manning crossed the roof to look over the edge. He could make out Barak's body on the concrete below.

He activated his tac com. "Roof clear. On my way down."

Manning was halfway down the access ladder when he heard the sudden crackle of concentrated autofire. It was coming from the advancing U.S. military who had received the signal from Hawkins to move in.

CHAPTER TEN

Presidential Helicopter, Over Texas

"No bull, Hal, what's happening? Update me," the President said.

"The last report I had from Phoenix was they were closing on Khariza. They have him located in a television studio in Baghdad. The way we read it, he intends to make a broadcast stating his demands and using his nuclear device to force the issue."

"What the hell is going on, Hal? Nuclear blackmail now. The man is threatening to set off a bomb in the capital city of his own country if we don't back away? What next?"

"Unsettled times, sir. They create unexpected situations."

The President sighed. "What about Able Team and this Gardener affair?"

"My people are taking a look at the tape Sergeant Luke Jacobi shot. If it does support his accusations, then we have another problem. This time it's a home-grown one."

"Chase Gardener has always been outspoken. So has Senator Justin. But I'll be the first to be disappointed if this story turns out to be true."

Brognola understood the President's feelings. The Man needed to depend on those around him to stay faithful to their declaration of loyalty to the presidency and the nation. They were the first and last line of defense against outside transgressors. If the President couldn't trust his government—or his military—who could he depend on?

Threats from outside the country were bad enough.

If those threats came from *inside* America, and especially from within the hallowed ranks of the nation's protectors and defenders, then freedom was on the slippery slope to anarchy.

"Hal, I need your people on this full-time. Show me a single shred of hard evidence and we'll act on it. So fast they won't know what hit them."

"You have my word, sir."

"While we're on the subject what about this man McAdam?"

"His association with Gardener and Justin has been established. So has his interference with information being sent into the CIA. McAdam's black-ops team is running its own agenda by the look of it. He's been utilizing the CIA to field his own directives and play his own game. My cyberteam has come up with money transfers coming from a Gardener Global affiliate to a bank account in Turkey that traces back to McAdam. It's a dormant CIA paymaster account they used to bankroll operations. That account hasn't been used for years. Ever since the Turkey station was withdrawn. Money started to be sent to that account a few months ago."

"This is a mess, Hal. Have I been naïve not to notice all this happening around me?"

"You can't act on something you don't know about, sir."

"Not exactly what I wanted to hear."

"At least we've closed one bolt-hole. Zehlivic isn't going to be providing sanctuary anymore," Brognola stated.

"Hal, I want that son of a bitch in U.S. custody sooner rather than later. I hold him as guilty for Bucklow as Khariza. No damn quarter for these people."

"Mr. President, Stony Man is behind you all the way on this. Our problem is Khariza has a big network. If he doesn't get help through loyalty, he goes for the money option."

"Then we play by the same rules, Hal. Get the result however you can. Upset who you like. I don't care any longer. This country is under siege from these people. They don't care who they deal with in order to hurt America."

The President turned to look out of the side window of the helicopter as they swung in over Bucklow. The great swathe of the bomb site lay black and dead below them.

"God save us from these madmen," the President whispered. "Look what they did to us, Hal. Thank God your people stopped the second bomb. Now let them stop the bastards who orchestrated it all. I want those people dealt with before they do anything else. You hear me, Hal?"

"I hear you, Mr. President."

Brognola peered through the window himself. He was used to dealing with tragic scenarios, the results of hostile action. In the normal run of things he handled transcripts of events. Video footage. Photographs. It wasn't every day he found himself confronted with the reality of some brutal happening, and as the Army helicopter made its touchdown on the edge of the Bucklow site the sheer awfulness of what had happened reached out to touch him. Brognola glanced sideways to where the President was staring out the window, his face tight with emotion, eyes scanning the blackened, burned patch of ground that had become Bucklow's shrine to the baseness of man against man.

"My God, Hal, they really did it."

The President's voice was low, halting as he pushed to get the words out. He cleared his throat before he could speak again.

"So help me, Hal. If I had those bastards lined up in

front of me right now I wouldn't hesitate to pull the trigger."

The chopper touched down, the roar of the engines starting to die as the pilot cut the power. Outside the area was ringed by armed police. Vehicles were blocking the approach roads to the site. One of the presidential aides slid the side hatch open and others moved forward to place the steps in position for the President to step outside. Secret Service agents moved from the rear of the helicopter, surrounding the Man as he walked forward and paused briefly in the open hatch to survey the site, then he was down the steps and walking across the grass to meet local officials. Brognola followed a few steps behind him.

The next couple of hours passed in a rush of meetings, the President barely given time to catch his breath. He met officials, spoke to survivors and the families of those who had died. He promised all the help and aid the administration could offer. It was a difficult time. Brognola, on the edges of it all, was able to observe and to see the hurt in the eyes of the survivors. They were ordinary, honest people, thrown into a world they barely understood. Terrorism was something that happened somewhere else, not in a small town like Bucklow. One of the questions they kept asking was why? Why had Bucklow been singled out? Brognola, a man who lived and breathed the business, could have told them. Bucklow had happened because it had simply been chosen for no other reason except that the date of *its* celebrations coincided with a date significant to Razan Khariza and his regime. It was cruel. Unfeeling. It was something Brognola would have voiced to the people of Bucklow, but in the cold, hard light of day, that was the fact behind the choice.

At the end of the President's visit, Brognola walked close behind as they returned to the waiting helicopter. The President turned and beckoned the big Fed to join him.

"What do you say to people, Hal? How do you make them believe in anything after something like this?"

"You do the best you can, Mr. President. Give them the truth and trust they can accept it. Coming here today has to count for something."

"I truly hope so, Hal. These people trusted me to run the country, and I let them down."

"No, sir. You can't take that on your shoulders. As hard as it is to accept, we can't prevent every indiscriminate act of terrorism. We do what we can, but some are going to get through."

They reached the helicopter and stepped inside, moving to their seats. The President's protection team followed. The hatch was closed and the helicopter's power increased as the pilot prepped for take off.

Brognola had just settled when he heard a scuffle of sound coming from the rear of the passenger cabin. He turned to see what was happening.

"Just stay where you are. All of you. Do something stupid and you will die."

A man's voice rose in protest. One of the President's Secret Service agents. His words were cut off by the sound of a brutal blow.

"I told you. Now let's see empty hands. Do it."

From up front a pair of uniformed figures appeared. They were armed with M-16s and covered the President and his group. Brognola glanced to the rear of the helicopter and saw other armed men appear.

He recognized one of them instantly, from the ID data Stony Man had located.

Rick Renelli, Gardener's man.

"Just sit tight, gentlemen, we won't be in the air for long."

"Do I assume that General Chase Gardener is responsible for this?" the President asked.

Renelli glanced at him. "You can assume whatever you want, mister. I suggest you sit back and consider what's likely to happen if you don't do what I tell you." Renelli gestured to his men. "Search them. I want every weapon cleared."

It didn't take Renelli's men long to disarm the President's group. They passed the weapons along to the front of the helicopter where they were dropped into a carry-all. The communications equipment worn by the Secret Service agents was also removed.

"This one isn't wearing communications," one of the uniformed men said, standing over Brognola. He reached inside the big Fed's jacket and pulled out Brognola's cell phone and ID. "He's just a Fed. Justice Department."

Renelli stood over Brognola. "Justice Department? You have anything to do with those snoopers we had following us around lately?"

"Way I heard it they did more than just follow."

Brognola regretted the words even as he spoke them. Renelli's lips tightened into a hard line.

"Son of a bitch."

He swung his bunched fist into Brognola's face, the hard knuckles catching him across the side of his mouth, then backhanded him on the return swing. Brognola's lips split and he tasted blood. His head rocked back from the blows and for long seconds the world went into shutdown.

War Room, Stony Man Farm, Virginia

ABLE TEAM, along with Grimaldi, sat around the table. The meeting was headed by Barbara Price, with Kurtzman providing the data link.

"We have confirmation on all the people on Jacobi's tape," Kurtzman said. "Took a little time isolating each face and running them through the database for a comparison, but we have them now."

He hit a button and a wall screen threw up an image. He flicked through the shots, each image from the videotape had its official photo next to it, with data about the person next to it.

"Army, Navy, Air Force," Price said. "Gardener covers the ground."

"So we have the goods," Lyons said. "Time to shut the man down."

"Does Hal know about this?" Schwarz asked.

Grimaldi was first to spot the quick glance that passed between Price and Kurtzman.

"Something you haven't mentioned?" he asked.

"Hal went with the President on his visit to Bucklow. They needed time to discuss the current situation."

"Hold it right there," Lyons said. "If they were suspicious about this Gardener plot, why the hell did the President go ahead?"

"Come on, Carl," Price said. "The President felt strongly about this arranged visit to Bucklow. Those people needed his face on the ground to show he hadn't forgotten about them. He refused to cancel. At the time we hadn't anything solid. And he said he wasn't going to hide behind the White House drapes. If the President showed he was too scared to go outside, what did that say about the administration?"

"The Man has a point," Schwarz said. He turned to Price. "So what's the current situation? Not good by the way you're looking at me."

Price sighed. "*Okay.* I tried to contact Hal just before we came down for the meeting. Couldn't get through to him. I checked further. The President's helicopter went off air shortly after it left Bucklow. Soon as that happened, a search went out. The helicopter was found abandoned in a clearing some miles short of the airbase where it was supposed to land. Search party found the crew dead and the President's Secret Service team cuffed and hooded. The President and Hal weren't on board."

"Looks like Gardener's made his move," Kurtzman said.

"We don't have all the details, but it looks like he got his people on board that chopper while it was waiting for the President to return from his meeting at Bucklow. Being military, they wouldn't have looked out of place at the landing site."

"How long before the search party located the chopper?" Lyons asked.

"Just over forty minutes."

"Long enough to put the hostages in a plain vehicle and head off in any direction," Blancanales said.

"This gets better," Lyons snapped. "Assuming Gardener has the President, do we have any ideas where they might be going?"

Kurtzman flicked another switch. A second wall screen flickered to life, displaying a selection of locations.

"Gardener-owned or -associated places," he said. "New Mexico ranch. Fort Leverton, Arizona. Gardener Global corporate HQ. Hunting lodge in Wyoming. I could go on for the rest of the meeting."

"Not likely Gardener is going to take the President to any of those places," Schwarz said. "They'll be the first to be checked once word gets out he's behind the kidnap."

"What about the senator?" Grimaldi asked.

"Too high-profile, like his buddy Gardener," Kurtzman said.

"McAdam," Lyons said. "The guy is CIA. He runs a damned covert ops team. He probably has safehouses even his own people don't know about."

Kurtzman leaned forward. "Good thought, Carl."

"Maybe," Price said. "But he isn't likely to tell us where they are."

Lyons didn't answer. Price was right. On the other hand, the Able commander thought, he might tell if he finds himself with no place to run.

Blancanales nudged Schwarz. "We could be in for a hard time."

"What?"

"He's thinking. Working something out."

"This could be tricky."

Lyons glanced across at them, shaking his head.

"Nothing come, boss?" Schwarz asked.

"Have we passed anything on?" Lyons asked.

"No." Price spread her hands. "We literally only just finalized the ID data."

"So we're the only ones with the information?"

Price nodded. "Carl, what are you thinking?"

"I'm thinking we ought to let Luke Jacobi make a call to the CIA and ask to speak to Agent McAdam."

"You'd better explain this slowly," Price said.

"It has to do with credibility," Lyons said. "If Jacobi can make McAdam believe him, get him to arrange a meeting, maybe we can get our hands on him."

"Take McAdam?" Price glanced around the table, then back to Lyons. "Go on."

"Out of the three, McAdam is likely to be the most useful."

"How?"

"Gardener and Justin are going to have their hands full with the President. McAdam is the most expendable. I don't have Gardener's timetable of how this takeover is going down, so I could be wasting our time. But I think it's worth a shot."

"You want to use Jacobi as bait to draw McAdam out? In the hope we can get him to tell us where the President is being held?"

"Carl, this is running close to the edge," Schwarz said. "Gardener might say screw Jacobi, I'm on my last mile, so what can he do."

"He might also still be organizing his troops and if the identity of his military conspirators was leaked too soon…"

"As a plan, it's thin," Kurtzman said. "But seeing as how we don't have anything else to go with, it's worth a gamble."

"Let's do it," Price said. "Now all we have to do is get Jacobi to agree."

Washington, D.C.

LUKE JACOBI, HIS ARM in a sling, sat in a booth of a diner situated on a badly lit street north of Washington's Union Station. It was an area bordering on a rougher edge of town and at this time in early evening, had an air of dereliction to it. The heavy downpour sheeting down out of the gray, clouded sky added to the chill desolation of the district.

The drab interior of the diner, far removed from its better days, wasn't relieved by the odors of overcooked oil and rain-damp clothing. The few customers, hovering over their meals and coffee, kept their heads down, avoiding eye contact for a variety of reasons. The atmosphere suited Jacobi as he waited for Rod McAdam to show up. He would have been the first to admit to being nervous. The situation was fraught with danger. The risk had been explained to him at the outset, but when he had been told of the President's disappearance Jacobi had said yes to the operation. It was a way to partly redeem himself after recent events, even though he had been told there was nothing he needed to blame himself for. Jacobi felt different. His betrayal by Gardener, the shooting of the cop and the deaths of his relatives had left him feeling responsible. If he hadn't run, subsequent events might not have escalated. So anything he could do to even the score was acceptable.

Earlier, using a cell phone, Jacobi had called the CIA number supplied to him and had asked to speak with Agent Rod McAdam. He had made it clear he wouldn't speak to anyone else, stressing that the matter had to do with a conversation McAdam needed to be aware of. To draw McAdam's attention Jacobi had added that the conversation had taken place in Arizona, in the company of two other individuals. He also added there was a tape of the conversation.

The call had been made from Able Team's battered panel truck. It had been parked across the street from the diner they were using for the meet.

"You think he'll call?"

Lyons shrugged. "If he doesn't, we'll need to go back to the drawing board."

"If he does, he might not be convinced I'm telling the truth."

"Luke, just give it your best shot," Blancanales said.

"Right now I wish I could call Cassie. Tell her I'm okay."

"They might still be monitoring her calls," Lyons said.

"Yeah. I forgot."

"Wait a minute," Blancanales said. "Maybe he should call her. Tell her the same story he's going to run by McAdam. How he's back on the run because he doesn't trust the people who took him. Let him pass her the word he's decided to hand over the tape to McAdam and ask for his protection. If Gardener's people are listening in, they'll pass the details to McAdam as proof he's genuine."

"You want to call her?" Lyons asked.

"I don't want to but I will. Jesus, she's not going to like this."

THE CALL TO Cassie Stone had lasted a full five minutes. When it ended, Jacobi had let out a sigh, slumping back in his seat.

"She buy it?" Lyons asked.

"You mean, you couldn't hear?" Jacobi held up the cell phone. "I'm surprised this thing didn't melt. She believed me okay, but she isn't happy. She thinks I'm crazy and she told me. Cassie has a way with words."

"You convinced me," Schwarz said.

"If I get back to Arizona in one piece, she is going to kill me."

"Sounds like love to me," Blancanales said.

JACOBI'S CELL PHONE had rung less than ten minutes later.

"Yeah?"

"You know who this is?"

"I recognize your voice, Mr. McAdam. I have you on tape. Remember?"

"So why have you fallen out with your Justice Department buddies?"

"Bastards were going to use me for bait. Wanted me on a fuckin' leash to draw you guys out in the open. Gardener. Justin. Renelli. They don't give a damn if I live or die. I heard them discussing it when they figured I couldn't hear. They're not as smart as they believe. I decided I was better taking my chances with you. I went along with them until I got the opportunity to duck out."

"Going AWOL seems to be your specialty, Luke."

"I want to make a deal."

"Who says you have anything I want."

"McAdam, I still have the tape. I told those Justice dicks I hid it for insurance. They haven't heard what's on it yet, which is why they don't already have your ass in a sling."

There was a pause. Jacobi could hear McAdam speaking off the phone. It seemed to be a one-way conversation until Jacobi realized the CIA man was on a second telephone.

"Let's say I believe you've got that tape. What's the trade-off?"

"You can have the damn thing for cash money and I get left alone. Tell Gardener I've had enough. He wins. Just buy me off and he can have his revolution. And I can move on. What the hell do I care anymore? You guys have turned my life into shit. I shot a cop, dammit, because of you bastards."

"Assuming we agree, what's to stop us coming after you and making this personal?"

"My risk. Look, once Gardener has the tape and puts his operation on go, I'm no threat."

"True enough. How do we know you won't be bringing your Justice buddies with you if we arrange a meeting?"

"Your risk, McAdam. But why should I arrange a double-cross? I've been on the run since this started. I'm tired. I've got a shoulder hurting like hell. It's raining. It's cold. All I want is to be left alone. McAdam, I've got the tape in my pocket right now. I'll be in a diner behind Union Station. I'm sure you can trace this call and find me. You want that tape come get it. I'm here for the next hour. After that I'm thinking maybe CNN might make me an offer. How do you think Gardener would like to be on prime time?"

Jacobi ended the call.

"I'm impressed," Blancanales said.

"If that doesn't drag him out of his hole, nothing else will," Schwarz agreed.

"Okay," Lyons said. "Time to hit that diner. And don't worry, Luke, we'll be around even if you don't see us."

"If I come out of this alive. I mean, what about the cop thing?"

"You won't have to worry about that," Lyons said. "We can iron that out for you."

SHORTLY AFTER HE'D ENTERED the diner, taken his coffee and sat in one of the booths, Jacobi noticed that the panel truck had gone from across the street. He had a fleeting rise of panic until common sense told him it had simply been moved so McAdam—if he showed— wouldn't be suspicious.

Jacobi sat through three cups of coffee and a couple of chewy doughnuts. He watched one of the diners get up and leave. Ten minutes later the door opened, letting in rain and a shuffling figure wrapped in a long, grubby coat and a sodden baseball cap. The figured had a thick scarf wrapped around his face. He ordered a coffee and took it to the far end of the counter, perching himself on one of the stools.

Twenty minutes later Jacobi spotted a dark-colored car roll to a stop across the street. He paid attention as the passenger door opened and a man dressed in a trench coat stepped out, turning up his collar against the rain. He crossed the street, making for the diner. Jacobi followed his progress to the door.

It opened and the man stepped inside, scanning the interior.

Jacobi had no problem recognizing Rod McAdam.

The CIA man moved to Jacobi's booth and sat across from him. "You have a nice feel for the dramatic, Luke."

"Dramatic is getting chased clear across the country by Gardener's hired goons."

McAdam ran a hand through his damp hair. "You caused us some problems. You didn't expect us to just let it happen."

"Was it necessary to kill my uncle and his wife? Jesus, McAdam, they weren't involved."

"That was down to Renelli's people. It shouldn't have happened."

"That supposed to make me feel better? It's one of the reasons I want to bail out. Before any more innocent people get hurt through me."

McAdam glanced out the window at the parked car.

"Did you bring my money?" Jacobi asked.

"Money?"

"For the tape."

McAdam cleared his throat. "Show it to me," he demanded.

Jacobi used his free hand to reach inside his coat. He pulled out the tape and placed it on the table.

McAdam stared at it, making no move to touch it. He had thrust both hands inside his trench coat pockets.

"There is no money, Luke. But I do have *something* for you…"

Jacobi could tell by the look in McAdam's eyes. The CIA man was about to cross him.

Out the corner of his eye Jacobi saw sudden movement. He turned his head and saw the coffee drinker at the end of the counter swing to the floor, throwing open his long coat. His hands came up wielding a Franchi SPAS combat shotgun that he thrust directly into McAdam's face.

"If those hands don't come out empty, I'll shoot your head right off your fucking neck," Carl Lyons said. He leaned forward to speak into the small microphone pinned to his shirt. "Dark Ford parked across from the diner. McAdam's backup."

McAdam's face darkened with anger. "You can't do—"

"Can't is a word we don't accept today," Lyons said.

Through the window Lyons saw armed men emerge from the Ford. Two turned to cross the street, making for the diner, while the driver turned to face the panel truck as it rounded the corner and came straight at him. The crackle of autofire reached those inside the diner. The shots came from the Ford's driver as he opened fire on the panel truck. The truck swerved, sliding broadside-on and hit the front of the Ford, lifted the wheels off the ground and scooping up the driver.

Lyons sensed time running out fast.

He saw a thin smirk etch itself across McAdam's face. The rogue CIA man had set his plan into motion, and he figured matters were once more back under his control.

He could still have been thinking that when Lyons hit him with the barrel of the shotgun, clouting McAdam across the side of the head. The force of the blow knocked McAdam out of his seat. He sprawled facedown on the floor.

The door to the diner was kicked open as McAdam's backup team crashed their way inside. They were carrying squat SMGs, and they were targeting Carl Lyons.

The Able Team commando wasn't in place to be targeted. The second he hit McAdam he followed the CIA man down, into a low crouch, the SPAS tracking the oncoming gunners.

Seeing Lyons's move, the lead gunner brought his weapon around, dropping the muzzle and squeezing off a burst that ripped splinters out of the diner's floor. Lyons felt one tug his coat, a six-inch sliver of wood that ripped through the cloth.

Lyons brought the shotgun on line and fired. The gunner was driven back through the door, clearing the steps and hitting the sidewalk on his back, his torso a ripped and bloody mess.

The second gunner, already clear of the door, swept the area with his SMG, slugs chewing at the booths and tables, filling the air with smashed crockery and shards of plastic.

If the move had been designed to unnerve Lyons, it failed. The Stony Man warrior maintained his position, returning fire with cool deliberation that was scary to see, especially in the face of the autofire. His second shot from the SPAS took the gunner in the chest, banging him against the wall. The man twisted, his SMG still firing, the diner's side window exploding, shattered glass spraying the street.

As the second gunner went down, Lyons pushed to his feet, the shotgun sweeping the immediate area. Out the corner of his eye he saw Jacobi pushing up from where he had thrown himself flat across his seat.

"You hurt?" Lyons asked.

"No."

Lyons dragged his badge folder out of his pocket and held it up so everyone in the diner could see it.

"Justice Department," he stated loudly. "Everybody stay put."

At Lyons's feet Rod McAdam stirred, groaning as he put a hand to his bloody head. Before the CIA man could recover fully Lyons crouched beside him and searched him. He found McAdam's sidearm and the backup pistol tucked into his belt against his spine. Lyons unloaded both weapons before he tossed them on the table. He caught hold of McAdam's collar and dragged the man to his feet, pushing him back into his booth seat.

"Time we had a talk, McAdam," Lyons said.

"Or what?"

McAdam reached up to feel the blood running down the side of his face. It was steadily dripping onto his trench coat.

"I could give you a matching one on the other side."

"You trying to scare me?"

"I think he's doing a pretty good job," Jacobi said.

Lyons's earpiece hissed briefly.

"All clear out here," Blancanales said. "You?"

"We're fine. Better call this in and have the locals informed. Then get in here and calm down the customers."

Lyons eased the shotgun around so it was close to McAdam's face.

"Listen up, McAdam. We've got you on tape discussing the kidnap of the President. It's over for you. No way of walking free and clear. Personally I don't give a damn what happens to you. So try not to piss me off. I'd as soon shoot you now."

McAdam stared around him. He saw one of his men down, blood and lacerated flesh in evidence.

"The rest of your crew is the same. I doubt they'll be in for coffee."

"You realize what you've done?" McAdam blustered. "Who you're messing with?"

"Quit the tough guy act, McAdam. I don't impress. We have you. We have the tape. No contest. There's only one thing I want from you."

McAdam began to accept his position. His mind had already spun through the permutations regarding his status and none was coming up with anything close to a winning hand.

"Where's the President?"

McAdam Safehouse, Northern Kentucky

"Do you really expect to get away with this?" Brognola asked Renelli.

"From where I'm standing, I'd say we already have," Renelli answered

"The President of the United States," Brognola said.

Renelli smiled. He glanced across the room at the President's seated figure.

"I know who he is. And *we* have him. Soon to be ex-President. Been a hell of a day."

"Do you really believe it's going to be this simple? Kidnapping the Man isn't going to get Gardener what he wants. It doesn't work like that."

"This isn't over yet. The general has it all worked out. Removing the President is just the start."

"And everything else is just going to fall into place? What about the Vice President? Congress? The Senate? Military Chiefs of Staff. You going to kidnap them all, as well?"

"The general—"

"Renelli, the general is living on Fantasy Island. Is the man so naïve he thinks this is all you have to do to take over? This is America. Not some Third World dictatorship where they change the CEO every other week."

"It's all been arranged. General Gardener has military allies. Men from every arm of the services backing him. When we commandeer the media and the utilities, he'll address the whole country and tell them—"

"Tell them what, Renelli? That General Chase Gardener is in control. That *he's* running the country now. That he's going to solve all their problems. Save us from the threat of terrorism and cure the Iraq crisis."

"People don't trust government anymore. They've been screwed over too many times. They need someone in charge who can give them what they want."

"And line his pockets with money from the Iraqi oilfields at the same time?"

"We need that oil to keep the military running. The minute we show we're weak we lose everything."

"Renelli, I'll give Gardener one thing. He can work his bullshit on you."

Renelli crossed to stand over Brognola. "I've had enough of your mouth, mister. Maybe I didn't hit you hard enough last time."

"Renelli."

Renelli turned at the sound of Gardener's voice.

"General."

"Don't fall for it," Gardener said. "He's just trying to get inside your head."

Renelli eased off.

"Have all your people checked in recently?"

"All accounted for, sir."

Gardener nodded.

"I'll try McAdam again," he said. He speed-dialed

McAdam's cell phone, heard it connect then ring out. "Damn you, Rod, pick up."

Gardener felt Renelli's eyes on him.

"Maybe I should go outside and take another look around," Renelli said.

Gardener nodded. He took a moment to stare across the living room. Two of Renelli's men stood guard over the President and Hal Brognola. Outside were six more on roving patrols. The two captives sat in low armchairs, wearing handcuffs and ankle restraints. Outside the early morning was brightening the sky. Pale mist lay in the timbered hollows of the Kentucky hill country.

"You look a little stressed, Chase," the President said. "This not working out as well as you hoped?"

"Early in the game yet," Gardener replied. He kept his tone light, perhaps a little too light, and turned away before his expression gave him away.

"I don't believe he's enjoying this as much as he was last night," Brognola said.

The President flexed his manacled wrists.

"Makes two of us, Hal."

"We'll get out of this, sir."

"Oh? Who have you got in mind? I don't see a big green guy in torn pants tearing up the trees.

The analogy with *The Hulk* made Brognola smile. That very moment he had been thinking about Carl Lyons.

"How many?" Schwarz asked.

"Enough," Lyons said. He lowered his binoculars. "I

counted four. Could be others around the front. They're carrying M-4s. Handguns, too. And they're wearing tac com units."

"Don't think they're up here hunting raccoons, then?" Blancanales said.

"We've got the right place. I just saw Renelli doing a tour. Checking out the guards."

Blancanales made a final check of his M-16, removing the magazine and inspecting the loads before he locked it back in place.

"Hey, I hear a vehicle coming," Schwarz said.

Lyons raised the glasses and focused in on the big silver-gray SUV as it crawled around the final bend in the rough approach trail. Just before it moved out of his vision he managed to get a close look at the man sitting beside the driver.

"Now we've got three jokers out of the pack. Senator Ralph Justin."

"Things could be getting close," Schwarz said. "Pity McAdam isn't here to join the party."

"That guy has enough on his mind right now," Blancanales said.

"Time for us to go be party-poopers," Lyons said. He activated his tac com. "You with us, Jack?"

"Just sitting here waiting for you chumps to shake the lead out," Grimaldi responded from *Dragon Slayer.*

"Add one more to the guest list," Lyons said. "Senator Justin has entered the building."

"Time to reel 'em in."

Lyons turned to his partners. "The only ones I give a damn about are Hal and the President. The rest of them are expendable as far as I'm concerned."

"How do you want to do this?" Blancanales asked.

"Fast as we can. I know McAdam is locked down, but I don't want to risk my life on that staying secret. If Gardener gets a hint his game is about to be canceled, he might decide to cut his losses and do something stupid. So we hit fast and we hit hard. Go for front and back entrances. First there goes in before our time runs out."

"Any preferences?"

"Give me two minutes then go," Lyons said. "If any shooting starts before time up, make *your* move. Don't wait."

They ran a swift time check.

Lyons pulled back into the dense shrubbery behind them and started his wide circling of the lodge and Renelli's armed guards.

"I HAVEN'T HEARD A THING from him," Justin said. "I tried every half hour on my way here."

Renelli turned to Gardener. "General?"

"I'm starting to get a feeling maybe that Jacobi thing was a trap. Those Justice sons of bitches got their hands on McAdam, and he told them where we were to save his own skin." Gardener spun to where Brognola sat. "You set this up?"

Brognola raised his cuffed hands. "How would I do that, General?"

"Isn't it time you reconsidered your position?" the President asked.

"Isn't it time you shut your damn mouth?" Gardener yelled. "You're finished."

The President glanced across at Ralph Justin and the senator had the grace to lower his gaze.

"The hell with this," Gardener said. "Time to make that call." He glanced at his watch. "The units should be in position anytime now."

He crossed to a black attaché case sitting on a small table. He opened it to expose a sleek satellite communication unit. The unit was programmed in to the Gardener Global network, the call he would make being simultaneously transmitted to each of his military commanders.

"This is our day, gentlemen," he said, picking up the handset.

From outside the lodge, at the front, came the crackle of autofire.

Renelli's earpiece burst into life. "Then stop them for Christ's sake," he yelled.

Gardener turned to stare at him. "What?"

"Intruders, General."

Renelli snatched up the M-16 propped against the wall and cocked the weapon.

Reaching inside his jacket, Gardener pulled out his holstered M-9.

More gunfire sounded, this time from the rear of the lodge.

Renelli pushed by Justin and made for the front entrance. There was a crackle of autofire and a stream of slugs thudded against the outer wall, extending on to shatter one of the front windows, throwing glass inside the room. As Renelli paused by the door, he glanced through a side window and saw one of his men on the ground, blood already staining the front of his shirt.

Renelli reached for the handle and yanked it free, swinging the door open and stepping out onto the wide wooden porch.

BLANCANALES AND Schwarz were four seconds short of the two-minute wait when they heard the crackle of autofire from the front of the lodge.

"Let's move," Blancanales said.

They broke cover and cut across the ground, their destination the rear door to the sprawling lodge.

Schwarz spotted movement off to their left, a dark-clad man raising an M-4 to his shoulder, tracking in on Blancanales's running figure. Schwarz hauled up short, raising his own weapon. He caught the distant gunner in his sights and fired a 3-round burst that hit the target in the chest. The man floundered backward, trying to maintain his balance. He managed until Schwarz hit him a second time and laid him down flat.

Blancanales almost tripped when his foot caught a snaking root. He stumbled, off balance for a couple of seconds. The near fall saved him as one of the guards fired on him. The slugs were close. Too close. Blancanales, aware of his luck, dropped to the ground, scrambling for what cover he could find while seeking the man who had fired. His fall had drawn out the guard, believing he had hit his target. He started in to check out the man he thought he had shot, giving Blancanales time to pull his M-16 into target acquisition and return fire. He caught the guard in the left hip, saw a burst of dark flecks erupt from the wound as the guy faltered. Raising himself on his elbows Blancanales fired again, punching a burst into the target's middle chest. The man gave a startled cry as he went down.

Pushing upright, Blancanales saw his partner engaging a third guard. As he came upright, he caught a flicker of movement close to thick brush. A man stepped into the open, rifle to his shoulder, as he drew down on Schwarz. Blancanales took a chance and fired from the hip, clipping the shooter's right arm, pulling his muzzle around a fraction and firing a couple more bursts. In the short time between his first and second burst the shooter got off a single round.

Schwarz put down his target with a keen head shot,

then turned under the impact of the fourth man's only shot. The slug burned across his left side, cracking a rib in passing. Schwarz fell to his knees, clasping his left hand over the wound.

Blancanales ran over to his partner, activating his tac com.

"Jack, get in here fast. No time for playing hide-and-seek any longer. Rear of the lodge. Gadgets caught one in the side. Come get him. I need to back Carl."

"Roger that," Grimaldi responded. "On my way."

"Go find Carl," Schwarz said. "Go."

LYONS EMERGED from the thick brush close to the front of the lodge. It lay to his right. The silver-gray SUV was parked alongside two black 4x4s.

There was an insistent, small voice inside Lyons head telling him to get this done before Gardener decided to set his game into action. If the general managed to press the button marked Go, and Stony Man failed to initiate moves against all the players, there might still be casualties.

Identification of the conspirators had been made. Stony Man had been forced to walk softly until they were sure the President and Hal Brognola were in safe hands before they gave the go-ahead to move against Gardener's people. It had become a stalemate, a period of biding time so that one call didn't galvanize a response from the opposition, while hoping that the same didn't come from the enemy. It took walking a fine line to extremes.

The ultimate decision about the right moment to strike was snatched from Carl Lyons as he emerged from the brush and made his run for the lodge.

Out the corner of his eye he saw a dark figure break from the trees to his right. The armed guy reached to activate his com unit even as he pulled up his weapon.

Lyons didn't hesitate. He triggered his M-16 and knocked the guy off his feet with a burst, following him down and laying in a second to keep him there.

A second gunner showed around the rear of the SUV, already speaking into his com unit, dragging his M-4 off his shoulder.

Lyons hit him on the run, the impact of the 5.56 mm rounds wrenching him off balance. The Able Team leader kept firing, his shots blowing out messy exit wounds. As the man went down, his M-4 fired from the end of his flailing arm, the shots shattering one of the lodge's front windows.

The sound of autofire from the rear of the lodge reached Lyons.

Blancanales and Schwarz.

The front door of the lodge was dragged open. Lyons turned toward it as he skirted the front of the structure and saw Rick Renelli step outside. The man spotted Lyons and opened fire. The stream of 5.56 mm slugs dug dusty furrows in the ground as the big ex-cop dropped, rolled and came up firing. His initial burst ripped chunks of wood from the porch supports, throwing them in Renelli's face. He stepped back, one hand reaching up to claw at the slivers embedded in the side of his face. The momentary hesitation gave Lyons his chance. Up on one knee, he steadied his rifle and jacked out repeated bursts that punched in through Renelli's chest and throat. The traitor hit the porch rail behind him and flipped over it. He landed hard on the back of his neck, his body going into spasm, blood erupting in a fountain from his severed jugular.

Lyons headed for the door, keeping low as he passed the windows and went through at a run.

THE LODGE'S REAR DOOR led Blancanales into the kitchen. It was all pale pine and gleaming copper pots, and he could smell traces of a recently cooked breakfast.

The Able Team commando continued on, his M-16 tracking ahead of him.

As he emerged into a short passage, he heard a hard footfall, then saw a man stepping through an open arch, rifle up. The guy opened fire as he caught a glimpse of Blancanales, sending a burst that shredded wall plaster.

Blancanales had ducked down the moment he heard the sound, then swept the passage with tribursts. The shooter yelled as he caught a slug in his ankle and calf, the slugs splintering bones. The guy stumbled against the wall, cursing against the pain of his shattered limb. All that achieved was to offer Blancanales a target source. He raised himself up, pulled the M-16 on line and placed his next burst through the guy's head. The close range gave the slugs added power and they took out the back of the target's skull.

Pushing to his feet, Blancanales moved to the arch, leaning around the edge to scan the wide expanse of the lodge's living room.

He saw Brognola and the President, cuffed and sitting in chairs at the far side of the room.

Senator Ralph Justin was caught in a frozen moment, his face registering the shock of what was happening.

Another armed guard was turning in Blancanales's direction, his weapon starting to rise in anticipation of a target.

And then there was General Chase Gardener, M-9 clutched in one hand, a telephone handset in the other.

Coming in through the open front door was Carl Lyons. He had cast aside his M-16 and had his Colt Python out of its holster.

The tableau held for a split second, then erupted in a round of gunfire that filled the room with its powerful noise.

Blancanales hit the guard with a 3-round burst. The man went down in a heap, blood spraying the air as he crashed to the floor.

Chase Gardener swung his M-9 toward Lyons, his face almost calm as he pulled back on the trigger.

The big revolver in Lyons's fist boomed three times, the heavy sound of the powerful .357 Magnum bullets drowning out all other sounds. The shots cored in through Gardener's chest, shattering bones and tearing organs apart. The force pushed the general back across the room. He collided with a heavy armchair and fell across it. He lay with his head hanging, eyes wide open and staring up at the ceiling.

As the rattle of shots faded, Ralph Justin gave a whimper and looked down at the blood that was starting to leak from the bullet wound in his right arm. One of the bullets from the Python had gone through Gardener, emerging between his shoulders. The misshapen slug had ripped into Justin's arm, a fraction of an inch above the elbow joint, taking out a sizable wedge of muscle and flesh. A jagged sliver of bone jutted out from the torn, bloody fabric of the senator's expensive jacket.

Lyons crossed over to where Brognola and the President were sitting.

"We'll get you out of those soon as possible, sir," he said.

"We can wait a little longer," the President replied.

Brognola caught Lyons's eye. "You guys okay?"

"Gadgets picked up a bullet. Jack's dealing with it." Lyons put away his weapon.

Blancanales had produced a cell phone and made

contact with Stony Man. "We're clear. Both hostages safe and well. Make your call. It's a go."

The President nodded his approval.

Blancanales listened as further information was passed to him, then he shut off the phone.

"Mr. President, we have confirmation that the Iraqi problem has been resolved. Phoenix Force located and neutralized Khariza. The nuclear device is in our hands."

"Now that is good news," the President said. "Any casualties on our side?"

Blancanales smiled. "Few scrapes, including a hip wound for McCarter."

"That's all I need to hear," Brognola said. "He'll make the most of that."

"As soon as we get back, Hal, I want everything on this affair on my desk. It's going to be a busy time clearing house on this one. Hal, I owe you."

Brognola raised his cuffed hands and pointed in the direction of Lyons and Blancanales.

"No, Mr. President, you owe these guys. Able Team and Phoenix Force."

"I stand corrected, Hal. Damned right I owe them. Once again."

TAKE 'EM FREE
2 action-packed novels plus a mystery bonus
NO RISK
NO OBLIGATION TO BUY

DEATH LANDS

Ritual Chill

Cursed in fathomless ways, the future awaits...

STRANGE QUARRY

A cold sense of déjà vu becomes reality as Ryan's group emerges from a gateway they'd survived before—a grim graveyard of lost friends and nightmares. The consuming need to escape the dangerous melancholy of the place forces the company out into the frozen tundra, where an even greater menace awaits. The forbidding land harbors a dying tribe, cursed members of the ancient Inuit, who seize the arrival of Ryan and his band as their last hope to appease angry gods...by offering them up as human sacrifice.

In the Deathlands, the price for survival is the constant fear of death.

Available September 2005 at your favorite retail outlet.